13 French Street and The Red Scarf

GIL BREWER was born in Canandaigua (New York) in November 1922. Self-educated following a poor childhood, he was based in England with the US Army during World War II, and later served in France and Belgium. Once demobbed, he worked as a warehouseman, gas station attendant, cannery worker and bookseller. His writing talents were discovered by the agent Joseph T. Shaw, previously the editor of *Black Mask Magazine*, who was responsible for selling over four hundred of his short stories to a variety of pulp and popular magazines.

His first novels were written in 1950. *So Rich, So Dead* took him only five days to complete and was soon followed by *Satan is a Woman*, which he wrote in fifteen days. But his third novel, *13 French Street*, was the first to be published, in 1951, and became a major bestseller with more than a million copies sold.

A prolific author for the paperback original market, Gil Brewer lived most of his life in Florida, where much of his fiction is set. Partly influenced by James Cain, Erskine Caldwell and Hemingway, his lean and suspenseful novels fit into the Southern school of hard-boiled writing popularized by Day Keene, Harry Whittington, Jim Thompson and principally John D. MacDonald. He wrote over fifty novels including war stories, gothics (as Elaine Evans), a western (*Some Must Die*, 1954), novelisations and ghosted memoirs. He also wrote as Eric Fitzgerald and Bailey Morgan.

His other crime novels were *Flight to Darkness*, *Hell's Our Destination*, *A Killer is Loose*, *The Squeeze*, *77 Rue Paradis*, *And the Girl Screamed*, *The Angry Dream*, *The Brat*, *Little Tramp*, *The Bitch*, *The Vengeful Virgin*, *Wild*, *Sugar*, *Wild to Possess*, *Angel*, *The Three-Way Split*, *A Taste of Sin*, *Memory of Passion*, *Play it Hard*, *The Hungry One*, *Sin for Me*, and *The Tease*.

Gil Brewer died in 1983.

Series Editor: Maxim Jakubowski

blue murder

Gil Brewer
13 French Street & The Red Scarf

David Goodis
The Burglar

Davis Grubb
The Night of the Hunter

Geoffrey Homes
Build My Gallows High

William P. McGivern
The Big Heat

Joel Townsley Rogers
The Red Right Hand

Newton Thornburg
Cutter and Bone

Charles Williams
The Diamond Bikini

Cornell Woolrich
Rear Window & Other Stories

blue murder

13 FRENCH STREET
and
THE RED SCARF

Gil Brewer

S I M O N & S C H U S T E R

LONDON • SYDNEY • NEW YORK • TOKYO • TORONTO

13 French Street first published in 1951; *The Red Scarf* in 1958
First published as a Blue Murder paperback by
Simon & Schuster Limited 1988

© Gil Brewer 1951, 1958

Simon & Schuster Limited
West Garden Place, Kendal Street
London W2 2AQ

Simon & Schuster Australia Pty Limited
Sydney

British Library Cataloguing in Publication Data

Brewer, Gil, *1922–1983*
    13 French Street; and, The red scarf.
    I. Title   II. Brewer, Gil, 1922–1983. The
    red scarf
    813′.54[F]
    ISBN 0–671–65279–6

Phototypeset in Ehrhardt by Input Typesetting Ltd
Printed and Bound in Great Britain by
Richard Clay Ltd, Bungay, Suffolk

13 FRENCH STREET

CHAPTER 1

PETRA'S LETTERS should have warned me. Those secret, smiling letters written in an overbold hand with violet ink on pale green perfumed paper, sealed in green envelopes. They should have been warning enough for anyone. And the house should have warned me. The minute I stepped through the doorway at 13 French Street, I sensed something wrong – something I couldn't nail down. But she closed the door before I had a chance to run. So, you see, it was already too late. Only I should have run anyway. . . .

'Alex. You've come!'

I nodded but I didn't speak. She leaned back against the door, one hand resting on the doorknob, the other fussing with the bottom of the long V neckline on her black dress.

The long, broad hallway was deeply shadowed, though some of the early-autumn twilight filtered into the house. I could still hear the lazy rattle of leaves outside against the porch. The bite of burning leaves had entered the door with me. I remembered the red winking of the taxi's taillight as it rounded a far corner, left me standing on the flagstone walk before the large, square, red brick house. Verne Lawrence's home, 13 French Street.

Yes. Already I sensed the beginnings of panic. The first hint of futility and hopeless outrage.

'Alex Bland.'

3

'Yes, and you're Petra?'

'What do you think?' She smiled. I knew her lips were very red, but they looked black, there in that hallway. Her right hand left the doorknob, and I took it. It wasn't shaking hands. It was holding hands. No, it was even more than that. Communication, from Petra to me. Maybe it was the last warning. Maybe it was the moment when they untied the rope and the cage door slammed down. Her palm was cool, her fingers long and strong.

'Where's Verne?'

She ignored it. She let go of my hand, stepped closer. Whatever perfume she wore was faint, elusive. But I remembered the letters. It was the same stuff. I'd smelled that perfume on her letters at least once a week for three years.

'It's queer,' she said. 'Never having seen you. Only the snapshot of you and Verne in uniform. The one you had taken in Paris. Your face was all in shadow, you know, so I thought you had dark hair. But you're a regular tow-head. And those gray eyes – ' She paused and shook her head slightly. 'You're a bigger man now, too. I'll bet . . . Well, never mind. Anyway, Alex, you look like I expected – only better.' She smiled. 'You don't wear a hat?'

'No.'

'Well, take off your coat, Alex.'

She helped me with my coat, held it in her hands a moment, then dropped it in a heap on a chair. I hadn't moved from beside my two bags. I could feel the leather of one of them against my leg. It felt substantial, like the beach does after you've been swimming for a mile or so.

We looked at each other some more. I guess we had that much coming. That much of it wasn't wrong.

She was tall, slimly provocative. All in black. Black hair, worn long, tumbling around her shoulders. Black eyes, all pupil, or all iris. Her skin was very white. Her black eyebrows arched slightly, making her eyes seem bolder than ever, and

4

her smile had shock value. Long-legged, full-breasted, and the neckline of her dress reached down. *Down*. She was a bold, beautiful woman.

'All right? I mean, what did you expect, Alex? We know each other, in a way. Of course, not . . .'

I didn't tell her I had expected a white house with a white picket fence. I didn't explain that I had always visualized her in a light cotton dress, maybe watering the flowers. Hell, there weren't any flowers.

I said, 'Verne could always pick 'em.'

'Yes?'

'He outdid himself. Where is Verne?'

She'd been speaking quietly, the tone of her voice soft, warm, full. Now it lost the softness, the warmth. 'Oh, yes, Verne. Upstairs. He'll be down. You didn't tell us you *were* coming, you know. We'd have met you at the station.'

'You told me you like surprises,' I said.

'You don't surprise me, Alex,' she said. 'I've known all along.'

'Known what?'

She smiled.

Somebody walked softly across the hall at the far end. I turned and saw a staircase leading upward and what looked like a white shawl vanishing through a doorway at the foot of the stairs.

Petra's eyes had gone metallic. Then they were molten again. 'Mother,' she said.

'Your mother?'

'My husband's.'

I wondered how much longer this was going to continue. I didn't sense that something was wrong any more. I knew it for sure. But what?

'How long can you stay?'

'A week.'

She smiled. Every time she'd smiled at me it had been

5

like the silent communication of her hand. She was saying, 'That's all you know about it.' She knew I knew what she meant. But I wasn't bothered too much. Yet.

She acted all wrong. I mean, I figured Verne would be there, pounding me on the back, cracking out a bottle, with Petra saying, 'Oh' and 'Ah.'

It wasn't like that. It wasn't like anything. But it was real as all hell.

'Alex, I feel I know you terribly well.'

I chanced a smile. 'Me, too.'

So that's the way it was. When she said something, you never knew what was going to come out. You never knew.

. . . and Verne would so much like to see you. It's been five years now and he still talks of the good old times. He seldom writes anyone, Alex, so he's left it up to me to keep at you until you visit us. He said you always did work too hard and that your fault is you're too honest. Verne says a man can't get ahead anyplace nowadays if he's like that. You're too serious. I know you don't think I'm too forward in saying these things, Alex. But, Alex – let that museum go hang. You need a good vacation. Please come, Alex. We'll have a grand time. I feel I know you so well, now. We've been writing each other for three years, Alex. . . .

Pages. Page after page, every time. As if all she had to do in the world was write to me. An archaeologist with no place to dig and with no one to give a damn if he did dig – but with a dream. And a philanthropic gentleman in Chicago had the foresight and interest to help me realize this dream. A museum for the future to end all museums. It would take years, probably my whole lifetime, but it was what I wanted now.

. . . so I keep asking you, for Verne, to come and spend some time with us here in Allayne. We have a fine home, just outside of town – nearly a mile – lots of freedom. Alex, really. I simply won't give up, Alex!

It sounded good. But there was the museum, and there was Madge, too. We weren't engaged, but marriage wasn't far off, either. Sure, I wanted that vacation. What the hell? So I finally decided to surprise them. I didn't let them know I was coming till I called from the station. Here I was. Great.

Verne Lawrence hadn't been out of the Army a week before he was married. I'd heard from him occasionally and we'd planned to get together after I finished some digging in Yucatan. But he never said much about his new wife, beyond the fact that she was beautiful and they were happy. After about two years he ceased writing, and Petra took over. I returned to Chicago and my dream.

I wanted to see Verne. He'd been a close friend and a good man – a good soldier, too. He was ten years older than I, making him about forty now. I wondered if he had changed.

I figured to spend a week with them. Verne and I would loaf and talk, while Petra mixed cocktails or opened beer cans. The hell with the museum, for the time being – the hell with everything. And Madge said, 'Why, certainly, Alex. I agree. You should do something like that. You've been working much too hard. Then, when you come back, maybe . . .'

So here I was. And already I wanted to run. I wanted to get away. It was all wrong.

'Here's Verne now.'

I turned toward the stairs again. I felt her hand on my arm and the fingers closed just once, not tentatively, but certain. Then her hand went away. I watched my old war buddy come toward us down the hall.

He looked as if somebody had machine-gunned his soul.

CHAPTER 2

'ALEX! YOU old fraud, you!'

'Verne, is that any way to – '

He ignored her, didn't even glance her way. 'Yes, by God! Sorry I kept you waiting, old man. Damned headache. Trying to– Well, say! You haven't changed.'

'Good to see you, Verne.'

The handshake. Flat out, once up, once down, release. He slapped me on the back. I don't know how I sounded; I'll never know. Verne Lawrence looked like hell. He was an old man, trying to suck in his guts and stick out his chest; trying to smile a smile that wasn't there. Obviously.

'You've met my wife?' He did not look at her.

I grinned. 'Lucky fellow. She's everything I – '

'Sure, sure.'

I was sick of it. I wanted to get out of there.

His eyes were haunted. Once he'd had blond hair; now it was a dirty, streaked gray. His face was lined, his mouth pulled down at the corners no matter how hard he tried to pull it up. His neck was wrinkled and his shirt collar didn't fit. He was wearing a tweed suit and it hung over his frame like burlap over a broomstick; like those scarecrows you see in winter-blasted cornfields.

And Verne Lawrence had once been a big man with broad shoulders, barrel chest, and with a face like a slab of beef.

8

Now his face was like breast of chicken, dried in a very hot
sun.

All of this in five years. . . .

'Should've let me come down and pick you up at the
depot.'

'Already had a cab.'

'How long you here for?'

'A week.'

'What the hell kind of vacation is that?'

'Best I could do.'

She was behind him, staring at me over his shoulder now.
She dampened her lips with her tongue and her gaze was
steady, patient.

'Five years,' he said. 'Five years.' He shook his head,
jammed his hands into his jacket pockets. Then he took one
hand out and pulled at his lower lip. 'You're tired,' he said.
'Jenny's got your room ready.'

I started to tell him I wasn't tired. But I knew he was. He
was tired of having me here already. As tired as I was of
being here.

'Here,' he said. 'I'll show you. Wash up. Change clothes.
Feel better. Here, I'll show you.'

'It would be best,' Petra said. She smiled at me over his
shoulder.

Great.

The room was all right. Better than that. It was a corner
room, on the left front. Big windows, with the late twilight
of autumn blowing in. The breeze was balmy, and I suspected
there'd be some warm weather coming. Not like Chicago.

Comfortable bed. Two chairs, a desk, a bookcase full of
brightly covered unread books, and a sparkling bathroom in
blue tile.

So this was how you met the guys you knew during the
war. This is what happened to them.

I went over and leaned out one of the side windows. Fields, trees, hills – and way over there was town. Allayne. I could see the road winding through the hills, dipping into the town. The hills were savage with color in the failing twilight. Almost as I watched, night began to creep along the sky, tugging a black blanket in its teeth. The wind began to die. It was very still out there, almost as if the evening were holding its breath.

It had been all Verne could do to carry the lighter of the two suitcases up the stairs. It embarrassed me. I would have carried them both, but that would have done more than embarrass Verne.

I walked around the room and rubbed my knuckles into my scalp. This was great, all right.

Some wife. Petra. Maybe . . .

But I didn't want to think of her. It hadn't begun to occur to me why I didn't want to think of her – yet.

I opened the two suitcases on the bed. Somebody whistled softly and said, 'I'm Jenny.'

I faced the door. It was partly open. She had genuine apples in her cheeks, a wealth of carrot-colored hair, the hint of a turned-up nose, bright, honest blue eyes, and one of those mouths that like to smile but are a bit hesitant about it. She was dressed in white: white apron, tiny starched white cap. She leaned against the doorjamb with her hands in the pockets of her apron, and I liked her right away.

'Mrs. Lawrence says to tell you dinner is served at six-thirty.'

'Thanks, Jenny.'

'That's all right. My job. You're Mr. Bland, from Chicago, right?'

I sat down on the bed. 'That's right.'

'Heard your name mentioned.' She smiled and her face lit up and laughed all over. Still there was that shy hesitancy

10

about the smile. It was the kind of smile model agencies would break budgets for.

'You've been here a long while?' I asked.

'Six months, Mr. Bland.'

'Oh.'

'That's all right. You can ask anything you want.'

'I see. Thanks.'

She cleared her throat. 'You have plenty of towels 'n' stuff?'

'Guess so.'

'That's good.'

We watched each other. She had something to say, but she'd decided not to say it. I wondered what it was. It was in her eyes. Somebody was coming up the stairs. Petra said, 'Jenny!' from down the hall.

Jenny winked and closed the door. She opened it quickly, stuck her head in, and whispered, 'You'd better keep it locked, Mr. Bland.' Then the door was closed and the house was silent.

I wondered if Jenny had finally said what she'd come to say. If she had, it didn't make sense to me.

Without a doubt there was something wrong between Verne and his wife. What it was, I didn't know. Petra was a very beautiful woman. Seated on the bed, I thought it over, and only came to realize more and more how truly beautiful she was.

And Jenny. A housemaid. Not a cook. So there must be a cook, too. And Verne's mother. I'd clean forgot to ask him about that.

The vacation I was supposed to be on was slowly becoming something else. I'm a guy who likes things orderly. If I lay my razor down on a certain part of a shelf, I want it to be there when I reach for it next time. Comes from living so long alone, I suppose.

So I got to thinking about Madge. I went over to the desk

11

and found paper. Using my own pen, I wrote Madge, and lied about how swell everything was. That wasn't good either, because some kinds of lying are all right, but others nag at me. This would nag. Then I told Madge I wished we were together, and that was no lie, so I felt better.

But after the letter was sealed I remembered Petra again. I tucked the letter under the blotter of the desk. Then I got out my shaving kit and shaved in the bathroom. I kept thinking about Petra, wondering what her last name had been before it was Lawrence. So I had to whistle in order to quit thinking about my friend's wife's black hair and the way her eyes got soft when she looked at me. I was finished shaving before I realized I'd been whistling 'Danse Macabre.'

Somebody rapped on the door.

'Yeah, O.K.,' I said. The door opened.

'It's me, Jenny, again,' she said. 'Mrs. Lawrence says not to go an' dress for dinner.'

'Thanks, Jenny.'

She closed the door. I took a shower and went downstairs in gray flannels and a white shirt. I felt good and not at all tired. When I reached the foot of the stairs I happened to glance up. An old woman in a white shawl was leaning over the railing, staring at me.

I went on down the hall and opened the front door, stepped through the vestibule, opened the door onto the porch. Leaves skittered around the threshold and over my feet. Lights from house windows winked between the flashing branches of trees. Verne's place wasn't so far from town. There were street lights out here. And there were some stretches of sidewalk. I stood there in the doorway. Behind me, the house was very still. As if nobody lived there at all.

A car went by out on the road with the radio playing. Music trailed off into the evening. Then it was quiet again. A cow lowed. It wasn't cold at all. The air was warm and still.

12

I turned to go inside and I smelled the perfume. She was standing in the vestibule. She didn't move, so I had to stop and stand there. It was dark, but her face was pale and I could see her lips and her eyes shone in the darkness.

'You like it here, Alex?'

'Very much. It's very nice.'

'Alex, if – if Verne seems peculiar, please excuse him. He's had rotten luck. Business, business, you know? He's a little worried, because he doesn't know how to tell you he won't be able to spend much time with you. He can't possibly take a week off.'

'I see. Well, that's all right.'

Her hand touched my arm, went away. Her voice was as soft as the breeze outside. 'That's what I told Verne. Don't you worry. I'll see that you have a fine time. We should have lots of things to talk about. And I know plenty of things to do.'

I tried to make my voice encouraging, but the panic had mounted another notch. 'Great. That's fine. I'm sure we'll – '

'So am I, Alex. Come, dinner's ready. And don't you dare let on I mentioned that about Verne.'

Already we were conspirators. Inadvertently I touched her shoulder. It was bare and warm. She was wearing a strapless dress. I jerked my hand away. I said, 'Don't you worry. Maybe I can talk him into feeling better.'

She whispered, 'I won't worry, Alex.'

For me there has always been something about the darkness of a house, a large house, of a hallway, just before dinnertime in the autumn. Something about the darkness, with the lights in another part of the house – something that excites me. Perhaps everyone has felt it. I felt it now. And she felt it. We stood there and the faint panic increased a bit.

Her voice remained a whisper, conspiratorial. 'And Verne's

mother. Don't pay any attention to her, either. She's quite deaf, by the way.'

'Yes.' I cursed myself because I had whispered.

She took me lightly by the arm. 'Come on, Alex. I'm famished. I'll bet you are, too. Nobody eats in this house but me. They're all – ' She ceased. We went on down the hallway. I was very conscious of her movements, her lithe grace.

They're all what? I asked myself. There was something so damned secretive about her. In spite of anything I could do, it was getting to me. Right then was when I began to fight.

Dinner was a wake. We sat for three quarters of an hour over a rare roast of beef. And I met Verne's mother. Yes. Really there were three corpses at that table. The old woman, Verne, and the roast of beef. Petra and I faced each other across the table. She still was the only one with an appetite. I'd felt hungry, but a few moments at the table took care of that.

Verne's mother. Verne had doubtless been born into her old age. She was very old now. Like those dried, withered vines clinging grimly to the side of a stone building. At first glance, you think they're dead, but then, way up there, you notice a tiny green leaf. You wonder how in hell it ever got there. You know the sap still flows, however frugally.

There wasn't much sap left in this old woman. She wore a gray dress, buttoned around her throat, like those World War I Army tunics, with a round diamond brooch in the middle. And above the collar, a small choker of pearls circled her thin neck. Her face was small, shrunken, and sly. Her eyes glinted and gleamed like the slowly burning tips of two Fourth of July punk sticks. The kind you light firecrackers with, or used to, anyway. One of these days those eyes would turn to ash. I wondered if she would find a fuse; she seemed to be looking for one.

Her dress was long, tight-sleeved, and a flower of white

lace handkerchief bloomed at her wrist. Her hands and fingers trembled like dried willow wands in a breeze. A white shawl, looking somehow too heavy for her to carry, sagged about her shoulders. She was quite deaf, and beyond a nod to me when we were loudly introduced, she didn't speak.

Petra hated her. I saw that from the first. Petra would glance at the old woman and Verne would, glance at Petra.

'She's afraid of the old folks' home,' Verne said, 'She believes they would kill her if she ever went. Don't know where she picked up the notion. I suppose it's just as well she stays here. She can't last too much longer.'

'She'll outlive us all,' Petra said. She cut a piece of meat, dipped it in gravy, and chewed with unconcern. 'She's in the way here. She's unhappy. She has nothing.'

'You take her out for rides,' Verne said.

'Yes, it's lovely.'

Petra ate for a while. The old woman fussed at her plate, believing that she ate, but actually all she did was play. It wasn't nice to watch. Verne drank water. I creased my napkin, and remembered how the red taillight of the taxi had winked around the corner, leaving me here – with this.

'You've noticed I look like hell, I suppose?' Verne said. His gaze touched mine, drifted away. Petra was watching me. The skin of her shoulders and throat looked soft, unblemished, warm.

I shrugged. 'A little tired, maybe.'

'No. I look like hell, Alex. Everything's going to hell. My business is shot, what with the government stepping in, taking over supplies. Can't get the things I need, have to be there every minute or I'll lose what I have.'

'What is it?'

'Building project on Long Island. Have to leave tomorrow, Alex. Don't know when I'll get home. I'm sorry. That's the way it is. Biggest deal I've ever had, and it's tumbling around my shoulders. I'll stand to lose what I've got. It would have set me – us on Easy Street. Really.'

Petra stared at me. Her lips were touched with disdain, her eyes hot and black. 'He worries too much,' she said to me.

'I never worried before in my life!' Verne's voice was harsh. 'Excuse me,' he said. 'Let's go in the other room and have a drink.'

'Haven't you been drinking too much, dear?' Petra said.

He ignored her.

The old lady was trying to carry a forkful of cole slaw to her mouth when she erupted into laughter. It sounded like dry leaves rustling against the basement windows of a house.

Verne stared at her. Petra glanced at Verne, then at me, and she smiled.

'Come on,' Verne said. He rose and started around the table. 'We'll have coffee in there.'

'Sure, fine.'

Petra watched me. We rose together and I couldn't tear my eyes away. Then I did and it was all right again. But the sense of panic, of the unknown, kept rising inside me.

Verne walked through an alcove into a small room, and on into the living room. I followed. Petra touched my arm. The lights went on in the living room, gleaming soft and slow and saffron, like a stage set. Verne called, 'You coming, Alex?'

'Yes.'

Petra leaned close and her breath was warm against my cheek. The faint odor of her perfume – was it jasmine? – mingled with her breath. 'Try to cheer him up, Alex,' she whispered. Only she didn't mean that.

It seemed as though she had spoken merely as an excuse to be near me, to touch me. My throat thickened and I couldn't speak. I nodded. For a brief moment, perhaps, we understood something between us. Then she sighed.

I went on into the living room.

Behind me the old lady commenced laughing again.

I knew I was going to have to cut the vacation short. It had to be. Maybe it was all right for some people, but not for me. I was born with a deadly conscience; something I detested, but something I couldn't override. If I made a mistake, it lived with me for a long while, and it was too much of a price to pay. Even a little mistake. I had long since avoided mental discomfort.

She was beautiful. Petra. My friend's wife. It was all I could think. My best friend's wife.

And there was Verne, leaning against the fireplace mantel, with his head in his hands.

'He's shot his bolt,' Petra said softly behind me. 'He's simply shot his bolt, the poor dear.'

I heard her quite plainly, but Verne didn't.

CHAPTER 3

AFTER TWO brandies I told myself I was a fool.

One thing I did know – it was true that Verne was deeply troubled about his business, but business hadn't marked him. It was something else. Petra? How?

'You'll have a good time, you two,' Verne said. He still stood by the fireplace. Petra sat directly across from me with her feet resting on an ottoman, ankles crossed. She watched me across the brim of her brandy glass. The old woman was perched like a stuffed bird on a chair in the corner.

'Sure we will,' I said.

Verne drained his glass, picked up the bottle, poured himself another, drained that, and set bottle and glass on the mantel. Petra's eyes followed his movements, then she began watching me again.

'Hell of a thing,' Verne said. 'Been asking you to come for years, and now you're here, I have to leave. Don't know how long I'll have to stay in town. I've only been coming home week ends.' He turned to the mantel and poured himself another drink.

I glanced toward Petra. She raised her glass, watching me, and emptied it.

'Wonder if I could have a little soda,' I said. 'Maybe brandy should be drunk straight, but I think perhaps I'd better have some soda.'

'I'll get it.' Petra left her chair and crossed the room. She had to pass my chair. My hand was over the arm of the chair, and as she swung by, her thigh brushed my knuckles. It could have been accidental. It was the merest contact. Yet I knew she'd meant to touch me. We were talking together by touch, by looking at each other. I was saying things to her against my will. I told myself again that I was a fool to think that way. Yet there it was.

All right. You say, laugh. But I didn't want it that way. Because something was wrong, dead wrong. It was in the house. In the way they spoke. In their actions. And already I was a part of it, without knowing anything about it.

There was a long silence. Then Petra returned. She had mixed me a drink, and as she handed it to me our fingers touched. She crossed the room, placed ice and a syphon on the coffee table. I glanced at the old woman in the corner. She was watching me.

Verne brooded at his empty glass, one arm sprawled across the fireplace mantel.

'Is it good?' Petra asked me with her back turned.

'Fine.' Her hips swelled beneath her dress, black again, but not the same one she'd met me at the door in. This one clung. Her back was bare to the waist. Her waist was slim, supple. She poured a drink of brandy into another glass she'd brought with her, went swiftly to the old woman, handed it to her.

'Thank you, darling,' the old woman said. It was the first time she'd said anything. Her voice was flat, dusty.

Verne's voice was low-pitched, but harsh. 'Damn it, you shouldn't have done that! I've told you.'

Petra faced him, brushed a heavy wave of black hair away from her cheek with her wrist. 'Don't be tiresome,' she said. 'The old girl doesn't have any fun these days. Let her have her little kick.'

Verne's face was red. The red deepened. He looked at me, tried to smile. I drank from my glass.

Petra settled in her chair again, flipped her feet onto the ottoman, and, glass in hand, watched me. It was nothing, perhaps. She didn't alter her expression; she didn't try to show her legs; she made no movement that wasn't entirely accepted and proper. But she said what she said, all the same. And I got it and I answered right back, because I couldn't help myself. I answered without speaking, just by looking at her. I answered, Yes, you're beautiful. But stop it, cut it out!

She smiled and sipped.

Verne said, 'I don't like to have Mother drink anything. It goes to her head. But if I reach for that glass now, she'll knock it down like a scared drunk.'

There wasn't anything to say.

'Wish you could see the job I'm working on,' he resumed. 'It sure is something – would have been. No, damn it! Will be!'

I grabbed at the straw. 'Maybe I could go in with you. Maybe we could – '

'No. Wouldn't hear of it. You're on vacation. Petra will take you around, show you the country. I've got a million things to do, Alex. Hell, it's a mess. I wanted to sit and talk. But either I go tomorrow morning, and try straightening things up, or I'm flattened.' He paused, gestured with his glass as I didn't look at Petra. He said, 'How's the new museum coming along?'

'It's all right. Coming along.'

'That's the trouble with you, Alex. You'll never get ahead. You'll go on from year to year, wasting your time. You won't get ahead because you're too damned honest.' He drank. 'Enough to make a man sick. Don't get me wrong, now. Just that in business today, you got to grab, you got to lie, you got to be there one jump ahead of the next guy. If you

20

aren't – ' He snapped his fingers. 'Like that. You want to get ahead, don't you?'

'Well – '

'Yeah, "well." What good is *well?* What good is a museum? What good is digging up bones all over the damned world? And now you've quit that to build a fool museum, and the man putting up the money must be a fool, too. Ye gods, Alex! Get into something hot!'

'Like you? You're into something hot, from what you say.'

'You're right. But listen, it *is* hot. No, damn it – it isn't. Not now. There's a war on. Damn it!' He drank.

Something bumped on the floor. We all looked. The old woman had dropped her glass. It rolled across the rug and onto the hardwood floor, *clink, clink, clink, clink. . . .*

'You're a sweet boy,' the old woman said. She was leaning awry in her chair and as drunk as a lord.

'I told you!' Verne snapped.

Petra didn't look at him. She smiled at me.

'Is she all right?' I asked.

'You're a sweet boy.'

I'd thought she was speaking to her son, Verne. But she was looking at me. There was a silly grin on her lips, and she nodded toward the right side of her chair, catching herself each time at the very instant of collapse.

'It hits her more quickly than it used to,' Petra said.

'He's a good man,' the old woman said. She pointed a quivering finger at me. 'Yes, you, sonny. Take care of yourself.' She went off into laughter. The dry leaves again, rustling against the side of a basement window, maybe with mice playing in the leaves.

'It's a vile thing!' Verne said. He faced Petra. His voice turned from ruggedness to pleading. 'Good Lord, don't you know she's an old woman? Don't you know the very smell of alcohol sends her balmy? You do know. You do it deliberately.'

21

'Oh, snap out of it,' Petra said. 'Stop and think. What's she got? Nothing. It won't hurt her. So she's drunk. So are you drunk.'

'Yes, but I – '

'It's no different.'

'You know damned well it's different.'

The old woman said, 'They're talking about me.' Only she didn't say it that clearly. It was thick, sickly, bad. 'But don't you worry,' she went on. 'I know what I know.'

Petra looked at her.

Verne said, 'Take her upstairs, will you?'

Petra rose, placed her glass on the coffee table. 'Will you excuse me?' she said, looking at me. She went over to the old lady. 'C'mon, Maw,' she said, 'let's go.'

The old woman couldn't stand. Her eyes were mere glinting slits, her mouth a tight clamp of chin to nose, and she kept saying over and over, 'I know what I know.'

As Petra half carried, half walked the old woman past me, she halted. 'Tell Mr. Bland good night.'

'Oh, God!' Verne said. Petra was shouting as loud as she could; shouting into the old woman's ear.

'Tell Mr. Bland good night.'

'Good night, Mr. Man,' Verne's mother said. 'I know what I know, but you're a good boy.' They reeled off into the hallway. I listened to them going up the stairs. The old woman was muttering.

'I'm sorry about this,' Verne said. 'Damn it. Seems like everything's going wrong. Naturally Petra doesn't like Mother. She says Mother's malicious, evil.' He ran his fingers through his hair and paced the room. 'I don't know, Alex. Sometimes I think I'd be better off dead.'

'Everything'll be all right.'

'Easy to say.'

'Don't let things get you down.'

He paused before me. I was trying to relax. My muscles

22

ached from being held rigid. It was like waiting patiently for some terrific explosion – waiting until the second of the explosion you know for certain will occur; then, no explosion. But it would come – it had to come.

Verne's mouth sagged at the corners. 'A bad evening. But you'll feel better tomorrow. Get Petra to take you for a drive around the lake. It'll do her good, too. Hell's fire, have some fun – somehow!' He strode to the mantel, poured himself a drink, drank it. His eyes were glassy, beneath heavy lids. I wanted to ask him what was wrong. Once I would have asked. Now there was something about Verne Lawrence that hadn't been there when I'd known him five years before. Some added something that prevented you from asking anything personal.

'Well, you have a beautiful wife,' I said. 'And a fine home. You have money socked away, I'll bet.'

'Yes.' Nothing more. Just 'Yes.'

'Look, Verne,' I said. 'I know something's bothering you. Everything's in an uproar. Why don't I go back to Chicago and you let me know when you get things ironed out?'

'No. Wouldn't hear of it. Never see you again. An evening like this is enough to scare anybody away.'

'I know you don't feel much like talking about the old days now.'

He looked straight at me, let his shoulders sag. 'Alex, I'm tired. I'm dead rotten dog-head tired. In the morning I've got to go into New York and start fires under a bunch of fat behinds. I stand to clear over two hundred thousand dollars if this thing goes through on time.'

'Why don't you get some sleep?' I hesitated, and the brandy talked. 'Maybe I *could* manage to stay over a couple of extra days. We could get together, drink some beer, go fishing. Might even get in some hunting. O.K.?'

'Alex, there's nothing in the world I'd rather do. Maybe

23

we can – maybe we can work out something. If I can just build hot enough fires.'

'This damn business – it's really got you down.'

'It's got me nuts.'

I looked at him and I knew it wasn't business at all. No. Verne was lying. He was afraid of something.

I heard movement in the doorway and turned. Petra stood there. Her left hand fussed with the waist of her dress. 'Well,' she said. 'The old girl's snoring fit to kill.' She looked sharply at her husband. 'Why, Verne! Do you know you're plastered?'

Then she looked at me and laughed.

CHAPTER 4

I SAT there on the edge of my bed with one shoe off. I took off the sock and wriggled my toes. It felt good, so I did the same with the other foot. Then I just sat there, wriggling my toes, contemplating my bare feet.

It had always been Verne's creed, I guess. From what I knew of him, anyway. And from what he'd told me of his early life, before the Army. Dig, dig, dig. Well, that much was all right. But he believed in elbowing the other guy out of the way. A little judicious lying got a fellow places. Be fast. Get in there and sock. Sock the other guy out of the way. Everything was business with Verne. There are millions of Vernes, and they don't honestly mean to hurt anyone, either.

He'd always kidded me about not wanting to do enough, go far enough ahead. Well, that was all right, too. Some of us don't. Some of us just want the satisfaction of an accomplished dream, enough money, a good home, and a loving wife.

Yes, wife. He was cutthroat about that, too. Find her – find the one that's right and marry her. She's got to have push and power, too. Yeah. Well, he'd sure made a discovery. Petra.

I finished undressing, flung all the windows up, and

climbed into the shower again. I got it just off cold and stood there with it blasting my back.

He'd socked his way out of a family of fifteen and finagled his way from a Nebraska farm to a possible two hundred thousand dollars. With God only knows how much in the bank now. Only maybe he'd used that. Could be. He'd gamble, too. Anything. All the way.

Petra of the long black hair . . .

I shoved my face into the needles of water with my eyes closed. When I tipped my head, it sounded like rain on a roof. Tin roof, maybe.

Well, I wasn't going to get snarled up in his mess. The museum looked good from here and it looked good from the museum, too. And Madge looked good. Now, take Madge and Petra.

I stood there. Then I turned off the water. I found a heavy towel and tried to rub myself pink like they say in the magazines. No luck. Never did have. I padded into the bedroom, finished unpacking my suitcases, and looked at the new pair of pajamas I'd bought special for my vacation.

Hell, I always sleep in the raw. I wasn't going to stop now. I tossed the pajamas on the bureau and sat down at the desk.

Take Madge and Petra, for instance.

Well, I loved Madge. We were going to be married. Chicago was a long way off. Seven hundred miles? Nearly.

I closed my eyes and saw the red taillight of the taxi winking around the corner.

Take Madge. I had, twice. Take Petra. . . .

I slammed my fist on the desk. The blotter moved, and there was the letter I'd written Madge earlier in the evening. I ripped the envelope open and read the letter. Then I went and got my pen and wrote a postscript. I wrote four lines about how nice it was here, addressed another envelope, sealed up the letter, andstuck it beneath the blotter.

His old man couldn't even write, Verne had told me. He

died standing between the handles of a plow. The horse was so old it didn't even move when the buzzards came. That's the way they found him. Standing upright between the plow handles, leaning back against the reins. There was a buzzard on each shoulder, plucking at his ears.

Verne said his mother found his old man like that. She shooed the birds away, unhitched the plow, loaded his father on the horse. When she got the body back to the house she dug a grave. Then she waited till the kids got home from school and she read from the Bible. Verne said he threw the first shovelful of dirt. It landed on his father's face. It made him so mad he walked off the farm in his bare feet and hopped a freight into St. Louis. He never went home again.

'Don't you ever wonder how they made out?' I asked him.

'Yes,' he said. 'Yes, Alex. Sometimes I do wonder.'

I went over and turned off the bedroom light. There was a moon. I stood at the open window, the side window. This autumn was still in the hands of the Indians.

Petra of the hot dark eyes. . . .

Another man's wife.

Why in all hell did I have to be born with a conscience?

So, then, maybe I was a fool all the way. I began to wonder. Maybe I was overtired. Imagining things. She probably hadn't meant a thing. I'd read what I'd wanted to read. Maybe it was me, not Petra.

Only none of this did any good. I could still feel it and the house was quiet. I went over and locked the door, like Jenny said. In my friend's home? I unlocked the door, and went to bed.

What was the matter with Verne? What kind of beast was gnawing at the already frayed edges of his being? What was eating away at him? He looked like an old oil painting that someone had carelessly spilled a small amount of acid on. It eroded and bit and gnawed away, making small traceries of lines, curlicues. . . .

27

The house was very still. Night and moonlight sighed in the windows, billowing the curtains. Somebody walked quietly down the hall. Whoever it was wasn't tiptoeing, wasn't trying to be especially quiet. But the footsteps paused at my door.

Then they went on down the hall. I realized I'd been holding my breath. I got out of bed and opened the door.

I'd recognize that perfume anywhere.

Plenty was wrong, cockeyed wrong. I had to get back to Chicago.

I went back to bed. The footsteps came back along the hall and paused at my door again. I held my breath again. She waited longer this time. Then she went on.

Chicago. Chicago. It was like the wild beating of surf against rocks. *Chi-ca-go . . . Chi-ca-go. . . .*

My door opened. 'Is everything all right, Alex?'

'Yes. Fine.'

'Just wanted to make sure.' Her voice was a whisper. She closed the door very quietly. Some of the perfume remained in the room.

CHAPTER 5

'VERNE? OH, he's gone long ago. I drove him into town at six-thirty. He caught the seven-o'clock train for New York.'

We were alone in the large kitchen. Petra was seated on a high stool at the lunch bar, drinking coffee. The red shorts and halter she wore were very tight and her skin was very white. Creamy, because it was not a sickly white. It was lush, warm, solid. I noticed how long, how perfectly formed her legs were. Her lips were dark red in daylight, and she looked fresh, wide-awake. In the bright morning, there were traces of midnight in her hair. It foamed about her shoulders, seemed so full of life I expected it to sparkle. It did, when she moved.

She sipped coffee. 'Verne said to tell you again that he was sorry he couldn't stay. He felt real bad about it.'

I wasn't really awake yet. I was in that blank, staring stage.

'Did you sleep well?'

'Fine, Petra.'

'Reason I asked, strange bed and all that, y'know?'

'Slept perfect.'

'Hope I didn't disturb you when I opened your door.' She wasn't looking at me. She rose, swung over to the electric range, took up the coffeepot, poured herself another cup, returned to the stool. All the time, I couldn't keep my eyes

29

off her. Like a magnet, a deadly magnet, even when I tried not to watch.

'You didn't disturb me.' I was tardy with that. She drank her coffee black. I suddenly had a strong desire to touch her hair. 'What's for breakfast?'

She smiled. 'I was waiting for you to ask that. Cook's day off.' Her eyes were black. Jet black.

'Oh?'

'But I can cook, my friend.'

Ten minutes later I was at the kitchen table eating scrambled eggs, country sausage, toast, and coffee. I'd managed to avoid the stool beside her at the lunch bar by saying I liked my feet on the floor when I ate. But it only made matters worse, because she was above me, looking down. She was perched on the stool, her legs crossed, leaning back against the bar, with a cup in her hand. Her breasts filled that red halter like nothing I'd ever seen before.

The food was perfect. The kitchen was as neat as a pin.

'Where's Jenny?' I asked.

'Gave her the day off.'

'And Verne's mother?'

She glanced at me and chuckled. 'Not up yet.' She drank some more coffee. 'We're all alone. Just you and me. But not for long. The old girl will be down shortly.'

I managed a weak grin. She grinned back.

'How long has Verne's mother been with you?'

'Ever since we were married, right after Verne left the Army.'

I finished off the last of the sausage. Petra poured me another cup of coffee, returned to her stool. I tried to imagine that old woman unhitching a plow, digging a grave, reading from a Bible. 'What happened to the rest of Verne's family? I mean, couldn't she sort of shuttle around? It'd make it easier.'

She stared at me, thinking. 'There were two sisters. The

rest were brothers. Two killed in the war. One sister
vanished. The other married, but doesn't want the dear old
girl around. Husband won't have it. One brother's in the
penitentiary for arson. Verne says he was a pyromaniac, a
fire bug, but nobody'd believe it.' She lifted her hands, let
them drop loosely to her thigh. 'Others just gone.' Petra
motioned her thumb toward the ceiling. 'She sold the farm,
Verne discovered. Then one morning the people who bought
it found her sitting against a fence in the cornfield, and they
contacted him. He took her in.' She shrugged.

Neither of us said anything for a few moments.

'Alex.'

'Yes?'

'You'll never know how glad I am to see you.' She got off
the stool, stepped over to the table, and leaned against it with
the front of her thighs. The table came to just below the rim
of her red shorts. She laid her palms flat on the table top, then
slowly moved them together until they touched. I smelled that
perfume and my heart rocked.

'Wonder how the coffee's holding out,' I said.

'Plenty where that came from.' She moved away. 'I'll heat
it up.' Her back was to me. 'Alex.'

'Yes?'

'Did you hear what I said?'

'Yes.'

She whirled, shouted, 'Good morning, Mother!'

The old woman entered the kitchen. She carried a cane.
She said, 'Good morning, Mr. Bland.'

'She'll never say good morning to me,' Petra said. 'She's
a witch. I wish to God – ' She stopped, went and looked out
one of the rear kitchen windows with her hands clenched
before her. I couldn't see her face. Her voice was low, throaty.
'She must be a hundred years old.'

Verne's mother staggered in a meandering line over to the
breakfast nook at the far side of the kitchen. She wore the

same gray dress, I thought at first. Then I saw it was fresh, unwrinkled. A different one of the same style and color. Her white shawl. On her feet were carpet slippers that folded out at her ankles. The only sound as she walked was a faint shuffle and the light rap of the cane.

'Petra, I'm hungry.' The old woman's voice was full of wavers; it trembled and it was very faint. 'I'll just have a little tea. Some soda crackers in milk.'

Petra watched her without expression.

'Warm the milk.'

I said, 'Petra, d'you get a paper?'

'It's on the front porch. I didn't bring it in yet.' As she looked at me, her eyes spoke, trying to say something. 'Go look around, Alex. I'll be with you in a few minutes.'

As I left the kitchen I heard the old woman say, 'Bet you gave Jenny the day off.'

'Shut up!' Petra said. But she didn't say it loud enough for Verne's mother to hear.

I found the paper and settled down in what looked like Verne's study, across the hall from the living room. He had a large desk, so I sat there and spread the paper out on the desk. The books in the bookcases looked somehow too neatly arranged to have been read lately.

I wondered what spot on the wall Verne beat his head against after he'd locked the door.

Beyond large windows, autumn was violent with color. A red maple stood close beside the study and its leaves looked as if they had been sprayed with blood. I tried to read the paper. It was no go.

The desk was clear save for a large, unstained blotter, a single pencil, and a framed picture lying face down. I looked at the picture and it was of Petra. A full-length shot. She was lying in a hammock, with one leg dangling, her hands behind her head. Without thinking, without realizing it for a moment, I suddenly knew I wanted the picture. She smiled

32

out at me. I had to have the picture. It was a strong, abrupt desire, and for an instant conscience, will, everything vanished. Then I laid it carefully face down again and stepped away from the desk.

'Did you like it, Alex?'

I whirled. Petra was standing in the door, leaning against the jamb. She held her arms up, tying a white ribbon around her hair, so it bunched at the back of her head.

'Yes. It's a fine shot of you.'

'Verne took it. The hammock's still there, too. Only nobody uses it any more. It stayed out there all last winter. It's faded now, but it used to be very bright.'

'I'm afraid the hammock doesn't count much in that picture.'

She knew what I meant, but she said, 'How do you mean?'

I smiled and she smiled. Her hair looked fine tied up that way and we stood that way staring at each other for a long moment.

I heard nothing, but I saw the listening in Petra's eyes. She turned slowly. The old woman's voice reached me thinly from the hall. 'That milk was sour, Petra. I don't like sour milk.'

'She spies,' Petra said. 'Oh, God, Alex. She's a witch.'

As she moved out into the hall, I noticed for the first time that she wore a red wrap-around skirt over her shorts. It swung at the hem, pendulous, as she strode off.

I went over to the desk and looked at the picture again. I had an overpowering desire to steal it, but I laid it back down on the desk and left the room quickly.

The hallway was dim. Madge Collins. A nice name. Chicago. Madge had blonde hair, dark blonde hair. Her eyes sometimes were blue, sometimes gray. Slim, she was always neat, crisp, quick-moving. She had thousands of sisters, in all parts of the world. Lined up, they would possibly be hard to tell apart. But she was mine and I wanted her always to be mine. Because I knew the woman beneath the crisp exterior. I remembered the letter I'd written to her, and headed for the stairs.

Petra. She stood alone. There was nobody like Petra. One image was made, then the gods shattered the cast. Why?

Halfway up the stairs, I glanced at my watch. Ten-thirty. I wanted a drink. Well, I was on a vacation, so why shouldn't I have a drink if I wanted one? I'd intended to see about mailing the letter to Madge. It could wait. I went back downstairs into Verne's study, because I'd remembered seeing a decanter of whisky on a shelf beside one of the bookcases.

There was no glass. For the first time since I'd left the Army, I drank straight from a bottle. It warmed me and I felt better. Some of the panic that had started growing with morning subsided.

The picture was not on the desk.

My hand shook as I replaced the glass stopper in the decanter and returned it to the shelf. Verne's study was directly beneath my bedroom. Somebody was moving around up there.

Now that I'd drunk the straight whisky, I wanted some water. There was another door in the study. I went over and opened it, expecting a closet. Beyond was a music room, with a baby-grand piano, a large leather couch, a record-player, and a case stacked with records. There was one window hung with crisp white curtains. The air was stale. I opened the window and autumn breathed on me. It was like summer, only the smell was autumn and blue skies and beyond the edge of an apple orchard colorfully splotched hills rose to a sharp horizon. There was dust on the window sill.

Dust powdered against my fingers when I touched the piano keys. The record-player had been shut off halfway through a now dusty record, the arm and needle somehow evocative of a contented past abruptly severed. The record was Debussy's Arabesque Number 1 in E Major. That was

not Verne. It might once have been Petra; it might still be.
Yes. It was possible. It was not haphazard selection; not with
the library of records in this room.

I went on through the door leading from the music room.
A small alcove with a small couch in it led into the main
hallway beneath the stairs. I felt myself wishing my own
record collection was one tenth as large as the one in this
house. I knew I was trying to force my thoughts into other
channels – anything so I would not think of that woman.

It was all foolishness. Less than a day ago I would have
laughed at anyone who had said he felt as I did.

Once, when I was very young, I had wanted to play the
piano; wanted to learn how very much. I saved money and
took lessons. But I knew my folks wouldn't hear of such a
thing. As I accomplished each lesson and sought out pianos
to play on – because we didn't have one – I knew eventually
I'd be found out. It would end. Something would happen.

That's how I felt now, only much worse, much more
strongly. It had been the same when I tried to paint.
I painted anyway, but my family talked me out of that, too.
Consequently, I never learned to do anything I really wanted
to do. Because I thought there was nothing left. And then it
was too late; I felt it was too late. My father died and
surprised me by leaving me some money. I'd always had a
slight interest in old relics and Indian mounds, so I went and
studied archaeology. It was, I decided at first, my way of
escaping the knowledge that I had failed to do what I wanted.
By taking an opposite. Picks, shovels, brushes, maps, mules,
bones, and rusty iron. But I had fun, too, and then I had my
dream about the museum and now that was my life. So I
had really found what I really wanted.

As I started up the stairs again, Petra called to me as she
came along the hall. 'Alex. Come on. We'll take a ride.' She
paused, smiling, and her knee parted the slit in her red skirt.

35

She was wearing red sandals. She painted neither her toenails nor her fingernails.

'I'd like to mail a letter,' I said.

'Yes. Well, we'll ride into town, how's that? Have to take the old gal along. Hope you don't mind.'

'Sure.' I could feel myself relax.

'Yes. Then we'll come back here and eat. I'd like to show you around. Tomorrow we'll go to the lake.'

'Be right with you.' I hurried upstairs and into my room to get Madge's letter from beneath the blotter.

The picture of Petra lay face up on the center of the desk. Something tense and slow tightened inside my chest, like black thread slowly winding on a spool.

I got the letter to Madge, found my pipe and tobacco pouch, and went on downstairs.

Petra and the old lady waited in the hall. 'Ready?' Petra asked.

'Yes,' I told her. 'I'm ready.'

The old woman watched Petra, and her eyes glowed in the daytime just as they did at night.

CHAPTER 6

WE DROVE between hills through autumn. Petra had insisted that I sit in front with her. Verne's mother was perched in the middle of the back seat. Twice I looked around at her expressionless yet sly face. I wanted to mention the picture. Several times I nearly did, but I couldn't, quite, I felt she knew. It was a large car, black, a Buick. Petra drove at a steady sixty.

'We couldn't talk so well with her up here, you see?'

'I guess that's right. If she doesn't mind.'

'She put up a fuss. But what the hell?' She glanced at me. Each time she moved her right leg, the skirt parted a bit more. I avoided looking toward her, but I felt compelled to.

'It's so nice to ride,' Verne's mother said. 'We take one every day, hey, Petra?' The laugh. The dry rustling of leaves with chipmunks or mice skittering among them. 'Hey, Petra?'

'Yes!' Petra shouted. She was biting her lip and the car's speed increased. Then we were in the small town of Allayne. A long, elm-shrouded main street. The business section was about four or five blocks long. We went to the post office and I mailed the letter to Madge. Allayne seemed a quiet, peaceful town. There was a courthouse with a silver dome and the sun gleamed on it. The clock on the city hall read eleven-thirty as we headed back out of town.

'Wonder how Verne's making out,' I said.

'Don't bother,' Petra said. 'I mean, don't trouble yourself about him. You're on a vacation, remember? Verne's had bad luck. He'll have to work it out himself.'

'I wish there were something I could do.'

'There's nothing. There's the lake, over there – see?' She nodded toward the left. A faint patch of blue water showed momentarily between two hills, like a sliver of glass. 'We'll go there tomorrow. We'll have to take her with us.' The car's speed increased.

'Probably her only pleasure.'

'No, Alex. Her pleasure is spying on me. She follows me around. She hates me.'

'Why?'

'I don't know why. She's bad, evil, Alex. I wish to God she'd die – die!'

'She will,' I said.

'Now, though, now.'

'She's just a harmless old woman, Petra. Sometimes old people become dominant, like that.' I wasn't saying exactly what I meant. I wasn't saying that I wanted to reach out and touch her hair. . . .

'She's vicious. I'm a nurse, that's all, a nurse. Left out here with that harridan.' She laughed and we didn't speak again until she parked the car behind the house by the garage. Then she said, 'You'll see what I mean about her. You can't help but see.'

We both helped the old woman out of the car. Petra leaned close to me with her arm outstretched, and for one long moment her right breast pressed full, round, and hard against my arm. At the instant of contact she looked straight at me and her eyes said, Yes, yes, yes!

I turned, went into the house. I wanted to run. I went into the study and had a drink and closed my eyes and saw the red taillight of the taxi winking around the corner.

'She saw that.'

I turned. Standing in the doorway, Petra watched me.
'Who saw what?'

'Mother. She saw that at the car.' Her eyes were bold.
She was too bold, yet at the same time oversecretive. All
wrong. 'You'll see now,' she went on. 'There'll be no rest.'

'I don't know what you mean,' I lied. She was making
something out of nothing.

'Yes. We touched and she saw it.'

'Oh, that. It was – '

She smiled. 'You *do* know, don't you? I was beginning to
think you were immune.' She unhooked her red skirt, ripped
it off savagely. 'It's too hot for this. Yes, you know, and she
saw it all. She's got eyes like a cat. There'll be trouble now.'

'But, Petra!'

'You don't know her, I tell you. She makes mountains out
of molehills.'

'Aren't you doing just that, Petra?'

She dampened her lips with her tongue, shook her head
slowly. 'I'm afraid not, Alex.' Turning, she vanished from
the study doorway. I heard her walking down the hall.

. . . and Alex, it's almost like writing to a lover. Because
I have no lover, you see. But then, I shouldn't talk like
that, should I? Verne says you embarrass easily.

. . . feel lonely? I mean, among trees, like, when even
others are around? Chicago can't be lonely, though, can
it? Funny you aren't married. Verne says you're quite a
guy with the gals! That why? I mean, I'll bet you have
some time!

. . . mind my writing so often? It's really nice here, but
it's rather quiet, though I like the quiet. There's a big
old apple orchard behind the house where I walk. Let
you in on a secret, Alex. I talk to you there. I mean, you

know what I mean. Verne isn't much for talking – much for doing some of the things I like to do. We do wish you'd come, Alex.

And that afternoon I saw the apple orchard.

'Take my hand.'

'What?'

'Take my hand, I say.'

Her fingers were tense, her palm slightly damp, warm.

'We'll cross the creek here, on these stones. We can both go at once. Come on, Alex.'

It was a small creek, twisting below a knoll at the edge of the orchard. Beyond was a grassy knoll sparse with hickory trees and, from where we stood, three pines.

'I thought you wanted to show me the orchard.'

'Come on, Alex. Cross the creek.'

We did. Twice our bodies brushed.

We started through the trees over the knoll. There were more pines and a large sycamore.

'We'll go on the other side of that knoll,' she said. There was something abrupt, terse, in the tone of her voice. 'It's cooler there. See? It's cooler already. A breeze comes down off the hills. Always that way. Hurry.'

'But Petra – '

She didn't release my hand. We reached the top of the knoll. From where we stood the house only showed in red-bricked tiny patches of distance between trees. It was cool and shady, which was good, because the afternoon sun was very hot as it sometimes is in Indian summer.

We paused and she turned to me and said, 'Kiss me, Alex.' Her hair streamed to one side of her head, thick and full of vagrant sunlight. Her lips glistened, her eyes were molten black.

'Petra . . .'

'Please, Alex. Don't wait now. Talk later, if you must, but

kiss me. Don't lie. You want to and I want you to. Don't wait, I couldn't bear that now, Alex!'

'Petra!'

She rushed against me. I stepped back, but I was against the trunk of the sycamore. She pressed against me, her hands moving slowly along my throat, her head flung far back, eyes wide, lips parted.

'Alex!'

Her lips were all-yielding, her body strained, tense, hot with nervousness; her fingers bit into my shoulders. I felt the moving curve of her back and the whole vibrant length of her as my mouth closed over hers.

Then I had her against the tree. Her mouth slid away from mine along my cheek as she pushed away from me, her hands pushing against my chest, and she moaned.

I stepped back. 'Petra, good Lord!'

She watched me, leaning back against the trunk of the tree. Her lips were parted as she breathed, her eyes heavy-lidded. Her hands lay on either side of her against the tree trunk, trembling. 'It's as I thought,' she said. 'Just as I thought. As I knew it would be.'

I should have struck her then. I should have struck her and run. Because the fuse was lit now – the long hot fuse that would blow me straight to hell.

CHAPTER 7

SHE DID not move from against the trunk of the sycamore. My own breathing was as sharp as hers. 'Petra,' I said. 'Why? What happened to you?'

'It was the waiting, I guess. That's all.'

'The waiting?' She was making too much of a kiss. But perhaps I was, too.

'Yes, the waiting. We both wanted that, we both want more. It's been silly to waste so much time. Time is too precious.'

'But you're Verne's wife.'

'Yes. Verne often said you were his best friend, maybe the only real friend he ever had. Because you disregarded things other men wouldn't put up with. So he never had any real friend, other than you. I'm his wife, yes. But you and me – that's something different again.'

'Then why did you push me away?'

'Because – not all at once.'

'Petra, this means I'll have to leave. It couldn't possibly go on.'

She laughed. Shortly. Then she threw her head back and laughed still harder. She sobered. 'You won't go, Alex. I won't let you.'

'Petra – '

42

'You wanted that. You want more – you want me, and you know it. Why be childish?'

We stared at each other. The sharp shadows of leaves lay across her bare legs, her red halter and shorts, her arms, and sunlight still sought and found her hair.

'You're very bold.'

'Am I? Listen, Alex. I've felt like this for over two years and you tell me I'm bold. Why did you come here? To play checkers with that shell of a man? With what actually never was, never will be? He's shot, Verne is.' She smiled. 'Don't tell me that. You read my letters, you aren't blind.'

She stepped up to me and took my hand, lifted it, laid my palm in her hair. My fingers clutched instinctively, but I jerked my hand away.

'There,' she said. 'You wanted that, didn't you?'

'Petra. That picture. Why did you put that picture on the desk in my room?'

'Because you wanted that, too.' She moved closer to me, stared at me, and the faint, elusive odor of her perfume recalled three years of jasmine-scented mail. 'I watched you,' she said. 'You ate it up with your eyes, Alex. It was all you could do to put that picture of me down on the desk – where Verne laid it face down after he picked it up from the floor, where he'd thrown it.' She paused. 'You know,' she said, glancing away, 'I think you really wanted to steal it.'

I grabbed her wrist and she chuckled. 'Really, Alex. I mean that. You were like a small boy all alone in a candy store.'

I flung her arm down, turned, and started down the knoll toward the creek.

'Wait!'

I waited. She reached me. 'Admit it.'

'I won't admit anything.'

'Verne told me about you – about how honest you are, to the point of mania, almost. All right, you're like that. You're

43

too serious and you're overhonest. Then you're probably being tortured right now. You admit it!'

I hit her. Across the face with the back of my hand. She moved with the blow like a boxer. I hit her again, the heel of my hand bouncing off her cheek.

'Yes,' she said. 'I was right. Do you see now why it was silly to wait? I was going to wait. Take my time. Because I didn't want to frighten you off. Verne being your friend, and all that rot. Go ahead, hit me again. It won't change anything.'

'Only one day,' I said.

'No. That's just it, Alex. It isn't one day. It's over three years. Two years, anyway, and that's long enough. Too long.' Something came into her eyes, something like tears, only they couldn't be tears, and she walked rapidly away down the knoll.

I watched her cross the creek, then I crossed. She didn't wait for me until she was nearly through the orchard. Then she waited and we walked through the ankle-deep grass together.

'Will you take my hand again?' she said softly.

'No. I won't take your hand. Now or ever.'

She looked at me and smiled. 'O.K. Straighten out now, Alex. I told you she had eyes like a cat. We're in sight of the house.'

I closed and locked the door to my room and sat on the bed. I could still taste her lips, feel them, tremulous, surrendering, and offering and giving all at the same time.

But this wasn't all of it. I felt this wasn't all. A kiss – a mere single afternoon kiss. Nothing more?

God, yes. Too much more always. The all-impending more that lay even beyond imagination.

As I stripped my clothes off, I realized I was soaked with perspiration. And I knew with a sensation of conscious guilt that the only reason I hadn't taken Petra out there this afternoon was because she was Verne's wife. I had wanted her, I wanted her now.

I had come that close to taking her – beneath the sycamore, on the knoll.

It was bad enough now. I had to leave. I couldn't stay on, not with that. . . . And yet, she pushed me away from her.

'Because – not all at once.'

I went in and took a shower and shaved and came back to the bedroom. I dressed. I put on a pair of crepe-soled shoes, the same gray flannels, and a clean white shirt. I looked through my shirts. They were all white. I wasn't a very colorful fellow. Just a guy who had damn near attacked his best friend's wife. No, not attacked. It wouldn't have been that. Or would it?

I was combing my hair when somebody knocked at the door. I opened the door.

'Hello, Alex. This came for you. It was in the mailbox. I guess nobody looked this morning.'

It was from Madge. In a white envelope. There was no perfume. Only a faint trace of powder, and a very faint smudge of lipstick where she had dampened the flap with her tongue.

I felt her hand on my arm.

'Don't,' I said.

'All right.' Her hand went away. She wore a white dress and it fitted like a white glove. With the black of her hair and eyes, and the dark red of her lips, and everything, she was a very beautiful woman.

'I'm sorry I hit you.'

'It's all right. Only swollen a little. See?'

'I don't want to see.'

'All right.'

'But I'm sorry. I shouldn't have done it.'

'You were talking to me that way, that's all. It was the only way you could tell me without committing yourself by voice.'

45

'Look out, or I'll hit you again.' I didn't smile and neither did she. We looked at each other, then I looked down at the envelope in my hand. I tapped it against my other hand.

'So her name's Madge?'

'Yes.'

'How nice. Is it too bad you had to meet me?'

'No. It's not too bad.'

'You're still trying not to admit it.'

'I'm not trying not to do anything.'

She smiled now and she was a bold, beautiful woman.

'I'll have to leave,' I said. 'I'm trying to be honest.'

'You don't have to try, darling.'

'Don't call me that. I mean it. I'd better leave now, tonight.' I really meant it. Just holding the letter from Madge was enough, and with Verne, too. 'Verne is my friend,' I said. 'I know you don't understand. I don't ask you to. I wouldn't have understood myself once. But I do now. Maybe it's wrong, but it's how I feel.'

'You have the most peculiar way of admitting things.'

'I told you I wasn't admitting anything.'

'Well, for the very reason that Verne is your friend — for the very reason that you two went through a war together, and saved each other's lives, and all that — that's why you can't leave, Alex.'

'Can't I?'

'No. Don't be thick as well as honest, damn you!' She wiped her palms on her hips, then pushed her hair back. When she released her hair, it flowed around her shoulders like black smoke. Something was happening inside me; something I couldn't control.

'What do you mean, "thick"?'

'What would Verne think if you left now? What would that old witch tell him? He's suspicious, Alex, as it is. He's kept me cooped up here. I've never been able to go anyplace. If

46

you left now, he'd know. How would you feel then? Your bloody conscience would knock you dead.'

She kept jamming that knife home. But all the time, I knew it wasn't that alone. I knew there was something else. But she was right about Verne – what he might think about us.

I said, 'I told Verne I should go back home.'

'But he said not to, didn't he?'

'You're crazy to try something like this.'

'I'm not trying anything. It's there, that's all.'

'What's the matter with Verne?'

'His business has got him down. He's knocked himself out. Listen, you don't know what I've been through. I'm watched by that old woman. Watched all the time. I never see anybody. I'm all alone in this lousy house with that crawling old woman!'

'Take it easy. Why don't you go out?'

'Because Verne says I have to be with her.' She placed both palms against the sides of her face and sucked in her cheeks. Her voice was very low; she was obviously keeping it under control with effort. 'Wherever I go, whatever I do, have done, for years, she's with me. I'll go mad, Alex. Oh, God, I'll go mad!'

'You must have done something to –'

Petra turned. The old woman was slowly climbing the stairs. Just the top of her head showed, ascending into our line of vision with an almost awesome slowness.

'Quick,' Petra said. 'Close the door. And for God's sake, forget about leaving!' She went off down the hall. I closed the door on her perfume, but some of it oozed in with me. A funny thing. She wore so little of it that if you tried to smell it, you couldn't. Yet it was always there, faint, elusive.

So now we were both hiding from the old woman.

I ripped open Madge's letter. There were two blank sheets

47

of paper. No. At the bottom of the second sheet in very small handwriting she had written:

Dearest Alex,
    Fill these pages in with all the things you'd like to have me say and write often. I will, too.
                                        All my love,
                                        MADGE

Great. The one time I needed every word she could possibly send and she played jokes. But I knew the letter had been mailed probably at the same time I left Chicago. It was just her way of saying, 'Have a good time.'

And she would write every day. So if I left now, letters would start arriving and keep arriving for three days after I reached Chicago. Probably. And Petra would read them. And Petra might reply to Madge. Yes, the return address was on the envelope. So there I was figuring myself into a mess, as usual.

I went over to the desk and wrote a two-page lie to Madge about how wonderful everything was and how grand she was, sealed it in an envelope, and stuck it under the blotter.

All the time I'd been writing the letter, Petra smiled at me from the hammock with her leg dangling.

She was right about Verne. If he'd been the way she said, then he'd be certain something had happened if I left now.

I went over and stood by the front window at the corner of the house and looked at the failing afternoon. It still wasn't late. A truck went by with some crates of chickens rattling in the back. Then two girls rode by on bicycles with one of them waving her hand and talking loudly. Then two closed cars went by. Then there was a roar and a hot rod fogged past and leaves rushed in wild eddies on the black-top road. As this last one faded away, the countryside seemed unduly quiet, like the sudden stillness after an explosion. The sky was clear and then somebody fired a rifle. The sound rattled around for a few seconds among the hills, then vanished.

I couldn't leave now. Outside, the red maple was very bloody.

All right, then why did Verne act like that, what had she done?

Cut it out, I told myself. All the excuses keep popping up and all of them are the ones you want because they'll make you stay. You want to go but you want to stay. You know it's not the right thing, but you make excuses so it *will* be the right thing. Then when it's all right, you'll believe it and your conscience will almost believe it. But not quite.

I put my hands on the window sill and leaned my forehead against the wooden bottom of the open window. It rattled slightly but it was cool and the pressure was good.

Once many years ago – many years as the leaves are crisped by time and the price of butter rises and other wars lurk in global focus – once many years ago, in a town in France, there were two men. Verne and Alex. The town was Argentan, wasn't it?

Yes. We had stumbled across this bomb-shattered hospital while other bombs burst beyond and around. We were tired of it. There had been nuns there attending the wounded, I could still see all the black cloth and white and the beads. Bloody bandages and a table piled with arms and legs and things and knives and odors. But one ward hadn't been ruined; it had two walls and part of a ceiling and some iron cots in a double row. The syphilitic ward, it was. Because we were tired, the beds looked good at the time.

Only we didn't stay there long, as it kept coming to us what the room had been, was. And whether or not the odor was, it seemed to be that, and so you didn't want to stay there long even if you could hardly walk for being tired.

Verne called as he ran into the ward where I had fallen alseep, 'Roll out, man. C'mon. I struck oil!'

So I dragged myself out of the ward and down the stairs, where I just missed stepping on a hand, and around back of the remains of the hospital.

'Through here,' Verne said. He climbed through a shell hole in the side of the building and dropped out of sight into blackness. I walked around and into the cellar door, down a dirt embankment, and found him sitting in mud, drinking from his helmet.

'They missed this one,' he said. 'They shot the others full of holes, but they missed this one.'

There were about eight of them. Barrels that held thousands of gallons. The mud was wine mud, ankle-deep. As he said, they had missed one barrel. Some of the wine was still coming from a couple of the broken barrels, so it hadn't been long ago.

I turned the spigot and filled my canteen cup. It was good wine and I said, 'This will hold us for a time.' We drank heartily.

It was red wine. We tried to figure out how they got the barrels down there, but gave up. Either they built the hospital without a wall, then brought in the barrels and sealed the wall, or they dug a cellar, placed the barrels in, and built a hospital around them.

'It's better than an emergency dynamo in case the lights fail,' Verne said.

'Yes. There'd be no need for lights.'

'Hell. I'm rubbing it in my hair, see? Imagine!'

'Very wasteful.'

'I suppose you're right.'

It was red wine and it was aged just right.

'Maybe they left this one barrel for a reason,' I said, taking a long drink from the cup. My cup was a plastic one so the wine didn't taste bad. It wouldn't have tasted bad anyway.

We looked at each other. 'You mean,' Verne said, 'maybe they put something into it, like Borgia?'

'Thou wert once too august for adoration,' I quoted.

I refilled my cup and Verne drank from his helmet.

We mused above the wine. It was an aromatic drinking place. After a while we were drunk. We were brothers. Sharing was wonderful.

'We share the wine,' Verne said. 'If I have a wife, we'll share her, too. Do you have a wife, Alex?'

'No.'

'Well, we'll share her, won't we?'

'Certainly. Are many wives better than one?'

'I think one wife is best.'

'One at a time.'

'Yes.'

'On a share basis.'

A piece of the hospital that we couldn't see went away with a loud noise and the empty barrels rocked. Plaster and dust fell into my cup. Verne dumped his helmetful over his feet and refilled the helmet from the wooden spigot. He couldn't stand very well. Whenever he got really drunk he fell all the time. It was bad when there was snow on the ground. Once I saw him crawl on his hands and knees for quite a distance along the Champs Elysées. He said the air felt cold, and since it was raining he'd take no chances.

We had been through a long war and there was still more to come and we were tired and drunk and we were brothers.

'You'll see,' Verne said. 'I will marry a beautiful wife. You'll visit with me and she will warm your bed.'

'Thank you, brother,' I said.

But he hadn't meant that, really. And he hadn't remembered, and here I was. I glanced over at the picture of Petra in the hammock on the desk.

How very much Verne had changed! He wasn't the same man now. Something terrible had happened to him. I didn't know him at all as he was now.

She smiled out at me from the hammock with her leg

51

dangling. I went over and turned the picture face down. Then I went out into the hall.

I walked around the stair well and down the upstairs hall toward a door at the far front of the house. This room would be opposite mine, but where my door opened just beyond the top of the stairs, this one opened next to the end of the hall. The door was open.

It was a large room, and the moment I hesitated by the door, I knew whose room it was. Hers. The perfume, among other intangibles, told me. Excitement and panic both crowded my chest. It was a feeling I had never experienced before. The room was empty. She wasn't there. I didn't want to enter, I forced myself against it. It seemed, as I stepped inside, that I was invading the privacy of her flesh itself. Everything in that room read Petra. To the left, along the whole front wall of the house, were huge windows, reaching from ceiling to floor, casement windows. They were screened on the outside, and their inside surface was hung with draped curtains of peculiar red-and-black color conglomerate. The walls were a deep shade of red-violet, the ceiling a rich, allusive midnight conventionalized by neither stars nor moon. A large room, made to order – ordered by a woman laden with sensuality.

I stared down at the rug's thick nap. It snuggled against the baseboards of all four walls, a heady, unbelievable auburn glinting in errant light like the coat of a freshly slain animal.

I was drawn into the room as I was being drawn to Petra. It was like standing in a vacuum that had become feverish, the airless air writhing against itself in a kind of savage, futile bewilderment, like two newly awakened lovers in the dark.

The bed was large, half again normal size, with thick brown leather headboard and footboard, the spread of the same deep red-violet as the walls. All the furnishings – a table, a desk, three chairs, a small couch to the right of the door, and an immense dressing table – were of the same glowing brown leather. Not masculine, either; feminine. Delicate and heady, like the fine-beaded whisky of the last century. The sprawling mirror over the dressing table was auburn-tinted and as clear as a tropical summer's twilight.

An exciting room. A sensuous and sensual room. A room of wantonness and lurking sin.

I turned and left, rapidly, and as I approached the stairs I found myself wanting more air, wanting above all to escape. But I knew then that I would not escape.

I had seen my face in that huge tinted mirror and it had been the face of a stranger – a stranger who was already running backward on a forward-racing treadmill; a stranger afraid.

We had supper that evening at a table on the flag-stoned patio in front of the house, directly beneath Petra's room. The patio was surrounded by tall hedges. Petra and I talked mechanically, but her eyes – and probably mine, too – spoke a different tongue.

She said only one disrupting thing, and that was as we rose from the table. Her arm brushed mine. She turned and said, 'I wonder what Madge would think, Alex.' Then she walked away.

I followed, and behind us both I heard the light, rapid shuffle of the old woman's carpet slippers and the abrupt tap, tap of her cane. I wondered about that cane. She didn't always have it with her, obviously didn't really need it. I began to feel watched, as Petra said *she* was.

Again, as Petra and I walked down the inside hall, she turned and said, 'Oh, God. I wish that old crow was dead!'

That night she came to my room.

CHAPTER 8

I HAD BEEN in bed about an hour wondering why I hadn't locked the door when the door opened. I knew then why I hadn't locked it.

Moonlight sprayed in the windows on the side of the room where the head of my bed was. As she entered, she said nothing. She simply closed the door. And I lay stiffly beneath a single sheet.

She turned. 'Hello, Alex.'

I didn't answer. She wore a thigh-length nightgown as thin as gauze. I later found out the color of it was red; you couldn't tell in the moonlight. She was the most gorgeous thing I'd ever seen as I watched her long white legs gleam toward me and the bed.

'I had to see you,' she said.

'Get out, Petra!'

The short nightgown folded inward beneath her thrusting breasts and fell to a rustling caress against her hips. She sank slowly to the bed, crossed her legs, and smiled at me. The moonlight was over my shoulder, full on her. The bed sank with her weight, and the full warmth of her hip pushed against my leg. There was that sheet between us. I hauled myself back against the head of the bed, pulling the sheet with me.

Her hand snagged the sheet, tore it down to my waist.

She chuckled. 'I sleep that way too,' she said. 'I only put this on for you.'

'Go away.' It seemed to me I could hear the shuffle of carpet slippers, the rap, rap, rap of a cane.

'No.'

'Petra.'

'No.'

She laid her hand on my arm. I didn't move. I could see her breasts clearly through the thin gown. Her thighs gleamed in an ivory curve. She later told me she liked the length of the short nightgown, that it felt like feathers tickling the tops of her legs.

'I didn't come to cause any trouble. I wouldn't worry you for the world, Alex.'

'Liar.' Her every breath was tantalization.

'You've got to listen,' she said, and for the first time tonight I noticed the strain in her face and eyes. She wasn't smiling now, and she seemed to draw her breath in almost fiercely. She wheeled on the bed, facing me, uncrossed her legs. It only made things worse. The hem of her gown was up as far as it could go without refuting gravity. I had a sensation of being completely trapped. I tried to think of Madge, to concentrate on her.

'It's about Verne,' she said quietly.

'Suppose his mother finds us here.'

Her fingers bit into my arm. 'Don't say it!'

I listened to her breathe.

'I want to tell you this. There's nothing wrong with me, only I'm too much for him.'

'Too much?'

'Yes.' She didn't say it, she breathed it. 'He couldn't keep me – happy. Now he doesn't even try.'

'You mean – ' I tried to move away from her on the bed, but every movement only brought her closer. 'You mean Verne's like that because of you?'

55

'Yes. He's sapped. He's a dead weight. He can't do anything any more.'

I thought of tales of the succubus.

'He keeps me cooped up here. Yet he offers me nothing – nothing of what I need. Must have. I'm not crazy.'

'Why are you telling me this?'

'Because I love you, Alex. I want you to know. And you love me, you know you do.'

'My God, woman, you're off your rocker.'

'Don't say that!' Her fingers bit into my arm again. 'It's not what you think. Verne tried – hard. But he didn't really love me, ever.'

My voice was hoarse; I hardly recognized it. The smell of her perfume, the warmth of her body . . . 'Why don't you divorce him?'

'And lose all this? His money? He's going to die. I could kill him myself, I think. Merely by – His heart is weak. He – '

I tore her hand off me, started up in the bed, grabbed the sheet, began to sweat. 'Get out, Petra!'

'Listen! You've got to listen. He wouldn't divorce me anyway. He wants me here, he wants to torture me.' Her voice was a shrill whisper now, her hands against my chest. She leaned closer. I felt her thick hair brush my shoulder as her face neared mine. 'I watched him fade away. Bad business lately has helped. He's losing weight steadily. I love you, Alex! Don't you see? Are you blind? I've loved you for months.'

'You've never – we never saw each other till yesterday, Petra.'

'We didn't have to. My letters told you.'

My hand brushed her thigh. I jerked it away and it struck her breasts. She grabbed it and held it there in the soft dark valley between her breasts. I could feel her breath, taste the odor of her perfume, hear the sound of our bodies touching.

'You wrote me regularly,' she whispered. 'You must have known. Don't pretend you didn't know. Don't pretend

56

anything. I can't bear it, Alex. We've got to face this thing. We can't escape.'

'Good Lord, Petra!'

'Yes.'

She came down against me then and my arms circled her, pulling her to me. Her lips brushed mine, then she tugged savagely away, her knee on the bed, pushing.

'Petra!'

'Not now. We can't. That old hag!'

My fingers clutched at her nightgown. She slapped my hand away. I had to have her now.

'We must wait for that!'

She was up, standing beside the bed, her breasts rising and falling in the moonlight.

'Petra. Is this true?'

'Yes. You saw my husband. He's a dead man already.'

I stared at her, wanting her, frightened, wanting her, wanting to run, escape.

She bent over the bed, over me, and her hair fell across my face as her mouth met mine. She fell away from the bed, started for the door. 'There,' she said. 'You may leave now, if you wish. If you can.' She stood by the door. 'But don't forget what I said about Verne. There have been no other men, though I tried once. I was desperate. Nothing happened, but Verne caught me. Now, leave, if you can.'

She was gone. The door was closed. The air was full of her presence. The sheets were damp and cold.

An instant later I heard her talking loudly in the hall. I went to the door. 'Get to bed, Mother!' she shouted. 'What are you doing?'

'Harlot! Harlot!' the old woman shrieked.

I opened the door a crack.

'I shan't tell him. Not yet,' the old woman said.

Petra was walking swiftly toward her room. Her door slammed. The old woman stood in a flannel nightgown in the hallway, her thin gray hair wisping about her tiny, sly face. Her arms quivered like reeds. She turned and shuffled off. I closed the door and returned to my bed.

I didn't sleep until the first faint gray feelers of dawn touched the floor through the front windows. And I had discovered that I no longer wanted to leave this house.

She was torturing me, but I'd have her. Somehow. If I had to take her by force. Perhaps that's what she wanted. I knew it was wrong. My conscience was like a rasping steel file sawing back and forth inside me. But I refused to listen. And I would refuse. I had to.

When I woke I felt different. I remembered, but I felt wrong. I decided to fight. I'd stay and fight. And though I knew it was the right thing to shut up about everything, I figured I'd have a talk with Verne.

But Verne might not be home for days.

CHAPTER 9

VERNE CALLED at ten. Petra spoke with him a few moments, then turned to me in the hallway. 'He wants to talk to you, Alex.'

The old woman was eating breakfast in the kitchen.

'All right,' I said. I took the receiver from her hand. She didn't move from beside me, pressed against me. Her hand smoothed my back. She smiled, then moved away.

'Alex! How's everything?'

I was startled at the tone of his voice. He seemed full of life, very different from the way he'd been when he'd left.

'Fine,' I said. 'Everything's fine. Only I wish to God you were here.'

'That's what I'm calling about. Sorry to hell and gone, but I won't be able to make it till sometime Saturday.'

Saturday! This was Wednesday. No, Tuesday. Not until Saturday. Petra was standing down the hall, nodding at me. She wore a black skirt, a tight white blouse, and a yellow ribbon in her hair. As I stared at her, she tucked the blouse more securely into the waist of her skirt, smoothed it out.

'I'm sorry, old man,' Verne said. 'But that's the way it is. Things are bad down here. I had a minor strike on my hands, had to increase wages. Got ten truckloads of lumber not fit to build an outhouse with. Had to return that. Found out my head man was knocking down. Had to fire him and

59

hire another, and the government's got some damned new clause . . .'

'Cripes,' I said. Then I realized this was my chance. My chance to leave and to explain at the same time. It would be bad enough that way, but it would be lots easier than staying and standing what might come. I looked straight at Petra and showed her my teeth. She sensed something. 'Look, Verne,' I said. 'It's great here and everything, but why don't I go on back home and wait till you get things – '

He interrupted sharply. His voice seemed snappy, full of power, aggressive. 'Wouldn't hear of it. Don't suggest it again. If anything, you're going to stay over longer!'

Petra was watching me. At first her eyes had narrowed, but now she saw my face fall and she smiled again.

I knew I couldn't insist. I felt I couldn't. I didn't want to make him suspicious in any way. So now I was thinking like that.

'All right, Verne. Get home as soon as you can. We haven't even got drunk together yet.'

'Yeah. Well, I've got to scram now, Alex. Keep the ball rolling. You get Petra to show you around.'

'Sure, I will.'

'How's Mother?'

'Fine. She's fine.'

'Say. I forgot to pay Jenny and the cook. Will you tell Petra we owe them two weeks?'

'Sure.'

'Thanks. See you Saturday.'

He was gone. The line was dead.

'You see, Alex?' Petra said. 'You wouldn't leave now, anyway, would you – really?'

We drove around the far side of the lake, a good twenty-five miles, ate lunch at a drive-in near Canyonville, and came up the near side of the lake.

We didn't talk much. The old woman perched as usual in the center of the rear seat. She gabbled about the scenery until it began to get me down. But just being beside Petra, watching her from the corner of my eye, and listening to the stirring tones of her voice kept me still.

'I forgot to tell you,' I said. 'Verne told me to tell you to pay Jenny and the cook two weeks' pay.'

She didn't look at me. 'Yes. All right. See, we'll park here a while. I'll take you down and show you the lake.'

There were pines, and a glen that fed shallowly across the road, but showed great depth on the hillside. The lake flashed blue in the sun beyond the treetops.

'All right.'

Petra turned and shouted to the old woman, 'I'm going to show Mr. Bland the lake. We'll only be a minute.'

The old woman moved her mouth in what looked like some kind of secret smile.

Petra's chin trembled. She opened the door on her side, ran around the car and down the slope into the trees. She ran toward the lake. Her skirt furled around her legs and her legs flashed in the early-afternoon sunlight.

She vanished into the shadows of the trees, whirled, and called, 'Come on, slowpoke!'

'Be right with you.' I turned to the old woman. 'Excuse me,' I said. 'We won't be a moment.' I had forgotten that she was deaf. She didn't hear me. She was watching the darker shadow of the woods where Petra had disappeared.

I went on down, following Petra's course. It was very cool. As I neared the water the air was still cooler and I could smell the water. It was a spring-fed lake, Petra had told me, and very clear and cold. Very fine for swimming if you like fresh, clear, icy water.

'It's a little late for swimming, isn't it?' I'd said.

'It's always whatever you make it.'

I went into the trees along the glen with the stream of

water from the glen running over black slate to my right. I came out on the shore of the lake. It was about a mile and a half wide. The larger of the three hills on the other side looked like some huge green monster, like a buffalo, perhaps, hunched over, asleep.

I didn't see Petra at first. Then she called to me from nearby. 'Hurry, Alex. Hurry!'

She was standing naked on the shore of the lake.

I stood still for a long moment because I couldn't move or couldn't think. The sun shone on her back over the tops of the trees.

She faced me.

'Come here, Alex.'

I took two steps, halted. 'The old woman!' I said. 'She'll – Petra!'

I stepped back as she ran gingerly toward me over the pebbled shore. Her hair streamed back on both sides of her head and she was beautiful, too damned beautiful. Her beauty struck me very hard without release.

'Petra!' The old woman's voice reached us from the highway, just beyond the trees.

'Oh, God!' Petra said.

I turned and ran back to the car. I stumbled and slipped over the water-black slate in the glen and once went in clear to my knee. Scrambling up the slight rise onto the highway, I reached the car. I looked back but Petra wasn't in sight. I'd never forget the way she had looked standing there on the shore of the lake with the sun gleaming like liquid gold on her white skin and her black hair flowing around her shoulders and throat like a dense, fiery fog.

Standing there by the car, I heard splashing sounds beyond the pines and other trees surrounding the lake. And standing there I cursed the old woman silently. Then I cursed her aloud, knowing she couldn't hear. I cursed her until I could think of nothing else to say. Then I climbed inside the car.

The old woman was still watching the patch of shadowed woods where Petra had vanished.

Pretty soon Petra came back to the car. She was breathing hard. 'Wasn't it fine!' she said.

'Yes.'

I looked at her, my hand brushed her leg. Her skirt was damp. Her hair was damp. She'd been in the water.

'I went for a swim,' she said. 'You should have, Alex.' She turned to the old woman and shouted, 'I went for a swim. Don't you wish you could go swimming, Mother?'

The old woman didn't answer.

The days flicked by like the shadow from a sundial's finger as you glance at it from hour to hour. Petra put me through hell and there was no way to combat it.

If we were near the old woman, she lured me with eyes of promise and surreptitious caresses. But the instant we were alone it was all I could do to hold her in my arms.

'You want me now, don't you?'

'I'll have you.'

'Stop. Here she comes.'

'Petra, let's go someplace.'

'We can't leave Mother alone. She'd try to follow. She's suspicious now. She's saying awful things to me.'

Wednesday, Thursday, Friday – Saturday. It was the longest day, Saturday. And it was the day I realized I hadn't written Madge, nor had I mailed the other letter I had written. I went to the mailbox on the front of the house. Above it in brass scroll I read the number 13; 13 French Street. How many times had I addressed letters here?

There were three letters from Madge. I took them upstairs and laid them on the desk in my room, unopened.

The old woman was everywhere. She had become a shadow. She carried the cane always now and she hardly ever spoke in my hearing.

I wanted Petra now. I didn't understand what she was doing, why she was acting this way, when she said she loved me. She told me that all the time. 'I love you, Alex,' her lips and her hands speaking too, but when we were alone she became an eel.

I couldn't sleep. I suddenly realized the decanter of whisky in Verne's study was empty. On Saturday morning it was full again. I hadn't seen Jenny or the cook since the day I'd come. I asked Petra.

'I gave them some time off.'

I knew I was a little out of my head now, and I looked forward to Verne's home-coming sometimes with distaste, but always a little later with the last bit of hope within me.

I didn't know what was going to happen, but I knew something was going to happen. I was slowly losing all control. Propinquity, whatever, I could not combat it. I wanted her. The gods could have thrown me women from on high, of all shapes and sizes, and they wouldn't have meant a thing. Only Petra.

When I thought of Madge, it was like another day, another year, a bygone something that had never occurred. Chicago was someplace without existence. Only Petra.

Save when my conscience ate at me. That was when I started for the bottle. Not much. Only a bit. Just enough to stave off the sudden touch of the knife edge of despair.

Once I tore Petra's blouse off. Once I fastened my fingers in her hair and told her I wouldn't let her get away.

'I'll scream, Alex. She's only in the next room. I'll scream!'

And, of course, she would have screamed, I think. I thought so then. We did not leave the house after Wednesday. The old woman wanted to take rides. Petra refused. She seemed to be trying to work Verne's mother into a rage, also.

She was succeeding. No matter what I said now, she would only smile and say, 'Wait, my friend.'

64

I felt cowardly. I told myself I should take her.

I didn't. I waited. And I couldn't stand being alone any more. I searched her out wherever she was. I was in love with her. As much in love as a man can get.

'I think you're weak, Alex. You'll never leave now, and you can't leave, of course.'

'No. I won't leave now.' I looked at her. 'I don't want to hurt you, Petra. But I'm going to.'

'It's only been a few days. You said so yourself.'

'It's been too long. Something's happened inside me.'

'You must want me as much as I want you.'

I grabbed her close and breathed the warmth of her hair, felt her hot red lips, and most of the time I was with her, I didn't know what I was saying. I watched her like a cat, and the old woman watched us both.

Verne came home at six o'clock on Saturday evening.

He was a changed man. He showed vitality, and some of the color had returned to his face. He would never be the man I had once known, but he didn't look wrecked now. He showed energy. His eyes were bright.

'Things went good?' I asked.

'Terrible, Alex. I only came home because you were here. Got to leave again Sunday night.'

A kind of hot rage of triumphant satisfaction hit me.

We went into the living room and Petra fixed drinks. She smiled at me from behind his back and touched me whenever she passed. I wanted to hit her, smash her. But I knew I wouldn't. To me she was becoming a woman who had been denied the things she wanted; a woman of great life and laughter who had been cooped up here, where she didn't want to be. Some of this feeling gradually died as I talked with Verne.

'The whisky's good,' he said. 'I want a lot of it tonight. And a good dinner.'

'I'm going to fix it myself,' Petra said. 'Steak. You like that?'

'How come?' Verne asked. He seemed slightly suspicious, and his eyes looked queer.

I said, 'Petra gave Jenny and the cook some time off.'

'Oh,' he said. 'Why, Petra? Did you pay them?'

'I paid them Monday morning.'

'They haven't been here since?'

'No.' She became defiant; her eyes darkened. 'If you must know, Verne, I fired them. Both of them.'

He said nothing. But from that moment on I watched him sag again. Inside of an hour he was a shell again, gray-faced and forlorn.

I tried to talk with him after we ate.

'I'm bushed,' he said finally. 'We'll make a day of it tomorrow.'

Tomorrow . . .

He went to bed, a tired, unhappy man.

'Why did you fire the help?' I asked Petra. We were in the hallway.

She put her arms around my waist. 'Why do you think?' she said.

Tomorrow . . .

66

CHAPTER 10

VERNE WASN'T up yet at ten-thirty Sunday morning. I had spent another night thinking of Petra. After breakfast I went into his study and began hitting his bottle of whisky. I got a little drunk, I think.

'Alex, come here. She's out in the kitchen.'

Petra stood in the study doorway. She wore white rayon shorts and a flimsy halter and her red sandals.

'You've been drinking,' she said softly as I took her in my arms. 'He's leaving tonight.'

'Did he come near you last night?'

She laughed. 'No. Goodness, no.'

My hands strayed along her hips; I held her tightly against me. Then she whirled away and ran up the stairs. I knew this was it. I started after her, the whisky pounding in my head. It was all right now. I'd found an escape. I would tell Verne the truth, tell him I was in love with his wife. That she no longer wanted him. It had to be that way.

She moved into her room along the upstairs hallway. I followed, and closed the door. The windows were open and a cool breeze blew in, billowing the curtains.

As she looked at me, something like fright came into her eyes. 'Go ahead and scream,' I said, as I came up to her. The whisky swarmed in my blood.

'I don't want to scream, Alex. Alex!'

Reaching out, I ripped the halter away from her breasts, baring them. She backed away, tripped on the leather couch, and sat down. I pulled her up against me. At first she tried to yank away, twisting in my arms. Then abruptly she was with me, helping me. We went wild.

'You see!' she gasped. 'The waiting. It's best!'

Her lips were against mine, she was talking around a kiss, and I didn't hear the door open, I heard nothing, wanted to hear nothing until the old woman said, 'I caught you! I knew I would!'

We sprang apart. Petra didn't try to cover her breasts.

'I'm going to tell my son,' the old woman said in her dry voice. 'Harlot – sinners!' She came further into the room, and shook her cane in the air. I wondered crazily how she managed to hold such a heavy cane in her vine-like arm.

'No, you won't!' Petra whispered. She rushed from my side across the room.

I watched, rooted to the floor – feet sunk in the thick, soft rug.

Petra grabbed the old woman by the front of her dress and they scrambled at each other. Verne's mother beat at Petra with the cane, her sly face twisted, eager. They tore at each other before the open casement window, then the old woman's body sprawled out toward the screen.

'Damn you, damn you!' Petra whispered savagely, striking at her again.

Verne's mother moaned and moaned. The cane fell, drummed against the rug. I moved then, fast, but I moved too late.

'Catch her!' I said. Petra's moving figure was between me and the old woman. The screen ripped, sang out. I heard Petra's breath indrawn on a gasp. A dry noise, almost like wind in an alley, followed by a faint thud, reached us.

Petra whirled and leaned against the window, wide-eyed, her breasts heaving. 'Alex!' she said. 'Alex!'

I grabbed her arm, hurled her across the room, looked out and down through the torn hole in the screen. The screen was rusted, old. Verne's mother was sprawled out in a mass of gray on the flagstones of the patio, two stories below.

A quiet wind rustled in the curtains.

'She's surely dead,' I said.

As I turned, Petra began to scream. She screamed three times. Then she stopped and looked at me.

Tomorrow and tomorrow and ... tomorrow.

CHAPTER 11

'WHAT'S THE matter?' It was Verne. I heard him running down the hall, his bare feet pounding.

'Quick,' I said to Petra. 'Cover yourself!' I started for the door. Verne burst into the room in his pajamas, white ones. I whirled toward Petra. She was on the other side of her unmade bed with a flame-colored robe wrapped about her.

'What's the matter?' Verne repeated. 'Who screamed?' His hair was mussed, his face haggard.

I started to say something, but Petra interrupted.

She pointed toward the window. 'I was just getting up when she came in,' she lied. Her hands went to her head. 'Oh, God, Verne! She reeled against the window. Alex beat you here.'

'What? What window? Who?' He stepped farther into the room and his mother's cane rolled beneath his foot. He stared at it, slowly awakening. His gaze moved to the window to his left, to the torn screen. He leaped over, stuck his head through the rent. I saw his shoulders shake.

Petra looked at me with genuine fright in her eyes.

Verne kept on looking down at the patio.

Petra said, 'She just went all of a sudden, Verne. She just fell, she just reeled toward the window. I don't know what she wanted. She didn't say anything. She just – she just – she just – '

It was a great act. she sat on the bed and began sobbing uncontrollably.

Verne turned slowly, stared at me, then at Petra. He suddenly ran from the room. I heard his feet pounding on the stairs.

Petra wheeled on the bed. 'Go with him, Alex!' she whispered. 'Hurry! It will look bad if you don't!'

'You pushed her,' I said. 'You murdered her.'

'No, no, no, don't be a fool. Hurry downstairs with him, Alex. Hurry, I say!'

I stared a moment longer at her beautiful face and felt the flames creeping up around my legs. Then I went after Verne.

He stood in the patio staring down at his mother. It took but a glance to know she was dead. Her head was shattered like an orange. She had landed flat on her back. Her face was in repose. Her right leg had flapped beneath her, and the toe of her right shoe projected over her right shoulder.

Neither of us spoke. Verne seemed unable to tear his gaze away, then finally he went over and sat at the round luncheon table and bit his lower lip. He ceased biting, looked up at the torn screen. Then he commenced biting his lip again.

I heard Petra behind me. She walked past me, without glancing toward the body, and stood by Verne. He didn't look at her, either.

'Verne,' she said. 'I don't know what to say.'

'Don't say it, then.'

I hadn't moved. She glanced at me, her face still, her eyes jetty and unamazed.

A fly came from nowhere, lit on the old woman's nose, crawled across her half-open left eye onto her cheek. It stopped then. Faint wind fingered the gray dress. The fly did not move.

Verne rose, stepped around the body, started toward the front door of the house. 'Phone,' he said. 'Phone.' He looked very forlorn in his bare feet and his haggard hair and his wrinkled white pajamas.

When I glanced down again the fly was gone.

I closed my eyes. The red taillight of a taxi winked around the corner.

'You killed her.'

She watched me.

'You killed her. You pushed her out of that window.'

She held her hair bunched at the back of her neck and watched me, unblinking, serene. She had on a soft black dress now, and a cloud-thin white scarf was tied around her throat. 'Don't be silly, Alex,' she said. 'You don't know what you're saying.'

She was denying it. 'You saw your chance,' I said. 'A natural. You took that chance.'

We talked across the corpse. The old woman's body was between us. I was numb inside; rigid, like a plank, like a sheet of cast iron. Then somebody struck the iron with a maul. I stepped over the body toward Petra.

She whirled, pushed through some hedges, and retreated around the side of the house. I followed her, caught up, flung her against the side of the house.

'You're a bitch!' I said. 'A murderous bitch!'

I held her back against the red brick side of the house. Her feet were in a flower bed, but this was fall, and things were dying. Flowers crisped beneath her feet.

'He mustn't catch us out here, Alex. Not like this.'

I tightened my grip on her arms. She didn't wince. That old bold quality was there in her eyes and the turn of her lips, and it seemed then that nothing could destroy it.

'I'm going to tell him,' I said. 'I'll have him phone the police instead of just the doctor. What good will a doctor do? She's dead, and you killed her.'

Her tongue tipped her lips and for an instant her eyes

dropped. But then she looked at me more strongly than before. 'No, you won't, Alex. You want me too much.'

'A proud bitch, too.'

'Yes, Alex. And not only that. If you started anything by telling such a story, what would they think? What would the police think?'

'You black beautiful bitch, you!'

'You love it!' She brought her hands up to my arms. I flung them down. She said, 'You're as implicated as I am in this. Don't you see that? She's better off dead. But if you say anything, you'll go where I go. If it could be proved. Which I doubt. And we've waited too long already. We've told Verne one thing – we can't change it.'

'Where do you get this "we" stuff?'

'Alex, if you don't let go of me and stop acting like a fool, I'll tell Verne something. I'll tell him you did it. Because she caught you trying to attack me.'

I grinned at her. Then I let go and stepped away. I started laughing. Bitter laughter. There was a defenseless old woman lying dead out there just because I'd decided to pay a visit to an old Army pal. I ceased laughing and stared at her.

Petra's fingers closed over my arm and she said, 'Use your head, lover.' Then she turned and walked rapidly toward the rear of the house.

I stood there and stared at the woodpecker-notched trunk of a tall pine tree in the yard. I knew I should leave now. Madge was waiting; a life that was becoming very remote was waiting. I'd been here a week, I should be planning to leave anyway. Only anyway I couldn't leave now, and I felt the stir of that inside me, too. Excuses. Reasons. Somethings. Put if off. It was easy.

I went on around toward the front again. Petra was all I'd called her and she had been right in everything she'd told me.

Verne was sitting on a chair by the circular luncheon table

staring at the body of his mother. As I broke through the hedge, he glanced up, then stood and started toward the house. I followed. On the doorstep he paused and turned.

'I phoned the doctor,' he said. 'A hell of a lot of good it'll do to have a doctor.'

'Yes. Of course. . . .'

'God,' he said. 'This is great for you, isn't it?'

'Good Lord, man, don't think of me.' The wind blew. 'I'm sorry.'

The dry leaves skittered about our feet. A maple leaf crawled humpbacked with burry noise across the flagstone walk and tipped over in the grass. It reminded me of a crab scuttling.

'Did you see her fall?'

'No,' I lied. He was still in his pajamas. This lie would pile on top of everything else.

'Do you think we should bring her in?' He meant his mother's body.

I didn't answer.

'I guess not. They'll – ' He paused. 'Alex, will you do something for me? We'll need some help out here. Take the car and run into town. Pick up Jenny, will you? She was our maid. Jenny Carson. In Allayne.' He told me her address. 'Will you do that, Alex? Then hurry back?'

'Sure,' I said. 'Can't you phone?'

'No phone.' He went inside the house. 'Petra's got the car keys.' He called her. She'd been in the living room. As she entered the hall, she didn't look at me, only at him. He told her what he wanted. He seemed very haggard, worn out.

'Why, I'll go,' Petra said. 'There's no need sending – I mean, why should Alex have to go?'

'Because I asked him. Give me the keys.'

Petra's eyes turned my way. She was a beautiful black bitch. 'Well,' she said. 'I'll just run in along with Alex, then.'

'I'll need you here,' Verne said. 'The keys!'

She got them and handed them to me. Verne started up the stairs. I headed for the front door. She ran ahead of me, got in front of me. I tried to pass her.

'Kiss me good-by,' she said. 'And hurry, hurry.' Her eyes were a little wild and then I had her in my arms. God, oh, God, I said to myself. Her lips were hot and good, her body something I wanted to crush up against the wall. I held her so tightly she moaned. Then I flung her away.

'Lord, Alex!'

I went on out to the car and drove to Allayne. I wondered whether we were praying or cursing. Both of us. Every minute that passed snarled me up in this thing a little more. I was wading in deadly quicksand. Already it was too late to back out. Death. Murder. Sure as God.

Me. Alex Bland. Colorless and common and with a conscience that would keep five people treading the traight and narrow. Nose-to-the-grindstone Bland.

She was a sickness. I was filled with the insidious sickness of her and the only doctor was time and I wasn't sure Doc Time would do so hot with this case. Pulled one way, yanked the other. She'd waited, all right – she'd held me off, and now this. . . .

I passed a couple of cars on the road to Allayne and wondered if one of them might be carrying the doctor Verne had phoned.

The black-top road dipped and Allayne spread out before me; gray-roofed buildings beneath a roof of gray sky, church spires, the courthouse dome, and all the rust-red-green autumnal trees.

CHAPTER 12

CHURCH BELLS tolled a solemn recollection of timeless Sundays spent in an apathy of occasional prayer tokening an afterward of roast chicken and mashed potatoes, stuffed stomachs and shirts, groaning couches and the geometric disarray of thick newspapers among the wailing havoc of snores, wet diapers, clanking kitchen sinks, or the shade-drawn sedate parlors where through rich cigar smoke they mumbled ritualistic weekly histories of business and how Oscar got drunk last night at the hotel bar. As I drove up Main Street people were congregating in front of the churches and it was a nice autumn Sunday for death.

The elms were disrobing now and seemed slightly ashamed of it, clutching to the last minute browning remnants of their wardrobe. I found Chapman Lane, where Jenny Carson lived, and turned down.

It was a tiny house with two tiny front windows and a very small door. There was a second story, but it looked as if you'd have to bend over to walk around up there. The house was tightly enclosed by an artificial cement-stone fence, which only made the house seem smaller still. There was a gate. The house dated way back, the broad, white-painted boards running vertical. There was a brass bellpull. I pulled. It tinkled.

I half expected a little old lady dressed in blue with a

teacup rattling in her hand. Instead, I got Jenny. She was a different Jenny from the Jenny I'd thought I'd met out at Verne's.

'I kind of expected you'd come, Mr. Bland,' she said. 'Don't stand there, come in.'

I followed her inside and she closed the door. A radio played quiet melodies from somewhere.

'In here,' she said, leading me into a small living room. It was decked out like a studio, very clean and neat. A broad studio couch up against the far wall, with a tired but colorful blanket sleeping on it, a couple of easy chairs, a large bookcase, filled, and in one corner an easel with a painting of a nude woman partly completed on it. There was a table by the easel cluttered with paints, brushes, rags, and bottles. There was a faint odor or turpentine. Jenny went immediately to the painting and tossed a piece of cloth over it.

She turned, smiling that hesitant smile. 'Simply because it's not finished,' she said. 'Please sit down. Why did you come?'

I stared at her, groping for a chair, and sat. Her carrot-colored hair was sort of all flung over to one side and her eyes were filled with patient questioning laughter. She wore a fawn-colored skirt and a white blouse, short-sleeved, that buttoned close around her throat. Turning, she moved over to the studio couch and sat down, crossed her legs, put her elbow on her knee, and cupped her chin in her hand. She had very broad hips and a very thin waist. One of her soft red slippers had a hole in the toe.

'Well, for goodness' sake, Mr. Bland. Don't sit there like that. What's the matter?'

'I came because of Verne, Jenny.'

'Oh?'

'He wants you back.' I told her about Verne's mother. I told her how she had died, only I didn't mention that Petra had pushed her. And I didn't tell her what Petra and I were trying to do at the time.

'I see,' Jenny said. 'Is Mr. Lawrence broken up?'

'Seems to be.'

'I'm sorry, of course. That was a horrible way for the old lady to die, but – '

'But what, Jenny?'

She glanced down at the floor, then up at me again. 'I rather expected it would be something like that.'

'How do you mean?'

'Did Petra push her?'

'What!'

'Did Petra push her out of the window?'

'Listen,' I said. 'Will you come with me?'

Jenny shook her head slowly. 'No,' she said. 'No, I wouldn't go out there again. I've had enough of that place. It was bad enough, just knowing – '

'Knowing what?'

'Mr. Bland, you know what I mean.'

'Please call me Alex, and I don't know what you mean.'

'All right, Alex. Yes, you do. She's got you, hasn't she?' She rose quickly, moved across the room to the corner by the windows. The radio – a small set – was on the floor. She turned it off, then stood there with her back to me, staring out the window. 'You're – you're stuck like a fly in the glue,' she said.

'Verne's waiting,' I said. 'Will you please come?'

The thought of Petra was like a cold knife getting red hot. I suddenly wanted to burst these walls and be with her. Jenny turned and looked at me.

'I'm not going with you, no. He'll have to wait.'

'He needs help.'

She tipped her head and smiled at me. 'Yes,' she said simply, 'he surely needs help. A pail of arsenic would do the trick.'

'Jenny!'

'I'm sorry.'

I rose and something went loose inside me as I found myself staring at a telephone on the studio couch. It was a dull ache.

'Verne said you had no phone.'

'Just had it installed. I have a new job now. I can afford one.'

'Could I use it?'

'Sure.' She didn't move. The couch was broad, as I said, so I had to crawl over after the phone and unsnarl the wires. I placed a call with long-distance for Madge Collins, at her home in Chicago. Then I hung up and sat there, waiting.

'You're sweating,' Jenny said. 'Running around in your shirt sleeves, sweating. I'll go get you a drink of water.' She paused in front of me. 'Don't peek at that painting.' She turned and left the room. I watched the sway of her hips and thought of Petra. Water. I needed something stronger than water.

Murder didn't lie. I looked at my hands and they were trembling. I was in it right up to here; and 'here' was a long way up. Jenny wouldn't return with me to 13 French Street. What would Verne say about that? The phone rang. I grabbed it up. And all the time I was thinking how I wanted to be back there with Petra.

Madge's slightly puzzled voice finally reached me.

'But why haven't you written? Only one letter, Al.'

'That's why I'm phoning.'

'But Al, I've worried.'

'I know, I know. Something's come up.' The couch sank beside me as Jenny sat down. She handed me a cool glass of water and I drank it down, all of it. Jenny took the glass, watching me openly, and smiling a little.

Here I was, thinking of Petra, sitting beside a very pretty girl called Jenny, talking to the girl I intended to marry,

Madge. And through it all I kept seeing a gray something smashed against stone, like a broken rag doll.

'Al – Al, say something!'

'I'm sorry.' I tried to think of nothing but Madge. It wouldn't work. I could taste Petra's lips. . . .

'Al – '

'Madge, darling,' I said, and I didn't want to talk with her. She was too far away, too far removed from me and the things that were happening. I told her about the death of Verne's mother. 'Madge. That'll mean I'll have to stay here a bit longer.'

'Oh, Al. It's been long enough already. My gosh, maybe they don't want you around there – with that going on, and all.'

'No, Madge. He asked me to stay.' Jenny's fingers touched my arm. I glanced at her. She shook her head and clucked her tongue. She looked somehow very clean and fresh.

In my mind's eye I could see Madge standing by the phone in her hallway, looking crisp and efficient and blonde. She was Madge and right now her eyes were gray, sure as anything. She'd never act like Jenny, of the country, of hay and summer and sunshine, or like Petra, of . . . She was Madge. Jenny quietly inspected the hole in her red slipper.

'I think you should come home,' Madge said.

'I can't, darling.'

'You can, Al. There's no sense in your staying on. Besides, what about me? What should *I* do all this time? Just sit around and stare at walls?'

'Madge, I can't help it. I don't know how soon I'll be able to make it.'

Jenny rose, went over to the paint table, and began fussing with her brushes.

'Well, all right.' Madge's voice was a bit crisp. 'Stay, if you must. When you can make it, let me know.' She hung up. I slapped the phone in its cradle.

Jenny and I looked at each other.

'She's a fine girl,' I said. 'You'd like her.'

'I'm sure. But she hung up on you, didn't she?'

I rose and said, 'I'll leave five dollars for the phone call. If there's anything left, buy a new paintbrush.'

'It's not necessary,' she said.

I found a five-dollar bill and put it on the table by her easel.

'You coming with me?' I said.

'I'm afraid not, Alex. I'm sorry, but, as I said, I've got a new job, beginning in a week or so. Meanwhile I'm just going to loaf. And I don't want any more of *them*.' She kept trying to smile at me. 'Why don't you stay and have lunch with me? This is supposed to be your vacation, isn't it?'

'Yes. But I can't stay.'

She watched me a moment, soberly. Then she smiled again. 'All right. Maybe some other time?'

'Maybe.'

We walked to the door. I opened it. She leaned against the wall, watching me. There were pockets in her skirt and she had her hands jammed in them.

'Good-by, Jenny.'

She smiled. She didn't move. I went out and closed the door with her still standing that way, watching me.

Then all of the terrible parts of my world fell on me with a silent bang.

As I drove out of Allayne the streets were very still. Everybody was at church. Everybody except Jenny. She'd been a very easy person to get along with, to know, to feel free with. She had accepted my coming as a fact. Why? I'd forgotten to ask.

The downtown section was completely deserted except for three parked cars, looking strangely alone. The sidewalks and street looked dusty and autumnal. Then, pretty soon, I was between the hills again, on French Street, and Allayne was out of sight and mind. I was thinking of Petra, when suddenly I remembered Madge. The phone call, talking with her, seemed to mean absolutely nothing. Yet I knew I should feel good, having spoken to her.

Then I knew something else. I was driving back toward trouble. But every bit of distance covered carried me closer and closer to the hell I wanted more than anything on earth.

CHAPTER 13

I NEARLY MISSED seeing the man in the middle of the road. The house was just a short way around another bend. The man stood nonchalantly in the middle of the road and flagged me down. I started to drive past slowly on his right, but he leaped in front of the car.

'What do you want?' I shouted out the window, stopping the car.

He grinned, lounged quietly up to the side of the car, and stood there. He was chewing tobacco, a man of perhaps thirty or so, raw-boned almost to the extent of cadaverousness. He turned, spat a long string of brown juice, then fastened slitted, bloodshot eyes on me. 'Mr. Bland,' he said.

'Yes.'

He grinned again. His lips were loose, his mouth broad, his teeth very square and outlined in black. His mouth trembled when he grinned. He wore ragged blue jeans, a pale-washed blue denim shirt, and a battered, sweat-stained felt hat of no color.

'Mister,' he said, 'drive the car in them bushes.' He pointed to some bushes off the side of the road.

'What the hell's the matter with you?' I said. 'Get out of the way.'

One big dirt-grimed hand, knuckle bones nearby showing through the skin, grasped the window ledge. He shook his head. 'Nope. I seen it. I seen it all. Now, ram your damn car in them bushes like I say.' He ceased chewing and stared at me with his mouth open, then he grinned again. 'Come on,' he said, slapping my shoulder. He hitched his own shoulders. His arms hung loose at his sides. He chewed and spat on the left front fender of the car.

We watched each other for a while.

'What was it you say you saw?'

He grinned. 'Hell, mister. The old lady. I seen that dame push the old lady out that there window. I seen plenty.' He winked grotesquely and hitched his shoulders. 'Hurry up, 'fore I get a wind up, damn it.'

I drove the car into the bushes. He came in after me. I got out of the car and faced him. He was about my height, with a slouch. He carried himself with a slouch. He smelled strongly of the barnyard, and a wet tobacco.

'Played a mite too, far, hey?'

'You'd better explain yourself,' I said. He looked wise and jumpy, overexcitable. He scrubbed a hand across the dirty stubble on his face and spat again. Some of it splashed on my shoes. 'Who are you?' I asked. I could feel everything tightening up, like when you swim down into very deep water and begin to want air in a hurry.

'She wouldn't never come across for me,' he said. He mused on it for a while.

I turned and started to get back into the car. He grabbed my shoulder, whirled me around. I slammed at his arm. He stepped off, blinked at me, and grinned. 'Wouldn't if I were you, mister.'

'All right. What do you want?'

'I'm the hired hand down to Corey's.'

'Corey's?'

He gestured. 'Next farm, down there a piece.' He chewed and spat. A car went by out on the road. The bushes moved and a fine settling of dust formed in the air. 'I seen it,' he

84

said again. 'They's a bunch of trouble at that there house, mister. Constable's there now. They taken the corpse off to town. It ain't no mind, though. I seen it all. I seen you rip the front offen her.' I stepped toward him. He stepped back, holding a hand up. 'Easy, now. 'At won't get you noplace. She got nice big ones, ain't she?'

I stepped in close, let him have one at the stomach. He caught my fist and wrenched, and I landed on my back. I looked up at him. He seemed very proud of himself, grinning, chewing, spitting, and hitching his shoulders. I knew I could take him; it had been a lucky grab.

'Get up,' he said. 'I'll finish what I got to say.'

I got up. 'I don't know what you're talking about,' I said. How could he have seen anything? Where had he been? 'But I'll listen. Talk and talk fast.'

He threw his head back and said, 'Humph!' Then he squinted at me. 'All right, mister. You're gettin' at that bitch in the red brick house. I been watchin' her for months from a little hill across the road. Watch her undress, watch what she does after that, too. Quite somethin', sometimes.' He winked. I sweated and waited.

He said, 'Like I say, I seen plenty all along. Caught 'er down the road once at night. Tried to take 'er, but she wouldn't have me. She called me a pig. Hell, she's the pig.'

'You'd better get to the point in a damned hurry.'

He spat. 'This mornin' I milked an' fed the stock, then I kind of wandered over on my little hill just to look an' think about that sweet piece across the way. They's a shade tree in the front yard, an' I could see plumb in them big windows. Just like at night. I seen you an' her havin' it good. All ready for the ride, you was, when the old lady come in.' He cursed obscenely. 'Seen what happened. The gal fought the old lady, an' she pushed her out the window. You was there, an' you seen it too. You know, mister.'

85

'You're lying,' I said as calmly as I could. 'You didn't see anything like that. You couldn't.'

He blew air through his nose. 'I'll show you shortly. Anyways, after you went off in the car, the rest of the folks come. The cor'ner, he come, an' ol' Herk Williams, newspaperman, he come. An' Constable Sturge. So I went on over, to sort of see what they's sayin'. "She fell out the window," they said. "Poor old lady, fell out the window." Well,' he said slowly, 'I know she was pushed.'

'You're a liar,' I said. I was soaked to the skin and I had to see Petra. But first I had to know if he was telling the truth. Yet he must be telling the truth. Because how else could he know?

'Come on, then,' he said. I followed him. We crossed the road, then a stubbled cornfield, a small creek, and started climbing a low hill from the near side. Pretty soon we reached the top. Brambles grew on the hill. Directly opposite us, across the road, sat the house. Three cars were parked in the driveway. Two men were talking in the front yard.

'Now, just squat down,' the man said, 'an' take these.' He fished a pair of small field glasses from inside his shirt. 'See? Fiel' glasses, hah!' He pointed with a broken-nailed finger. 'Look in the big window of her room. See? At night mebbe it's better, but it's good right now, ain't it?'

He was right. If the big casement windows had been closed, it would have been impossible to see much. But with them open, and the field glasses, the screen seemed to vanish and I was looking straight into Petra's bedroom. I saw the couch where we'd been sprawled when the old lady caught us. A man was bending over by the torn screen, looking at it. I rose, handed him his glasses, and started quickly back down the hill.

'Ain't I right?' the man cried behind me, his feet crashing through the brush. 'Ain't I right?'

I didn't say anything. We reached the car.

86

'Well,' I said, 'what about it?'

He grinned. 'Figure I might's well be plain. Them little fiel' glasses, yes, *sir!* You pay me, an' I'll shut up. You see I get what I ask you for, see? Otherwise I go to Verne Lawrence and tell 'im what I seen, or mebbe the police, or Constable Sturge. All the same. You'd be a cooked goose an' so would she.' He paused. 'I sure would miss seein' 'er undress, an' all.'

'That's blackmail,' I said. 'Do you know what they do to people for blackmail?'

He spat. 'D'you figure you can give a damn? You think mebbe they wouldn't believe me if I told 'em? Huh. Listen, man, everybody in the county knows about her, an' how she had to tote that old woman wherever she went. A pretty dame like that.' He shook his head. 'If the money don't agree with you, then look at it this way. Talk with the gal, there. Tell 'er if she'll shack up with me one, two nights a week, O.K. I'll work it that way, too.' He faced me, and tobacco sprayed from his lips. 'But by God, it'll damn well be one or the other!' He spat at the ground. 'An' mister, you better look out it ain't both!'

I hit him with everything I had, flush in the face. I felt my knuckles bite and blood spurted as he flailed backward into the bushes. I stood, staring down at him.

He brushed his hand across his face, where he lay, and looked at the blood. then he propped himself on his elbows and grinned up at me. 'It ain't no matter,' he said. 'You can't hurt me. An' mister, you best show up right here tomorrow night, say about nine. Don't bring no money, just bring a yes or no. We'll see about the money later on.' He spat his entire cud to the ground beside him. He lay there, grinning up at me, his lips trembling.

I climbed into the car, backed onto the road, and drove ahead. My knuckles were sore, but they didn't bother me at all. It was too late to worry now. It was too late to back out.

It was all piling up and I knew it hadn't finished. There was more to come, a hell of a lot more, because through it all, through all this rotten hell, I still wanted her. I still wouldn't give her up. And I was in it now, in it all the way. . . .

There was only one car parked in the driveway when I reached the house. I drew up behind it.

Petra's voice reached me from the house and I glimpsed her at the doorway. 'Oh, here he is now. Alex! Alex! Hurry up. Sheriff Reynolds wants to see you!'

Yes. There was a sheriff's star on the rear bumper of the car up ahead, and it looked as big as a ferris wheel.

CHAPTER 14

FOR A minute I couldn't move from the car.

Petra ran down toward me across the lawn. I watched the movement of her body, the way her hair swung out behind her, the anxious light in her eyes. Behind her, standing in the doorway, I saw a larqe man in a gray suit wearing a blue tie and a gray hat.

Petra's hands gripped the window ledge. 'It's the sheriff. He just wants to talk. It's all right.'

'I'm going to tell him. I've made up my mind. I mean, after the sheriff goes, I'm going to tell Verne. He can do what he wants.' I didn't know when I'd decided, but I had, suddenly.

Her hand reached in and briefly touched my face. 'No, Alex. Don't talk that way. We have much too much in store for us.'

'Just the same – he's watching us.'

'I know, I know. Now, come on. Get out of the car and meet the sheriff. He says it's just routine, that's all.'

'Was the constable here?'

She opened the car door. 'Yes. Just a damned hick fat fool, that's all. He just wanted to look at me, that's the only reason he came. They've already taken the body into town.'

'I know.'

'How? Never mind now. Come on.'

I got out of the car and we walked toward the house. She talked loud enough so anybody could hear now. She was very beautiful and I wanted to feel her against me. But I knew I had to tell Verne. I couldn't weaken. My God, was there nothing left to me?

'Where's Jenny?' she asked. 'I thought you went in for Jenny.' We approached the porch and the man stood there, watching. 'Verne feels terrible. Where *is* Jenny?'

'She couldn't come just now,' I said. I didn't want to tell her now because the sheriff might think anything. Sometimes these country sheriffs were something to deal with – lots of times.

'This is Mr. Bland, Sheriff Reynolds.' She went on inside. His hand was cold and hard.

'Pleased to meet you,' the sheriff said.

I nodded.

'Let's go inside,' he siad.

We went in and the door closed again. The hall was cool and dim, and in the living room Verne was seated drinking brandy. He was dressed in shirt and pants, but his hair was still uncombed.

Petra stood by Verne's chair, one hand on the back of the chair. Whenever her gaze touched mine it was like a current passing between us. I'd never had it like this before. And now it was all mixed up with murder and blackmail; hired hands who sat humped in the cool darkness of brambled hills staring bug-eyed at a bedroom window.

The sheriff was a plain man, from head to toe. His face was something like a wad of dough with mouth, nose, ears, and eyes carved in it. But his eyes were little black oily beads and they watched.

'Just wanted to ask a few questions,' he said, 'then I'll run along.'

Verne glanced at me. 'Where's Jenny?'

90

I started to answer, but Petra spoke up. 'She couldn't come just now.'

'Oh,' Verne said. He drank from his glass and stared at his shoes.

'Reason is,' the sheriff said, 'in a case of this kind, and all. Routine. Did you happen to see Mrs. Lawrence fall?' He turned to Verne. 'Verne, why don't you go into the – '

'No, it's all right,' Verne said.

'No,' I said. 'I didn't.'

'Well,' the sheriff said. He sighed. He was holding his hat in his hands now and his hair was very sparse, plastered tight to his skull. It was straw-colored hair. 'Well,' he said again, 'would you tell me what happened, so far's you know, Mr. Bland?'

I hated it. Every word was like yanking a tooth out of my head with a pair of pliers. Because it was all lies, and I was saying it before Verne and she was standing there watching me and knowing with whatever it was in her eyes telling me, Yes, yes, yes, yes.

'I heard a scream,' I said.

'*A* scream?'

'Several. Two or three, maybe. I don't know. I was in my room. I ran down toward Petra's, Mrs. Lawrence's room, and went in. The door was open. Petra was standing over on the other side of the room, by the bed, and she – well, she was rather troubled.'

'I see. Yes, certainly,' Sheriff Reynolds said.

'She told me Verne's mother had fallen out of the window and right then Verne came into the room.' I spread my hands. 'That's all, Sheriff, that's all.'

'Yes. Well, thank you.' He turned to Verne. 'Now, Verne, you get some rest. You take it easy. I had to do this, you understand? Routine and all. Not many window fallings. . . .' He glanced at Petra. She smiled. He looked at me, jammed his hat on, and went out.

A moment later he returned. 'Pardon me,' he said. 'But if you could move your car, so I could get out of the drive?'

'Sure.' I went out and moved the car and he drove off. As I walked back to the house across the lawn, I glanced over at the hill beyond the road. Then I looked down the road. It was the man, the hired hand from Corey's; he was leaning against a tree just beyond Verne's home, watching. He saw me looking and waved. I went into the house.

I wanted to tell Verne everything, the whole stinking business. I wanted to tell him, and yet I was pulled the other way, too. I wondered if I'd be able to tell him. If she would just stay away from me long enough, maybe I would tell him.

CHAPTER 15

SHE DIDN'T stay away from me.

It was like a relighting a fire that had guttered down some, refeeding it with fresh dry fuel, the way she looked at me and spoke to me between normal conversation. And Verne sitting there in the chair in the living room staring at the floor. Now and then he'd shake his head.

'She had to go,' Verne said. 'It was time she died. She'd expected it herself, and I know I did. It was the way. The way she died. That's what gets me. She never had a damned thing. Never had any rest, any peace, until she came here. She didn't know what rest was, or peace. She'd never known.'

'Buck up, now,' Petra said. 'Take it easy, Verne.' And while she said it, she looked at me, standing there by Verne's chair, with one hand by his head, looking at me with her eyes, her lips, her whole body.

I didn't say anything, just waited.

'And then, when she did come,' Verne said, 'when at last she had a chance at some rest, she went deaf. Not that it mattered much. She didn't seem to mind that. It isn't that I feel so bad about her dying. Death isn't much, not to an old person anyway. It isn't that. It's the way. The way she died.'

'Darling,' Petra said, 'you better have a drink.'

'I don't want one.'

'It might help.'

'I said I don't want a drink.'

She shrugged, standing there behind him, where he couldn't see. I had been standing. Now I found a chair across from Verne and settled down.

'I should have left her sitting in that damned cornfield,' Verne said. 'Leaning against the fence, like they found her that morning. She was nearly dead then. It would have been best.'

Petra said, 'Are you going to – are you going to bring Mother back here?'

'I was, but not now. Only the funeral will start from here. The funeral procession will start from this house. Where she at least found a remote hint of happiness.'

I watched Verne. There was something wrong with him. Some men would dwell on a thing like this, but it wasn't in Verne's make-up to sit there talking about it the way he was. It seemed almost a kind of morbidity.

'Should have left her in the cornfield,' Verne said. 'It was winter, too. Dead winter with the snow piling up against the fence. Nobody knows how she got there, either.' His eyes looked burned out.

I tried to catch Petra's eye, so she'd pour him a drink of brandy, but she only smiled at me.

'She was wearing a straw hat,' Verne said. 'The kind you wear in the summertime – pitching hay, too.'

'Where will she be buried?' Petra asked. She went over and sat in the chair the old woman had been sitting in that first night when she got drunk. Verne stared at the floor. There was no sunshine outside and the room was gray and still.

Verne glanced at me. 'I wanted to bury her with Pa, out at the farm. Where she buried Pa.'

Petra said, 'Oh, but *Verne!*'

'In Nebraska, you mean?' I said.

He nodded. 'But I don't think so. It's too far, and when

94

you get down to it, one piece of ground is as good as another.'
He poured himself a small drink and drank it, then said, 'Or
maybe not.'

There was a long silence. Petra drummed her fingers on
her knee. Then she said, 'Well, then you're going to bury
her in town? In the cemetery in town?'

'No. I don't know, yet,' he said. 'The funeral procession
will start here, though.'

'There won't be any procession,' Petra said.

I glanced at her sharply.

Verne saw me. He said, 'That's all right. She's right, Alex.
There'll only be us. Nobody else knew her.'

'But Verne,' Petra said. 'Where will you bury her?'

'I think I'll bury her out on that knoll, the other side of
the orchard. You know, up by that sycamore. It's a nice spot.'

'Aren't you being a little – well, I mean – ' Petra stared at
me.

'I know,' Verne said. 'No, I'm all right.'

'But no hearse – ' Petra said.

'That's right. We'll have to carry her. Damn it,' he said.
'I'm all right. I don't know why I think this way, but I do.'

'But who will you get for pallbearers?'

She was watching him as she spoke, a little apprehensive,
maybe. She had a right to be. My insides were knotted up
like a tangle of barbed wire, and I kept wanting to tell him.
But how could I tell him?

'There should be six,' Petra said.

'Four will do,' Verne said.

'Won't people talk?'

'What do you care how they talk?' He turned in his chair
and looked at her without any expression. Then he turned
back and stared at the floor some more. I decided the best
thing to do was to let him get rid of whatever was inside
him. then maybe he'd be all right.

'I ordered a light casket,' Verne said. 'She'd almost fit in a child's casket. So four will do.'

'Verne, if you don't stop it!' Petra said.

'Stop what?' He seemed slightly startled.

'Nothing.'

I couldn't seem to get comfortable in my chair. It was hard, bumpy all over. I knew it wasn't, actually, but it seemed that way.

'Yes,' Verne said. 'Up on that knoll.' He rose and walked into the hall. I heard him at the telephone. Petra rose quickly and came over by me.

'He acts funny,' she said.

'He's been working too hard. Any kind of shock might make him act this way. He'll be all right in a little while.'

She stood very close to me. She leaned over, and without volition I put my arms around her, felt the firm swelling of her hips. Her lips descended. I shoved her away. 'Look out,' I said.

'Yes.' She went back to her chair. 'You're excited, aren't you?' she said. 'I am, too. I wish it were over.'

My hands were gripping the arms of the chair so hard the tendons and muscles in my wrists ached. It seemed as if little voices were shrieking and screaming in the back of my head. When I looked at Petra, her eyes were like black holes. They were pointed at me, but I don't believe they really saw me. It was all going on in her head, behind the eyes. I began to perspire.

Verne returned. He stood in the center of the room and ran both clawed hands through his hair three or four times, briskly. 'I talked with them,' he said. 'Two men will be out to dig the grave up on the knoll.'

I sat rigid with my hands gripped around the ends of the chair arms.

'You can hire professional pallbearers,' Petra said. Her voice was little more than a whisper.

'Listen,' Verne said. 'Don't think anything's the matter with me, for God's sake!' He turned to me. 'I'm sorry, Alex. It's just the way I want to do it, is all. No. I'll get old Herb Corey and his hired hand to help. You and I will make up the other two. She knew them; they're the only ones she knew around here. The only ones ever spoke to her. They'll be glad. You'll help, won't you, Alex?'

'Sure, Verne.' My voice was a raven's croak.

Corey's hired hand. . . .

I wanted a drink, but I couldn't trust myself to pour one because my hands would have trembled too much. Corey's hired hand. God. Up there on that brambled hill in the quiet nights of passing seasons, squatting, with those damned field glasses sweating against his eyeballs.

It was murder, that's what it was. And I was in on it. It was hard to believe, to comprehend. It always is, I guess, when things get close to you, like this.

Just after a lunch of sandwiches and coffee prepared by Petra, and during which no one spoke, I met Verne in the hallway by the stairs. Petra was in the kitchen.

'Alex, what about Jenny?' He tried to hold himself straight, to act all right, when he looked like death itself.

'She said she couldn't come, Verne. She has a new job. She was very sorry to let you down. Sorry, too, about your mother.'

'Oh.' His mouth twisted down at the corners.

'She has a phone now. You could talk with her if you like.'

'No,' he said. 'I understand, Alex. I don't blame Jenny, either. Hell with it all. Let Petra take care of things.'

I said nothing. Just stood there looking at the man who had been my comrade through a lot of hell-roaring days. A man I'd been able to depend on, as he'd been able to depend on me. We'd drunk together, and fought together, and raised hell together. Once we'd been brothers. And now

I had seen his own mother murdered – yes, been a party to that murder. But I didn't have the guts to tell him. I didn't have the guts because his wife had her hot hands snarled up in my brain. Too late. It's always too late.

'Going up and take a nap,' Verne said. 'Sorry about all this, Alex.' His smile was ghastly.

'Sure. Take it easy.'

I watched him climb the stairs. He looked very, very old.

CHAPTER 16

THE PICTURE. Petra in the hammock. She had returned it to Verne's study, laid it face down on his desk, the way I had first seen it.

'Only while he's around, darling,' she said. 'He might notice it was missing. No use taking chances. Not that it means much.'

She was standing close to me when she said it and the faint odor of her perfume seemed to choke me. I agreed with her, without speaking. And that afternoon the gravediggers came.

I walked out into the orchard and watched them up there on the knoll. Two men. Their shovels scraped and flashed in the gray, cooling light of autumn. The sky was a tent of gray and their voices joked upon the air between the rasp of earth against steel.

The sun was dead.

'Boy, will I be glad when this is done!'

'Ain't it a fact?'

'They buryin' a dog? Hell of a big dog.'

'Naw. Old woman kicked off.'

'Wish my old woman'd kick off.'

'Damn that root. Hand me the ax. Why in hell anybody'd wanta dig a grave up here ... What they make graveyards for?'

'Nutty. Went to Buffalo last week.'

'Hot dog!'

'Did somethin' I'd always wanted to do.'

'What's that?'

'Had two of 'em in bed with me the same time.'

'Hell, man. Ain't you ever done that before?'

I left the orchard and walked around the front of the house. Somebody rapped on a window. It was Petra. She motioned for me to come in. I went on inside the house.

'He's asleep.'

'Good,' I said. 'Petra . . .' I had to tell her about Corey's hired hand and what he knew, but I didn't know how to begin. It seemed I wasn't able to tell anybody much of anything these days.

'Never mind,' she said, 'Just hold me.'

'No.' We were in the hall. 'Stay away from me, Petra. We were seen.'

She still wore the thin black dress and the white scarf knotted about her throat. Her eyes were very black. 'What do you mean?'

'Somebody saw you push her out of the window, Petra. Not only that, but he saw us – what we were doing when she came into the room.'

She was very quiet. She stared at me for a long moment. 'You're serious, aren't you? But you can't be. How could – '

'He did, I tell you. Corey's hired man. He's been sitting on top of that hill across the road with a pair of field glasses watching you for God knows how long. He stopped me on the way back from town and told me. He wants money, or – '

Her lips had parted, but otherwise her face hadn't altered expression. 'Go on,' she said. 'Or – what?'

'Oh, God. Or you – once in a while, twice a week – nights. Or – or both,' I said.

She was wearing a thin silver bracelet. She took it off one arm and put it on the other.

She said, 'And the funeral's tomorrow and he's going to help. He's going to be here.'

'Yes. So the funeral's tomorrow.'

'Well, how much does he want?'

'I don't know. I have to see him tomorrow night.'

She became bold again, the way she always was. With both hands she bunched her hair behind her head, then let it sprawl out over her shoulders again. 'Well, we'll pay him something. I can just about figure his price. He'll be dirt cheap.'

'My God,' I said. 'Don't you see?'

'Of course I see. I'll think of something. Meanwhile, we'll pay him. You say he was watching me from across the hill?'

'That's right.'

'He couldn't prove a thing.'

'Sure. All right,' I said. 'Maybe he couldn't. But if he said anything, it might start the ball rolling. What if he spoke to Verne?'

She socked me with it. 'What if Verne were dead, Alex?'

'What?'

'Oh, nothing.' She moved in close and it all came in on me like a kind of white heat, dry and stifling. She moved in my arms and brushed her lips across mine. 'Alex, Alex,' she said, 'I love you so much.'

'What did you mean — what you said, there?'

'What?'

'About Verne.'

She leaned away from me, from the waist up. 'Nothing, darling, honest. Nothing at all.'

'You're lying.'

'All right, I'm lying. Kiss me, damn you! Come on, darling, kiss me!'

'Don't call me that. You'll slip.'

'You're getting to think right, aren't you? You're admitting it to yourself at last.'

I grabbed her close and pushed my mouth down on hers. My hand was fumbling at her dress when I heard footsteps in the upstairs hall. It was Verne. I let go and pushed her away from me.

She headed for the kitchen. I went into Verne's study and drank from the whisky decanter. I choked the stuff down. But it didn't help. It didn't stop my heart from whacking in there and it didn't stop that sense of being stifled, of being wound tighter and tighter and tighter.

CHAPTER 17

THE FUNERAL was at ten o'clock the next morning.

Sometime during the night it had started raining and it didn't let up with morning. A slow, cold drizzle that seeped into you, into your bones. The sky was a gray pall, splotched with black, as if it had some kind of disease that was spreading. And the rain kept slowly coming down, whispering in a steady hush over the cold country.

The Reverend Waugh was the first to appear at the house. He was a small, tight man in a tight-fitting suit, with tight eyes and a close-lipped mouth. He walked as if he were strapped together with leather, and when he turned, he turned his whole body. Maybe there was something the matter with his neck.

He had been talking with Verne in the living room after we'd been introduced. I had gone into the study. Petra was with Verne.

The Reverend Waugh's voice went on and on, droning monotonously from the living room. I kept sampling the whisky decanter. It was the only thing that would help pull me through. I tried not to think. But all I could think of was Petra and that our time was a little closer.

The Reverend cleared his throat in the doorway and walked tightly up to me.

'This is highly irregular,' he said. 'Highly, you know.

I don't mean to – of course, Mr. Bland – friends and all. But the officials won't like it. Burying out here when there's a cemetery in Allayne. There's an ordinance, you know.'

'We're outside its jurisdiction,' I said.

'Yes, but it's highly irregular.'

'Would you care for a drink?'

He looked startled, blinked tightly at me, with his small eyes. 'No.'

I heard a rustle at the door. Petra glanced in, blew a kiss at me, and vanished. Inside I began to tremble. You don't fool around with death like this. I kept telling myself that. Only it didn't do any good.

The Reverend Waugh went to the study window. 'Here comes the hearse.' He turned, looking at me. He seemed happy.

I heard Petra call to Verne, 'Here comes the hearse, dear.'

I didn't move. The Reverend Waugh scurried tightly from the room.

A funeral service was held in the house and after that we started with the casket for the knoll.

Verne had the left side and I was behind him. Herb Corey – a red-faced, embarrassed, stout farmer – was opposite Verne. Behind him, across from me, was Corey's hired hand. I'd been more or less forced to shake his hand when we were introduced, watching the loose smile play across his lips. His name was Cecil Emmetts.

Petra followed behind us, walking with the Reverend Waugh through the dripping orchard. All of us wore rain-coats. Petra carried an umbrella, beneath which the Reverend Waugh leaned tightly.

The coffin was not in the least heavy. The rain dripped and we walked slowly through it, through the wet grass and across a makeshift board platform bridging the creek.

Then we climbed the knoll. There were two other men from town up there to help lower the casket into the ground.

As yet there was no headstone, but I'd heard Verne speak of getting one.

I refused to look toward Emmetts. But I knew he was watching me.

Herb Corey and Emmetts had come just after the arrival of the hearse, and Emmetts' eyes stayed on Petra, watching her with a kind of harsh amusement. He was chewing tobacco, and as we trudged along, he occasionally spat.

I wondered if the old woman moved much inside the casket. We were very careful. Verne's back was straight and he walked stiffly. Climbing the knoll was bad, though, because the grass was slippery. Once Herb Corey, rather ungainly to begin with, dropped to one knee. He wrenched himself erect with a gasp and an embarrassed word of apology.

The Reverend Waugh muttered something to Petra behind us.

I heard Petra say, 'It can't be helped.'

We reached the top of the knoll by the sycamore, where the dark grave yawned. It was all I could do to keep from jabbering like an idiot. The whole business was horrible, and it was ripping me apart inside.

The rain struck the freshly wounded earth at the sides of the grave and, diamond-bright for a brief instant, vanished.

They whispered and mumbled while the casket was arranged on the slings over the grave.

Then Verne stood on one side with Petra and her umbrella. I was on the other side, facing her. Herb Corey and Emmetts and the other two men from town stood off to one side while the Reverend Waugh began praying.

It rained slowly, the fine mist of rain drifting down straight and almost as if a cloud were descending over the earth. Water dripped from the sycamore and fingered the shiny black surface of the casket. I didn't hear a word the Reverend said.

105

I looked into her eyes and she looked into mine.

I couldn't tear my gaze away. I felt Emmetts' eyes on us and panic knotted nauseously inside me and the Reverend Waugh's voice rambled on and on in prayer.

My friend, I thought. My friend's wife.

We looked at and into each other. I saw her lips part, and her breasts rose and fell more quickly beneath her coat and the umbrella's filmy shadow.

I wanted her. I wanted to leap straight across the grave and take her, bend her body to mine. She wanted me to.

We were both damned. . . .

Beneath us in that glistening black casket lay a murdered woman, and I'd been a partner to her death.

Returning to the house, Emmetts suddenly elbowed my side. His shoulders hitched and hunched beneath his raincoat and he smiled broadly, lips trembling. 'Body's buried, but the thought lingers, hey, Mr. Bland?' he whispered.

I turned on him, close to flying apart.

'Easy, now,' he whispered. 'See you tonight, hey? You ain't forgot, have you?'

'Get the hell away from me before I kill you.'

He chuckled quietly. 'Figure you done enough killin' for a time.' He spat. 'Only thing you'll be killin' now is yourself, on her!' He nodded toward Petra's back, where she was walking beside Verne. Just then she turned and glanced at me. For an instant her gaze locked with Emmetts'. He nodded and grinned at her. She turned away quickly.

His voice was low. ' "Pig," she says. We'll see who's the pig.'

None of them stayed at the house for long. They all seemed in a hurry to get away. And then we three were alone in the house and the slow rain continued to sift along the eaves.

Ten minutes later, Verne said, 'I'm going into town. Try

106

and pick out a headstone for the grave. I feel better now all this is over with.'

I glanced at Petra. I couldn't help it. She was staring at me and her face was pale.

She said, 'I'll go see if I can't fix something good for dinner.'

I knew I had to say something. I knew I had to say what I said. I was shaking all over inside and was afraid my voice would tremble, but it didn't. I just sounded a bit hoarse. 'You want me to go in with you, Verne?'

He hesitated, put on his hat, shrugged into his coat. 'No, I guess not. You stay here.' He smiled, the first smile in quite a while, but I wasn't seeing it, wasn't interested. 'Keep Petra company.'

He strode down the hall and the door slammed behind him.

Petra had started for the kitchen. She whirled.

'Keep me company, he said!'

The car wasn't even out of the driveway before we were at each other like two crazy animals.

I fastened my hands in her hair, jammed my mouth down on hers. She writhed away.

'Upstairs!'

I let her go. She ran for the stairs, undressing as she went. By the time we reached the door to her room, her dress was off.

I grabbed her in the doorway and we fought against each other, staggering wildly toward the bed. She was moaning now and beginning to cry a little.

We never made the bed. We fell to the floor and the house shook and her jetty hair spread out like a broad black fan on that thick auburn rug.

CHAPTER 18

WE FINALLY did reach her bed, and, lying there now, Petra suddenly sat up. Then she leaped to the floor and hurriedly dressed.

'He may be home any time. I've got to fix something to eat, like I said. Good lord, it's been almost two hours.'

'Yes.' I didn't look at her. Then I felt her hair fold heavily across my face and her lips brushed mine.

'See you later,' she said, and I listened to her feet hurrying down the hall, down the stairs.

There was only sickness inside me now, sickness over what had happened. I tried to fight it off, but it wouldn't go away. Lying there, I stared up at the dark midnight ceiling, and it seemed I was lying at the bottom of that grave with the damp walls pushing in on either side and with the dripping coffin slung over me. There was Verne's haggard face. A trusting guy. Why didn't he know better?

And then the pile of broken gray on the stone of the patio. . . .

Dressed, I went over and looked at the window. The torn screen was still the same. It would always be the same, too, in my mind. It wouldn't change; the jagged edges, and down there on the bare stone the broken gray mass.

I turned and went down the hall into my room and closed the door. Even closing the door didn't help, but it did start the thought, I've got to stop now. It can't go on. Something's got to be done.

I stripped and stood in the shower with the needles of cold water blasting on me, and I kept thinking of that grave out there on the knoll by the sycamore. And the pines were dripping beneath the forlorn gray half-light of an autumn sky. And when we had returned down the knoll to cross the creek, the creek was filling slowly, the grass along its edges soggy with an ability to draw more water from that mist than seemed probable. And the boards the men had put across the creek were swamped slightly, and in the orchard the mist jeweled brightly among thick spider webs.

Wild, she had been, wild, there on that auburn rug.

Rubbed down with a thick towel, I went back into my room and stood staring at the front window, beyond which the shank of the hill leaned against the road. Squatting among the brambles . . .

Madge was in Chicago, wondering what was the matter, or maybe with a chip on her shoulder. And there would never be any way of explaining to her. If I wanted to explain.

Murder.

The sound of a car turning in the drive told me Verne was back. A moment later the front door slammed and I heard him going down the hall. Then voices very faint from the kitchen, probably.

There had been no rules. Just an acceptance of what was to come. She'd resisted, put up a barrier of sorts, held me off.

She'd held me off until the old woman was in the ground. Then she'd exploded. And it hadn't been sane, either. And me without guts enough to go to Verne, or at least to run. Yes. Without guts enough to run.

There was a rapid tattoo of knuckles on the door. I turned. The racket ceased sharply, then commenced again. I slipped into a pair of pants and hurried to open the door.

'Alex, Alex! He's had an attack!'

She stood there momentarily in the doorway, then sprang at me, not touching me, but standing there with her hands out and her face dead pale with passion. She wore a black house coat, belted tightly at the waist.

'What?'

'A heart attack. Verne. When he was in town. He said it happened in the car, just as he started out of town. He stopped the car and waited, then drove on in.'

I started past her. She clamped her hands on my arms, shoved her body in my way. 'No. Let him be. He's lying down. Don't you see?'

I tried to shove by. For a moment we pushed at each other and she began to curse. One look in her eyes was enough. I ceased.

'Don't you see?'

'Did you call a doctor?'

'He won't have a doctor. Simply won't have one.'

'Call one anyway, Petra. For God's sake. The man may be bad off. He might die.'

'That's right. Don't you see?' She flung herself against me. I grabbed her and swung her around at the bed. She sprawled to her knees beside the bed, still talking, gesticulating with her hands. 'Don't you see, Alex? This is our chance. I told you his heart was bad. He'll never admit it's as bad as it is. The doctor told him he can't smoke or drink, but he doesn't care. He's down there now, with a bottle of brandy.' She paused. She spoke so rapidly that her voice seemed to run over itself, as if she were talking against time. 'All that money, Alex. He's worth plenty. It would be mine – ours.'

I stared at her without comprehension really, not even believing I heard straight. 'Petra. His mother's just buried this morning.'

She rose to one knee, imploring, her mouth a bloody gash

almost as black as her eyes and hair against the pallor of her face. 'Yes. Yes. That's right. The shock of his mother's death. It could kill him. We could see to it. Don't you understand? I can't bear it any longer, it's been too much. We could . . .'

I stepped in close, brought the flat of my hand, the heel, sharply against her jaw. She lifted backward against the bed. I wanted to hit her again but I couldn't. It was like striking water, because when you drew your hand away nothing had changed. She lay there watching me, breathing harshly. The house coat was half off her, her legs spraddled out, her breasts bared, with only the dark belt holding the flaring house coat around her.

She watched and watched while little beads of bright scarlet purled from the corner of her mouth.

'You love me,' she whispered. She nodded slowly as the spoke. 'You love me and it's hard for you to prove it, but you say it when you do things like that. You can't stand hearing me tell what's true; what's in your own mind. You can't stand it because you know I'm right and you love me.'

I couldn't answer.

'It's you. You're still fighting against yourself,' she said. 'Why don't you stop, let yourself go? Admit it to yourself, why don't you? Because you struck me now you'll want me more than ever. You won't sleep, because you can't stand it. I've heard you pacing the floor at night. You keep thinking about that girl in Chicago. Was she as good as I am. Alex? No. I can see it in your eyes, she wasn't. She couldn't be. She doesn't know what love is – the need. Even to kill for it, how better to prove it? How could you – '

I walked out of the room and hurried down the stairs. At the foot of the stairs I glanced back. She was leaning in the doorway of my room, looking down at me.

Verne lay on the couch in the living room with a bottle of brandy cradled in his arm. He was extremely pale and his face and shirt were bathed with sweat. He didn't move as I stepped up, but his eyes followed me.

'How do you feel?' I asked.

'Fine. I'm fine.' His voice was hollow, and when he smiled it wasn't a smile at all, just a torturing of the muscles around his mouth. There was something like fright in his eyes. But that went away as I stood there.

'Let me call a doctor, Verne. Petra said you had a heart attack.'

'No doctor, Alex. I'm all right. Had these damned things before.'

'Hadn't you better lay off the bottle?'

'No. It's good for me.' He grinned. 'Hell. You know how I always drank cognac.'

'Yes.'

'Well, this is cognac.'

'Fine. How do you really feel?' I kicked the ottoman over by the couch and sat on it.

'Tired. Outside of being tired, I feel fine.'

'Did it hurt much?'

He grinned this time, took a swallow from the bottle. 'No. It's not bad. You just wonder how many more you can stand. Or if this is the one, or what. Have some?' He offered me the bottle.

I took it and had a couple of good swallows. It was really good. I hadn't drunk any in a long while, and the flavor of it brought back flashing memories of times and of lots worse cognac.

As I sat there beside my friend, it began to get very bad. The realization of what had happened of the things I had done in this house began to eat at me. It was the beginning of the really bad time ahead. No matter what I said to Verne, it was shaded on some side by a lie.

'I think I'd better call a doctor,' I said.

He looked at me. 'No. give me the bottle.'

I took another drink and handed him the bottle. I knew I should phone the doctor anyway. But I didn't. It was a minor thing, but maybe there was that much trust he could place in me.

'Petra's had a bad time of it with my mother,' he said. He closed his eyes. The beads of sweat stood out on his forehead as large as field peas. 'What will I do now?'

'What do you mean?'

'Nothing.' His eyes stayed closed. 'Alex, will you stay on a while yet?'

'Yes.'

I heard the piano from the other side of the house. It was exact, brilliant, passionate playing. At first I didn't catch the music, then I did, and glanced quickly at Verne. His eyes were still closed.

'Petra,' he said. 'She certainly can play. It's been a long time since she's touched the piano.'

I stared at him, wondering how he could have such a small knowledge of music as not to know what she was playing. It was patent that he didn't know.

It was Saint-Saens' *'Danse Macabre'*; the very well-known Dance of Death. I wondered if she had taken time to dust the keys. I remembered how I'd caught myself whistling the melody the first night I'd been in the house. The way she played sounded a little mad, and a chill touched my shoulders. It was foolish and maybe melodramatic, but I felt that this was a house of death, of evil. Standing away from it, I wondered if it would be possible to detect any humor in it. All I could feel was horror at my own faults.

And I knew that I couldn't leave without telling Verne everything. I wondered how much he knew, how much he guessed.

Cecil Emmetts. The afternoon would go fast, and then the evening, and he would wait beside the bushes on the highway.

I could tell him only one answer. There was only one.

113

The piano ceased. I looked at Verne. He was asleep, the bottle beginning to slide from his arm. I took the bottle and drank deeply. As I set it on the floor by the couch I knew it was taking hold and it helped. But not much.

I went to the music room. The door was closed. I opened it, went in, and shut the door.

'Hello, darling.'

She was seated at the piano. She still wore the black house coat, but she also wore stockings now and high-heeled shoes. As she turned and looked at me there was an instant when I couldn't believe all that had happened. Then I could.

I sat in the chair by the window. The window sill was damp from the rain, but she had closed the window. She rose and came over to me.

'Look,' she said. 'I forgot to show you.' She smiled. 'Guess you were too busy to notice.'

She undid the belt of the house coat and, lifting her left leg, placed her foot on the left side of the chair cusion. She unhooked the garters from her stocking and peeled the stocking down her full thigh. 'Here,' she said. 'See what you did when you grabbed me yesterday?'

There was a large black-and-blue mark on her thigh.

She took my hand and ran the palm across the mark.

'You're getting excited,' she said. 'I can tell.'

I stood quickly and walking over to the piano, felt of the keys. Most of them were still partially gritty with dust. 'Why did you play that?' I asked.

'Because I felt like it. It was suitable. Why do you fight yourself?' She was fixing the garter on the stocking. Her legs, all of her body was white, voluptuous; and like fire to my heart and blood – just watching. Her eyes gleamed darkly and as yet the fighting within me was no good.

The brandy had gone to my head completely. 'Damn you.'

She put her leg down from the chair. The house coat

draped open. She wore nothing beneath it but the garter belt.

She smiled and her scarlet lips glistened. 'You love me,' she said. 'Why deny it?'

My voice said it. It wasn't me, yet it was me. 'Damn you. Lock that door.'

She did.

'Come here,' I said.

She did. The smile had changed from a smile of amusement to sudden passion.

'Why can't we forget it all? You, I mean,' she said. 'Why can't you forget it? We could have fun, then. We could be like we should.'

I was sitting in the chair again. She was perched on the arm of the chair, one hip against my shoulder. The house coat was in a heap on the floor.

'Dress,' I said. I rose and unlocked the door, peered into Verne's study. The house was silent. I closed the door but didn't lock it and watched her as she slipped on the house coat. She did it carelessly. Her breasts were large, perfectly formed, upthrusting, and firm. Her body was flawless, as if she had been carved with some lusty godlike precision from a warm, utterly unblemished slab of pure alabaster.

She drew the black belt tight around her slim waist. 'Why can't we?' she asked again. 'We never joke, it's just fire. Of course, I like the fire, too.'

'Shut up,' I said.

'I won't. You're still fighting yourself. How long will it go on? How long before you'll admit it?'

I didn't answer aloud but I said, Never, to myself.

'It's him – it's Verne, isn't it? You keep thinking about a foolish friendship that no longer exists. About a man who is no longer a man, but a machine. A machine with a broken part, at that – one that'll quit any time.'

115

I rubbed my hand across my face and the smell of her was on my hand like some acid eating into the skin, burning, until it could not be removed – ever.

I left the room, walked through the study, and looked in at Verne on the couch. He was awake. He blinked at me.

'What'd you do with my bottle?' he asked.

'I drank it.'

His hand had dropped down beside the couch. He grinned as his fingers touched the bottle. He took a drink. Then he sat up on the couch.

'Feel a lot better,' he said.

I stood in the doorway.

'Since you've been here,' he went on. 'I've felt better, somehow. A lot has happened, but maybe it'll calm down now. Maybe everything's ironed out.'

I didn't answer right away. Calmed down, ironed out. 'It's been fine,' I said. 'Only don't let anything get you down.' He looked better, all right.

'I feel good with you here,' he said. 'Like old times. It's good to know you can depend on somebody.'

His words slashed me, cut into me, dug at me. And he didn't know. There was nothing I could say or do. If I'd never met despair before, I had now. And what in hell was I to do? You weak-willed coward, I told myself. You gutless wonder. Not alone taking your friend's wife, but murder, too, and now blackmail, and all that wonderful clean world of yours gone.

'Alex, is something troubling you? You don't look right, the past couple of days. Somehow.'

'Nothing. I'm all right. A little tired, maybe.' A little tired, I thought. A little tired.

'I know it's been rough. I'll make it up to you.'

I laughed. It sounded like the last note of a funeral dirge. 'Forget all of that, will you? I'm going up and take a nap.'

He didn't say anything this time, just stared at me, puzzled, maybe.

I went on upstairs to my room and closed the door and stared at the bed.

Panic was nothing to what I began feeling now. Panic was like a mosquito bite on a dying leper.

I went and washed my hands, then smelled of them. The odor of her wouldn't go away. I poured rubbing alcohol on them, then suddenly looked at myself in the mirror on the medicine cabinet. Something lurked in my eyes that I'd never seen before.

'You're going crazy, you damned fool!' I said. 'You're out of your head.'

But the smell was gone from my hands.

CHAPTER 19

I WAS WELL on the way to being good and drunk by eight-forty-five. It was the first time I'd seen Petra slightly worried. The more she frowned and watched me, the more I drank.

We were in the living room. Verne was still resting on the couch. He had drunk some, but sparingly, and was quite sober.

'Alex,' Petra said, 'you're getting pie-eyed.'

Verne said, 'He's on vacation. He ought to stay drunk all the time.'

Only it wasn't that kind of drunk. Things kept getting clearer and I knew I'd have to drink a lot before I reached the stage where I could forget, or become careless enough not to give a damn about what I thought.

Petra said, 'It's ten to nine already,' and threw me a meaningful glance.

'So what?' Verne said. 'I'm not going to work tomorrow. Let the damned job take care of itself for a few days. I'll handle it by telephone. Least I can do for Alex.'

'Thanks,' I said. 'It'll be good for you, too.' I rose a bit unsteadily. 'Think I'll get some air, take a walk.'

'Sure,' Verne said. 'I'm lazy, myself. Go ahead with him, Petra.'

I cut her a look that said, No!

'No,' she said. 'But don't get lost and don't be long, Alex. It's still drizzling. Verne's raincoat is in the hall.'

I was already in the hall with the raincoat half on. I walked toward the rear of the house and found an unopened pint of whisky on the liquor shelf in the kitchen. I put it in the deep raincoat pocket and went out the back door.

In the back yard I opened the pint and took a good drink, capped it, and put it away again. Then I went out to the highway and started walking down toward the bend. The rain was still a mist, but slightly heavier, and it felt good on my face and on my bare head. It was clean. It came straight down from the sky without touching anything at all.

I kept thinking. Maybe it will wash out my brain, get the smell off my brain. That had been bothering me. My hands didn't smell of her right now, but how could I wash my brain? I decided the rain couldn't do it because it couldn't get inside.

It was very dark and the hills blended into the dark but the trees didn't. The trees were like flat deformed black hands against the streaming sky. Actually the sky was not black but more of an extremely dark violet, and somewhere there was a radiance because the vibrant puddles in the road gleamed. A single bird piped fitfully up in the brambles on the hill.

Cecil Emmetts. It didn't bother her at all. It didn't reach her. Murder didn't. So nothing would. that's what I knew now.

I was waiting for something. Every day. What was it? Strength? Will? The driving will that had always kept me on the straight and narrow, forsaking me like a lost hat when I most needed it? I was waiting.

Something was going to happen. It had to. Because it kept on mounting and getting worse all the time. Something had to break. I had a feeling it would be me.

It was getting a lot colder now. This was the coldest night

since I'd been here. I got out the bottle and had a good one. Then I was by the bushes.

I walked around the bushes on the soggy pasture grass. He wasn't here yet. I went and stood on the shoulder of the road. A car hissed by, whipping a spray of rain and exhaust into my face. I thought of Chicago.

I wrote a letter in my mind to Madge.

Dearest Madge:

   I am an accessory to murder, or maybe in some eyes an accomplice. I am sleeping regularly with my best friend's wife. We are being blackmailed for the murder of my best friend's mother. Right now I am drunk. I am also wet, and believe me, sick with despair. Whenever I see her I want her. I am rotten with desire for her. Yet I am certain that I love you. I will always love you, no matter what happens, and it probably will.

I began to laugh. Finally I stopped and had another long drink from the bottle. I looked at my watch and it was nine-fifteen. I laughed at nine-fifteen.

It began to rain harder, hissing on the highway.

All I wanted was to get away, back to Madge. Get away from the house and Petra. But now there was more to it than just that. Whatever way the dice turned, I had to stand up to their reading. It wasn't enough now just to get away and exhibit some bones and relics in Chicago. And not only murder, either. Somehow I had to face Verne and tell him. It was the only way for my own freedom.

I had another drink.

When I next glanced at my watch, it was nine-thirty and I was pacing in the rain. 'Hell with Cecil Emmetts,' I said aloud. I started off down the highway.

'All right, mister. Stay put.'

I stopped, turning. Emmetts came out from behind the

bushes. He lounged up to where I stood and snorted through his nose. 'Been watchin',' he said, punctuating his words with a stream of tobacco juice from the side of his mouth.

'You've been here all the time?'

'Not quite. Just thought I'd figure to give you a worry.'

I started walking off again. He grabbed my arm. 'Set tight,' he said. He wore a poncho and his hat, and he was very wet, but his eyes and mouth laughed. His shoulders hitched and hunched beneath the poncho.

In my left raincoat pocket I had one hundred dollars, just in case. I kept crumpling the money between my fingers.

'Give me a drink,' he said. 'I seen the bottle.'

I didn't move.

'Y'hear?'

I handed him the bottle. He uncapped it. 'Beggars can't be choosers,' he said. 'You ain't holdin' out nothin' from now on.' He drank and smacked his lips, then he threw the bottle cap away.

'You're worried, ain't you?'

'This will be the last time you ever pull a stunt like this,' I said.

'Think so? I don't figure you got much to say 'bout that, mister.'

'What if I go to the police?'

He grinned. His teeth gleamed. He tilted the bottle.

'Bet you must've felt funny carryin' the old woman to her grave, hey?' He blew air through his nose and slapped rain from his hat brim with his left hand. His eyes were like wet agates.

'Well,' I said.

'Must feel dandy,' he said. 'Your friend's wife, too. Figure mebbe I'm doin' him a turn, this way. Trusts y' like a brother, don't he? Ol' Herb says Verne told 'im you're th' one man in the world he can depend on.' He made a noise through his nose.

121

'You better shut up,' I said. I wasn't going to be able to stand much more of this. It was hell. Every bit of it was hell and inside me I was cramped up.

'Ain't y' got no shame? Figure mebbe the gal had reason, plenty reason, t' shove the ol' gal out the window. Cooped up like she was. Had t' carry the ol' woman ever'place she went. I seen it comin' in her eyes. Could tell what would happen someday. You show up an' things pop, hey? Bet she's red hot, hey?'

The whisky had worn off. I trembled beneath the raincoat and my guts knotted and writhed like a nest of snakes. Nobody could ever know how it was. It was something you read about in the old novels, where the hero crawled white-faced and weak back to his mistress' bed – throwing honor and pride and courage in the gutter, then crawling in after them, not even trying to find them again. You laughed at it today, because things had changed. You laughed if there was laughter with it. Only when it turned sour and you saw it was really evil, you were scared stiff. But you still crawled back toward those wanton gleaming eyes.

And maybe she was like the gatekeeper Milton wrote about, with the scales and the hell hounds running in and out of her womb, snarling and snapping, and you didn't care. Maybe that was it. Maybe you were subduing the hell hounds.

I began to laugh.

'Startin' to get you, hey?'

I ceased. I wanted Madge. God, how I wanted to see Madge, to be with her with all this done and over with. No matter what happened, and anyway, I'd have to take whatever came my way. And it would come – it had to. I knew that.

And now she wanted to kill Verne. I couldn't think clearly any more and it wasn't the whisky now. My mind felt like a smudge of smoke. She wanted to kill Verne, so we could have his money.

She had already nearly killed Verne. There wasn't much left now.

He finished the bottle, tossed it to the side of the road. It struck a stone and the glass shattered.

'All right,' he said. 'Make up your mind?'

'What do you want?' I said. I said it from the front of my mouth without thinking at all, trying to hold myself away from the thought.

'Figure to tread easy for a spell. Later on, I'll clamp down. fifty dollars now. Told you no money tonight, but I figure you got fifty on you. Next Sunday you bring the gal. Same time, right here. I want to see her face.'

'Fifty dollars?' I said. 'You're scared, aren't you?'

He shook his head. But he was scared. It was in his eyes. He was lousy cheap.

'No,' he said. 'I ain't scared. I figure to have me a regular income from now on. Easy at first, so nobody suspicions.' He paused and grinned. 'Sunday bring the gal. I'd kind of like to see her close up.'

He had asked for the money now. When I gave it to him he was in all the way. It might have been five thousand. It was all the same. And he knew it. That's why he was scared. but he was fairly sure of himself.

I gave him the money. He put it away beneath the poncho and spat. 'I'll be watchin',' he said. 'You step outa line, or don't show up with the gal, I'll make my move. Count on it.'

'You haven't got any guts,' I said. 'Why don't you make a big haul and leave?'

He snorted, thrust his face close to mine. I smelled the wet barnyard and tobacco and his eyes gleamed. 'You're a fine one to talk about guts,' he said.

I turned and walked away before I hit him again, because what good would it do? Maybe I'd feel a little better, but it wouldn't change anything.

'Don't forget to bring the heifer Sunday night.'

I walked faster. The rain had ceased.

My God, she wanted to kill Verne. It was just getting to me. So much had happened I was getting numb to shock.

I turned, looked back. He was standing in the road, watching after me.

'Sleep easy, mister,' he called. 'Thanks for the drink.'

Fifty dollars. Fifty lousy dollars' worth of silence. Silence I didn't want. That was it.

But the closer I got to the house, the more I thought about her, and when I reached the house I wanted a drink. Because as the alcohol wore off, it was much worse.

In the kitchen I found a bottle and drank it down like water. There wasn't a sound in the house, although a light was lit in the living room. As I drank I thought of Petra, and with every drink I wanted her a little more.

I draped the soaking raincoat over the lunch bar and dried my hair on a towel. I knew then I was quite drunk. The panic didn't go away, but neither did thoughts of her. It was like hot iron, being jammed between dry hot iron flanks – stuck to them with the skin searing without odor but with a kind of exquisite pain. Not love, even. If there had only been love with it, real love, or whatever it is – maybe like Madge and me – then it would have been all right. I could have killed then, maybe. No, not killed. That wouldn't have happened, none of this would have. Because it would have been all right then. We would have gone to Verne and told him. It would have been complete because it would have been right.

And whatever sorrow there would have been would be honest sorrow, not secret or hidden. And the despair wouldn't have been there.

But it was not love. Not lust, even. Something else. I was unable to fight back because there was nothing to get a grip on. All the sharp edges were worn round and smooth. But there was hope. There had to be hope, and all through this

I knew there was hope. Without that subconscious realization
of eventual hope after the blow-up that had to come . . . but
to kill Verne. Even the thought. In my friend's home I stood
drunk in the kitchen wanting his wife, knowing she had
murdered his mother.

There was nobody in the living room. I turned off the light
and felt my way upstairs. Taking a chance didn't matter now,
nothing mattered. In the back of my head I wanted him to
find us, so it would be finished.

I went directly to her room and she was waiting.

'He's asleep,' she whispered. 'We'll have to be quiet.'

We stood there in the cool darkness and she closed her
bedroom door. Her bare feet hissed on the thick nap of the
rug.

'I paid off our keeper,' I said, and my voice not only
sounded bitter, it tasted bitter. I told her what silence cost.

'I knew it,' she said. 'He's that cheap.' She stepped closer
and her perfume struck me like a blow.

'He's cheap,' I said. 'But he'll get expensive.'

'Let him,' she said. 'My God, you stink of whisky.'

'Do you care?'

'No. I don't care.'

The room was dark, which was a shame for anyone who
lingered across the road up on the brambled hill. . . .

It was three-forty-five when I dressed to return to my room.
I don't know why I dressed, but I did. Petra pleaded with
me to stay until dawn, but the whisky had worn off and I felt
rotten. Her passion didn't cool with time, it grew hotter.

'Stay with me, Alex. Stay. Verne's asleep. He'll never
know.' She was lying spread out on the bed, her hair black
against the pillow.

Without the whisky to hold me up, it was hell, plain hell.
I was living in a fire and she was the one who kept hurling

gasoline on the flame. Being with her had been a kind of hellish heaven. It was maybe like trying to drown yourself in pleasure, hoping to God that you would drown, but hoping that the pleasure would continue and in the back of your mind hating every second of it, but never wanting to let up, either.

We hadn't talked much, I had nothing to say to her. When she mentioned Verne's heart, I told her to shut up.

She had chuckled.

We'd been talking enough without using vocal chords. I didn't reply now, but left the room.

The house was still and dark. I went quietly on down to my room and opened the door. Moonlight flayed the shadows into soft light.

'Hello, Alex.'

It was Verne, seated on my bed.

CHAPTER 20

I WENT ALL to pieces. I shook like crazy. I couldn't control any part of me, just stood there shaking, unable to speak. Somehow I managed to close the door.

Then suddenly it was all right. He knew and it was all right. The relief was so great I wanted to laugh.

'You took a hell of a long walk,' Verne said. He was in his pajamas on the bed. 'But I don't blame you. I would too. This must have been hell for you these past few days. I just woke up a few minutes ago. Thought I'd see if you were awake. Felt like talking.'

He didn't know. He didn't even suspect. There wasn't a tinge of suspicion in his voice.

'I brought a bottle,' he said. 'Have a couple with me?'

'Yes,' I said. 'Sure. I'll have a couple with you.' Then the lies came out. It was simple, and my voice was calm even though the old torture was worse than ever inside. 'Been sitting downstairs,' I said. 'Turned off the light when I came in a couple of hours ago. I didn't feel very sleepy.'

'Yeah. That's the way I feel. This has been a rotten vacation for you.'

I went into the bathroom, closed the door, and lit the light. I looked as if somebody had squeezed me through a sieve and then tried halfheartedly to put the strings together again.

127

I washed, then went back into the bedroom and turned on the light.

'You do look kind of tired,' he said.

'Yes.'

'We'll just have a couple of short ones. Then I'll let you get some sleep.'

'I'm not sleepy.'

He handed me the bottle. It was cognac again. When I drank, it again went down like water. It seemed weak.

'I'm worried about Petra,' Verne said.

I glanced at him. He looked as sick as you can get.

'There's something the matter with her, Alex.'

'I hadn't noticed anything.'

'Well that's natural. You wouldn't, not knowing her, and all. But there's something the matter.'

'What seems to be the trouble?'

It was easy, a cinch. You just talked along with a kind of savage politeness, not knowing half of what you said. But you knew you must be saying the right things. Because convention had taught you that long ago. So you didn't have to think and you could see her all the time lying on her bed in there. And none of the pain inside you showed, either. None of the conscious guilt showed while you stood there and lied like hell to a man who obviously trusted you completely. You were just like one of those talking machines, robots, where somebody pressed the keys and the voice came out.

'She's not happy, Alex. She hasn't been for a long while. I can tell. Of course, Mother, and all that . . . But like now. Suddenly she wants to run the house all by herself. It's a big house and she's never taken any interest before. but suddenly she doesn't want any help. Wants to cook all the meals – everything else.'

'Sounds good to me.'

'Yes. Only you don't know her like I do.'

'Maybe you're right.'

'Firing Jenny like that. And the cook. All right about the cook, but Jenny was swell – a swell girl.'

I knew what he meant. But I didn't know how much longer I'd be able to stand there facing him and lying, even with the help of the bottle.

It wasn't anything you could just escape from, it was something that held you until it was done and you couldn't be free until the time came. God. To think. That beautiful goddamned bitch in there with the black hair not even knowing enough to know that she didn't know what was anyway partly the matter with her, or that she was cockeyed crazy and headed for doom.

All she knew was Get in bed with me, I love you. Kill. And money. And her husband suspected that something was the matter with her. I took a long drink from the bottle, glad that I was getting drunk again.

'I met her in a bar in New York,' he said. 'She played the piano there. You know what her last name was? It was Jones. Billed Pet Jones, and she sure could play.'

Jones. It rocked me. Petra Jones.

'And she was so damned beautiful, Alex.'

'Sure.'

'We got married and bought this place and we were happy, too. For a while. Anyway, until Mother . . . I didn't mean too – ' He ceased. 'Give me the bottle.'

He took a good drink.

'I'm going back to bed,' he said. 'Good night.'

I watched him leave the room. He left the bottle on top of the bureau in my room. He had tried hard to tell me something but he'd found himself unable to. Maybe it was something he couldn't even tell himself and believe it at the same time. Or just tell it, even; maybe he couldn't even do that.

I got undressed and took the bottle to bed with me and by five o'clock I was really soused and not a bit sleepy.

The next day I stayed that way. Every time I felt myself beginning to sober up I'd take a couple of good drinks. Not staggering drunk, just brain-helpless drunk, not-care drunk, hell-with-it drunk.

I kept trying to tell myself that it was just that Verne had kept Petra cooped up too much and running around with his mother, and now she was blowing her top. Only it was no good.

At noon Verne went up to look at his mother's grave. The headstone was supposed to be ready in a day or so, he told me.

Petra was washing the dishes from lunch. She was a good cook. Almost as good in the kitchen as she was in bed.

I went upstairs and into her room and started going through the drawers in her dresser. Then I went over to her dressing table. There hadn't been anything. That's the way it would be with her. Only in the top right-hand drawer of her dressing table there was a .32 Savage automatic. A deadly little thing. I stared at it. There was a full clip in it.

Lots of people keep a gun around.

'It's just like you,' she said from the doorway. 'Especially the way you've been drinking.'

I dropped the gun back into the drawer and closed the drawer. 'What have you got that for?'

'What do you think?'

'What difference does it make?' I said.

'That's right.'

She was close to me. She had her hair tied up with a ribbon in back and she wore a white apron over a black dress. Her eyes were clear and her smile was something you could watch for a long time – if you didn't know her.

'We won't have time now,' she said. 'He might come back.'

'I wasn't thinking of that.'

'Like hell you weren't.'

'Suppose I beat it and leave you with this mess in your lap?'

'You won't,' she said. 'But, Alex, if you do try anything, I swear I'll go to Verne and tell him you killed his mother. I'll tell him you've been making love to me. I'll tell him anything, you hear? I mean it, Alex.'

We watched each other. She was quite serious.

'He'll believe me, Alex. You may be his friend, and all that rot, but he'll believe me. Because I've never told him how I felt.' She smiled slowly and her eyes glistened. 'I just sort of worked on him.'

He would believe her.

'He kept me cooped up here, I tell you. With that damned . . . And I want that money. He's no good any more. It's us now, Alex – us, you hear?'

'Yeah. Us.' I started past her, but I didn't get by. It was like passing a magnet, one of these huge electro-magnets they use to hoist junk. Like trying to pass one of those with twenty pounds of steel buttoned inside your shirt.

Holding her tight against you with her moaning a little. Then both of you tearing, trying to get away, because you knew he might come back any minute from up there on the knoll by the sycamore.

I made it and got downstairs and found a bottle.

The next day the headstone came. And while Verne was up there on the knoll with the men and the headstone, Petra and I were on the living-room couch.

And the days went on like that, Wednesday, Thursday, Friday, until Saturday I was still drunk and maybe a little out of my head. Verne was concerned about me. He well might be.

But he suspected things now. I knew he did; it was in the

way he looked at me. He suspected but I couldn't allow myself to think of it.

I locked myself in my room, and paced the floor and wrote letters to Madge that I tore up. I couldn't get away from Petra.

She was everywhere. It was a mad hot hell from which I couldn't escape even by crawling into a bottle. And through it all Verne strolled, amiable, smiling, saying, 'Couple more days and I'll be feeling tops. You stay on, Alex. Then we'll get out and do things. I just want to be feeling right.'

Saturday night at six o'clock I got up from the dinner table.

'I'm going to take a walk,' I said. Neither of them paid any attention. I'd walked out into the orchard or along the road several times. This time I took a pint of whisky and my topcoat and started down the road toward Allayne. There was one way left. Hair of the dog. The antidote. Bounce one woman out of your mind with another. If I could do that, if I could stay drunk enough so I wouldn't turn around before I got to Allayne . . .

It was a windy fall night and the sky was black and moonless but with a million lazy stars blinking up there.

Hell was nearby, all right. But I only thought I knew what it was like. I hadn't seen any of it yet.

CHAPTER 21

SATURDAY NIGHT in Allayne was the big night. It was the night when those from the surrounding country came to town and when those in town went to town. The main street was jam-packed with cars and trucks, parked diagonally in toward the curb, fender to fender. The stream of traffic up and down the street was continuous and erratic in movement. Farmers and townspeople mingled in a bobbing, elbowing stream on the sidewalks, and the brisk autumnal wind blew dust in their eyes. The cheaper bars were loud with booming juke-box songs, loud red-faced laughter, the tinkle and clash of glass.

This was everywhere:

'Feller Lawrence. Out on French Street, there. Dug himself a hole in the ground an' stuck his old mother in it.'

'So I hear. Guess she was dead, anyways.'

'Dead, all right. Know what I think? Think she committed sewerside, by damn. Taken it into her head an' jumped plumb outen the danged winder.'

'Seen 'im on the street the other day. Looked peaked. Walked like he was in a trance, like.'

'Mebbe you'd look dangle-eared with a wife like her.'

'She sure is a whingding, ain't she?'

'Give us another beer, Charley. Say, I'd pay to get peaked over that.'

'It wouldn't take long, neither. But you ain't got enough.'

'Feller stayin' out there, now. Cece Emmetts says he met up with 'im at the funeral. Says he packs a pint ever'where he goes.'

'Say, you don't suppose . . .'

In three different bars where I stopped for a beer, such conversation reached my ears. Verne Lawrence was literally the talk of the town, and Petra was the added spice. Doubltess the exact truth was spoken more than once, all unknowing.

Without drinking too much during the past few days, I had managed to keep myself in a light haze. There was no sign of its catching up with me. I'd eaten regularly and I hadn't overdone it. But now I felt like blotting it out. The haze was all right, but every day I had to increase the dosage to prevent descending clarity of mind.

There were two hotels in Allayne, one a rather rundown establishment with a loud, roaring bar, on the main street. The other, Allayne Hotel, was more imposing, a block off the main drag on an elm-shrouded street.

I drifted that way and found the cocktail lounge. There was a juke-box here, too, but it wasn't quite so loud and the selection of recordings was of the sirupy rather than the bang-slap-bam type. It was cool, rustic, and obviously frequented by some part of the town's elite. Men and women conversed over highballs and cocktails rather than beer and wine. They dressed differently and the men had haircuts. They probably said the same things as in the other places, and they certainly got just as drunk – or drunker.

I had a bottle of beer at the bar. In another room off the bar there were tables with chatting couples beneath a low-beamed ceiling.

I stared at her for perhaps a full minute before I knew who it was. Jenny. She didn't see me. She was with a broad-shouldered man who sported a hand-painted tie but very little chin.

Turning, I went out the side door of the bar into the parking lot and tilted my pint. I drank as much as I could without retching, pocketed the bottle, and returned to the bar. The whisky was taking hold fine now. I had a glass of water at the bar, then went in and approached Jenny's table. I didn't know whether it would work, but I was going to try. I didn't feel bad about it, either, because the guy with Jenny didn't look like her type. Besides, the whisky was taking hold fine.

I came up to them from behind the man's back and winked at her. 'Miss Carson,' I said. 'Something important's come up, and!' I turned to him and said, 'No, sit still,' although he hadn't moved. 'You'll have to come with me.'

Jenny frowned, her eyes puzzled. She looked fine with her carrot-colored hair and a grey dress with a thick silver chain around the waist. 'What do you mean?' she asked.

'I mean, something's come up. Very important. I'm sorry, but – '

'Say,' the man said. 'What is this?'

'It's nothing at all,' I said. 'Merely something Miss Carson has to attend to.'

Jenny looked from the man to me, then back again. She was obviously puzzled. She started to say something and I shook my head slightly. She began to play along.

'You mean the house?' she said.

I nodded. 'Yes, and you'll have to come along right away. Can't afford to lose any time.'

I reeled slightly.

The man said, 'But Jenny – ' What chin he had positively vanished.

Jenny said, 'I'm terriby sorry, Tom. I didn't know this would come up.'

Her coat, also gray and light, was over the back of her chair. I held it up. The guy looked at me. I looked at him

135

and nodded. He stood. Jenny stood. I slipped the coat over
Jenny's shoulders and took her arm.

'I know it's tough,' I said. 'But you know you'd better see
about it right away.'

'But, Jenny – ' the guy said. 'Listen here,' he said to me.
'What is this?'

'You're spoiling the record,' I told him. I guided Jenny
carefully away from the table. The guy took three steps.

'Will you be back?' he said. 'Jenny!'

'Tom, I don't know,' she said. 'I'll try. I'm terribly sorry.
You can have my drink, I didn't touch it.'

He stared at her drink. We left by the door into the hotel
lobby and a moment later we were in the street. I wondered
if he enjoyed her drink.

I glanced back through the large glass doors. The guy was
coming down the length of the lobby with a determined
stride.

'Now, listen,' Jenny said. 'What's so important?'

'Me,' I said. 'Me.' There was a taxi stand and two minutes
later we were turning onto the main street of Allayne.

I looked back toward the hotel. The guy was standing out
in front, lighting a cigarette.

'You're drunk,' Jenny said.

'Yes.'

'Why did you do that?'

'You looked unhappy.'

'That was a mean thing to do, Alex.'

'You went along with it.'

'Well, I – '

'Sure. Never mind. But you weren't happy, were you?'

'No.'

'All right. How'd you like to take a walk? It's a beautiful
fall night and we could take a walk.'

She sighed and stared at the back of the cab driver's head.

136

He had a fat neck that bulged over his shirt collar. 'All right,' she said. 'We'll take a walk. Is something the matter?'

'Not something. Everything.'

'I didn't think you drank like this.'

'I don't.' We were coming near the end of the main street, and traffic was thinning out. 'Look,' I said. 'We'll get out here. Can you drink warm Martinis?'

'I never tried.'

'I'll get a bottle of it already mixed,' I told her. 'And some paper cups. We can drink it that way. It may not be fine and there won't be any olives, if you've got to have olives, but it will be something.'

She watched me and broke into a grin. 'All right.'

When I paid the driver I slipped him what was left of the pint of whisky. He said he didn't drink. I told him not to be foolish.

After we bought the bottle and the paper cups, we started off down the street. I felt fine. I knew there was Petra and the house out there and murder and that I was impaled on a hook, but I didn't care so much. I knew that when it wore off I would be in a complete hell, but right now it was all right.

'Where will we walk?' I asked.

She hesitated. 'Let me carry the cups,' she said. 'Well. We can walk to the end of this street and then cross the park to the lake. Will that be all right? It'll be chilly, but the lake will be nice tonight.'

'The lake it is.'

We stopped. It was a dark corner. I drew her close and she looked up at me and she was fresh and clean like a summer's wind. Her lips were warm and sweet and for a single moment she responded, then I felt her stiffen.

We walked on. 'Jenny kissed me,' I said.

'All right.'

We went on through the dark shadows of the park to the

edge of the lake. She was right. The lake was something to see beneath the star-freckled night with the dark hills humped and leaning over against the living mirror of slowly broken water. The water was very cold, so I put the bottle between two rocks in the water and we sat on a bench close by.

The wind smelled of pure clean autumn and pine and water. We sat very close together now because it was rather cold.

'We could have gone to your house,' I said.

'Yes. I guess so.'

'But it's nicer here.' I took her hand. I started to put my arm around her but then I remembered the bottle. 'We'll try a drink,' I said. 'It won't be cold but it'll be cooler.'

She smiled hesitantly but her eyes were bright and I told myself I must be very drunk because I thought her eyes reminded me of the stars. I did need a drink. She sort of reminded me of Madge, too.

'I have the cups,' she called to me.

I thought for a minute I'd lost the bottle, but I found it. It felt cool. The water was so cold my hand ached just reaching for the bottle. I remembered how only a short while ago Petra had gone in swimming. It certainly hadn't cooled her.

'It tastes good,' she said. 'Really.' She was lying.

'After the first few swallows it'll taste all right.' Then I noticed something and remembered. 'We'll have to drink each drink quickly.'

'Why?'

'The gin softens the bottom of the cup. See?'

'Oh.' She stared at me for a minute, holding the hair away from the side of her face with her hand. 'It's a fine way to get a girl plastered, isn't it?'

'Yes.' I touched my cup to hers. 'Drink up.'

We had another.

'What's troubling you, Alex? What is it?'

'It's nothing,' I said. 'Kiss me.'

'No.'

'Why not? We know each other, Jenny. You know we do.'

'Yes. I do know you, Alex. Maybe better than you think.'

'Then come on.'

'You really want to?'

'The other one doesn't count.'

She moved closer to me and her body felt warm even through both our coats. Maybe it was something more than just warmth. I kept thinking of Madge and Madge was all mixed up with Petra when we kissed. She drew away. 'Please,' she said.

I poured us each another drink. She drank hers fast.

'The bottom of the cup,' she said. 'It's come out.'

I started to hand her another cup. 'It's getting colder,' I said. There was a large thick clump of bushes beside the bench, and a few feet beyond the bushes was a large tree trunk with thick well-mowed grass between. 'Wait.' I got up and took off my coat, spread it out between the bushes and the tree.

She sat there looking at the coat. The park and the lake seemed very still but the wind blew stronger.

'Alex,' she said.

'Come here,' I said. 'We'll sit on the coat.' I put the bottle and cups down. 'It's warmer here, very good here.' She didn't move. I walked over by her and took her hands. She stood up against me, watching me, not smiling.

'Please,' I said.

'All right.'

We went over and sat on the coat. For a while we sat quite still and with perhaps a foot between us. The bushes did break the wind and on the ground it was much warmer. I was very warm. I was drunker now but doing O.K.

Every now and then I'd remember Petra and it was like a

black sack dropped over my head. I wanted to yell. Because there was no release. The sensation of despair and panic cropped up inside me. And when I thought, Tomorrow is Sunday; Sunday night we have to meet Emmetts by the road, I wanted to get up and run. It's that way sometimes. It's a complete helplessness that you feel, knowing all the time that the helplessness is only yourself. That you should be able to stand up to it – act. So you take another drink sometimes.

I looked at Jenny and for a moment I thought she was going to cry. I felt bad about tonight. Then I saw she wasn't going to cry and I felt all right.

I was kissing her and we lay down on my coat.

'I think I'm a little tight,' she said. 'Alex, don't.'

My hand moved down across her hip beneath her coat, down across her thigh.

'Let's take your coat off. We could put it over us.'

She didn't say anything. I helped her out of her coat and we lay there with her coat over us. We lay on our sides, facing each other. pressed tight.

'Alex,' she said. 'This isn't right.'

'Why not?'

She didn't answer. But I knew she was right, too, and something inside me began to draw away. She burrowed her face into my neck. I moved my hand along her leg across the hollow in back of her knee, and suddenly she moved against me, reached up, and unbuttoned the front of her dress.

'You don't love me, though,' she said. 'It's nothing like that.'

I couldn't answer.

'The coat doesn't cover us very well,' she said rapidly.

'There is one way it will.'

'Yes, Alex, only – ' She ceased. Her arms were tight around my neck.

'Only what?'

'Only hurry up!'

I held her very tight, then, very tight, and it was perhaps the most difficult thing I ever said in my life when I whispered, 'I'm sorry, Jenny. We've made a mistake.' I kissed her and rose. She lay quite still, her face pale.

Jenny sat on a large boulder beside the lake and stared at the dark water with errant starlight moving in it. I had thought wrong. I didn't want and wouldn't have anyone but Petra.

I went over by Jenny. I was still drunk, but I didn't want any more to drink right now and I felt bad about everything.

'It's all right,' Jenny said. 'I understand. You didn't love me or anything, really. I suppose I should curse you, or kick you. Anyway, it's all right. There's nothing you can do and you don't want anybody but her. I'm not sorry.' She turned and looked at me. She smiled.

I didn't say anything.

'Tell me about it, Alex. You can tell me.'

I tried to tell her something about how I felt. But not about the murder. I didn't tell it to her straight, but I knew she understood. Then for a minute I busted loose and said, 'I can't get away!' My voice was loud.

'What about Madge?'

'Oh, God.'

'I'm glad you love her, really.'

'If I could only see her, be with her for a little while, it might help. But everything's all messed up now.'

'You're shaking all over, Alex.'

'I can't help it.' I wanted to tell her I was scared, really scared. But sometimes you don't speak of that.

Then it all piled on me hard. I couldn't wait to get away from the lake, from Jenny. I knew it was the liquor wearing off. But that didn't help, the knowing. I had to see Petra, had to get back there to the house. What was she thinking?

'I'm frightened, Alex, the way you act.'

I touched her shoulder.

141

'You really love this Madge? What's her last name?'

'Collins.'

'You really love her, but Petra's got you stuck?'

'Yes.'

'Only there's more to it than that. More you're not telling me.'

'Yes, there's more. Let's go, Jenny.'

We walked to her house and we walked fast. I kissed her. 'I've got to go,' I said.

'I know. Don't worry. It's all right about tonight.' She didn't smile. She seemed almost as worried as I felt.

I squeezed her hand. Ten minutes later I was on French Street in a taxi. Then we had stopped in front of the house.

My hands shook so I dropped change on the floor of the taxi. Then I was out, running toward the house. A light was lit in the living room.

I went in the front door. Right away her perfume struck me and she was there in the hallway.

'He's upstairs,' she said. 'Where have you been, Alex?'

'In town. I walked into town.'

Then she was against me and I breathed against the thickness of her hair.

'You wouldn't try to run away from me, would you?'

'No, no.'

'I didn't think so.'

I broke away from her, ran for the stairs. Reaching my bedroom, I locked the door. I heard her coming up the stairs.

I barely made it to the toilet. I blacked out in an agony of retching, tearing the stuff up, trying to vomit all the crazy hell out of the bottom of my guts.

CHAPTER 22

SHE RAPPED on my door several times during the night. Softly. She whispered my name. I knew she waited for me just beyond that thin panel. I kept the door locked. I didn't answer. Somehow I stayed in bed, cold with perspiration, staring through the dark at the filmy outline of the door.

'Alex, Alex, are you all right? Alex!'

Was Verne deaf? Was he blind not to realize what was going on in his own home?

Finally she went away.

This was my first victory. Then I knew how small, how truly petty a victory it was. Because I kept seeing her in her room. Maybe pacing the floor. Waiting, waiting. . . .

The pulse of my emotions ran up and down a crazy scale. I wondered if I were thinking right any more – if I could think at all. I couldn't sleep. I was exhausted but I couldn't sleep because the whole business ran through my head.

Thinking of Jenny, I knew that consciously or unconsciously I'd got her drunk and taken her in a vain effort to knock the rot out of me. The clash of her sweetness beside Petra's savage evil kept reminding me that I'd done Jenny a wrong.

Instead of helping matters, it only made everything worse. It added another bit to my own personal agony of mind.

The mental torture was something I would never have

believed possible. To be any kind of criminal one had to be conscienceless. The ones who had a conscience, the ones who went through despair afterward, were those who did the screwy things. Like running out on the street, shooting up the town, going hog wild.

I could never do it. But it would be a pleasure to kill her. Not with a gun – not even with a knife. With my bare hands. Choke her, strangle the putrid life out of her, watch her writhe, make her scream for release.

It was like being chained. Better than that. That would be something you could fight, knowing what it was. It wouldn't be something in your head, in your body, uncontrollable.

I'd read someplace that there was one woman like this for every man. One evil bitch, or not evil, but one that could scar your soul, shred it to a bloody pulp, just with a glance. With a thought, even. Snare, trap you, talk you into anything. One you'd do anything for, knowing you didn't even love her. Knowing it was only want, desire. One that could drive you into black madness, into a deathless, grinning glassy-eyed hell.

Madge. It was like a name mentioned in some cool beyond I couldn't reach.

My hand lying on the sheet clenched. I yanked and the cloth ripped, stuttering in a violent agony of sound.

Getting out of bed, I went over by the window and stared at the black outline of the brambled hill and waited for the dawn.

Anything to stay away from her.

At noon I was standing in front of the house watching the dirty sky piling up in the east. I was sick in every way a man can be sick. All morning Verne had watched me, puzzled. I had avoided Petra as much as possible.

Deep in thought, I didn't hear the approaching horses until they were almost opposite me on the road.

'Whoa!' It was Emmetts. He was driving a team dragging an empty stone boat along the shoulder of the road. Standing on the boards of the stone boat, he spat and watched me. His mouth loosed itself in a grin, but he appeared nervous. His shoulders hunched and hitched beneath a threadbare jacket. 'Nice day,' he said.

I didn't answer. It seemed as if every way I turned I ran against a hot iron wall.

'Don't you think? Don't you think it's a nice day?'

I still didn't reply.

'Ain't talkin', hey? They're talkin' in town,' he said. He glanced quickly toward the house. There was something in his eyes now that hadn't been there before. His hands were nervous, fussing thickly with the leather reins. 'C'mere,' he said quietly.

I stepped closer.

'They's talk in town,' he said. 'Plenty.'

One of the horses jerked forward, the other pulled back. 'Whoa, you walleyed sons-o'-bitches!' The horses ceased, ears twitching. 'Listen,' he said. 'Bring five hundred tonight.' His mouth jerked loosely.

'Scared?' I said.

'Y'heard me.' His voice went loud for an instant, then quiet again. Turning, he spat a wad of yellowed tobacco into the road. 'Five hundred. An' bring her. Don't forget, damn it. Bring the gal!' He lashed the horses, ran beside the stone boat a few paces, then leaped on.

I watched him go along the road. He didn't look back. His shoulders were hunched and there was something about him that had changed. He was nervous and he was over-anxious.

Five hundred dollars? Five hundred dollars. . . .

'Verne's going up to the grave. We'll have time.'

'No,' I said. 'Watch out. Watch out, damn you!'

'Alex, what's got into you?'

145

'Nothing. Stay away, that's all.'

She reached up and opened the front of her dress. She wore no brassiere. Her face was full of defiance. 'There,' she said. 'Come here, Alex!'

The kitchen door slammed.

'Oh, god!' she said. She ran upstairs. I watched her go and something went through me that I didn't recognize as yet.

Verne came into the hallway.

'I thought I heard Petra,' he said.

'No. I don't think so. She's upstairs.'

'Oh.' He came up to me. 'Alex, you look like hell. What's up?' He wore a gray sweater that once probably fitted him, but it hung on him now, like the rest of his clothes. His face was gaunt, his eyes unclear and sunken.

'Nothing,' I said. 'Guess I hit the bottle too hard.'

'Go into Allayne last night?'

'Thought I'd look the town over.'

We watched each other for a while. He frowned. He shook his head. 'Alex,' he said, 'things have changed, haven't they? Those days back there in the war – it's all sort of unbelievable, isn't it?'

'Yes.'

'Alex, you sure you feel all right?'

'Just hung over.'

He stared, frankly puzzled. 'It hasn't been such a hot vacation for you, has it?'

'It's been fine. It'll be O.K. Think I'd better have a little drink. Hair of the dog.'

'Sure.'

I turned and walked toward the kitchen. I could feel his eyes boring into my back.

CHAPTER 23

SHE TRIED to corner me.

I stuck by Verne. I stayed out of her way. I didn't know what was happening. She had changed somehow. She acted different. She was still excited, but not excited in the way she had been.

Verne didn't talk much and he watched me a lot. I began to wonder if I were coming apart.

It went on like that all day. It was the worst day I ever spent in my life. Late in the afternoon it started to rain again. It rained softly at first, but hour by hour it increased, until by eight o'clock it was a steady downpour.

'We could all go to a movie,' Petra said in the living room.

I grinned at her. Verne glanced at me and said, 'Would you like to?'

I shook my head. 'Let's save it for another night.' I wasn't sure what was going on in my mind, but it was something.

The minutes marched along to the sound of rain.

The silence that descended was horrible. All three of us tried to break it, but it was like howling in the wilderness, shouting into a hurricane.

At ten to nine Verne went into his study.

'How are we going to leave?' Petra said.

I watched the faint tightness around her eyes and wanted to laugh. She came toward me as I got out of my chair.

'Don't,' I said. I stared at her, at her body, at the gleaming black eyes and the thick jetty hair. I let my gaze linger on the rounded thrust of her thighs against her black skirt and the full curve of her breasts.

'Alex – '

I didn't say anything. But I knew – I knew. . . .

'Stay here,' I said. I went through the back of the house, picked up a raincoat, and left by the rear door. As I glanced toward the house, a light came on in the kitchen. The curtains parted and I saw her face pressed against the glass.

Then I heard Verne call, 'Petra. Petra.'

Her face vanished from the window. I sloshed through the driveway that had become a river until I reached the road. Then I started down toward the bend. The rain gusted in blinding sheets, driving in a vicious splattering across the road.

Already I was soaked to the skin. The raincoat was no help in this weather. As I neared the bend in the road I began to run.

This time he was waiting.

He stepped back as I reached him. 'Where's the gal?'

I laughed and rain washed into my mouth. 'Here,' I said. 'Here she is, damn you!' I feinted with my left, then slashed him with my right. He stumbled back into the bushes.

'Did you feel her?' I yelled. I dove at him, dove into the running mud and the streaming bushes. He sprang aside with a curse, then leaped at me.

As he leaped I kicked. My foot caught him squarely in the face. I felt his nose crumble and he let out a yell. Blood spurted from his face. He groped blindly for me.

'Go ahead,' I said. 'Go ahead. Here's your five hundred dollars!' I grabbed him by the front of his poncho at the throat, and put everything I had into the blows. Five of them, straight to his face, feeling the bone grit. He was senseless before I finished.

148

I held him up. It wasn't only the bone of his face; the bones in my hand were broken. Pain lanced up my arm. Still I hit him with a kind of blind, groping despair.

Then I let go. He sprawled at my feet. For a long moment I stood over him with the rain tearing at us. He began to moan. His face was covered with blood. He tried to push himself up, moaning and trying to talk. Only he couldn't talk very well, with the blood streaming from his mouth.

I gripped my right arm around the wrist with my left hand, but it didn't stop the pain. Then I whirled and ran back toward the house along the highway. A tearing brilliant white streak of lightning slashed through the sheeted rain. Thunder cracked and slammed overhead and the world rocked. And all the time I ran I was laughing, laughing like hell.

I dropped the raincoat on the back stoop and entered the house as quietly as possible. My shoes squished water, but I walked softly into the living room. Nobody was there. I headed for the stairs. As I passed the study, I saw Verne hunched over his desk.

I hurried quietly on up the stairs, still gripping my right arm. My whole hand was smashed. Two white, crimson-flecked spears of knuckle bone jutted through the skin, and at the slightest movement of my hand they gritted with bright-iced pain.

I had to keep choking back laughter. It burst in my throat and I gagged with it, choking it back, my chest filled and heaving with laughter.

She was in her room. I entered and closed the door.

She came at me from the other side of the bed, wearing white lounging pajamas. A beautiful black-eyed devil straight from the fires of hell. Then she stopped, clapped one hand across her mouth. Her eyes widened, staring at my hand. I held it up, clenched before her eyes, and blood dripped to the floor, mingling with the thick auburn-tinted rug.

My voice was little more than a hoarse whisper and I sounded mad, even to myself.

'It's done. It's all over with, Petra. It's finished.'

'Alex! Alex! What's happened?'

I looked at her, wanting to laugh, but not wanting to make any noise yet. Stepping in close, I lashed out with my left hand, snagged the front of her flimsy pajamas, and tore the cloth away from her breasts.

And it *was* done. I could look at her now. I could be near her and nothing happened. It was done. Something had snapped inside me and she was nothing but a painting: a picture of a frightened woman. She began to talk rapidly.

'Alex, what have you done? Did you see Emmetts? Did you see him? Tell me what happened, Alex. You know I love you. You're acting foolish, Alex. What's happened?' Her voice was getting shrill.

'Shut up! I just wanted one last look at you before I go down and tell Verne. Tell him everything.'

'Alex – ' She stepped toward me.

'Don't,' I said quietly.

She stopped, both hands half raised, her fingers trembling. 'Alex,' she said weakly.

'Yes. You killed her. And you damned near had me help you kill him. Only not quite, not quite.'

'Alex, we could. We could have it all – all his money. The house, even. The house is in my name. He's nothing but a – '

'Shut up!' I watched the scheming behind her eyes. 'You killed his mother,' I said. 'You murdered her.'

'What if I did? Sure I did. I hated her. She was in the way. Oh, Alex.' Her voice dropped a key, scheming, planning. 'You don't know what you're saying. You've hurt yourself. Here, let me see your hand.'

'Get back, you bitch!'

Her head began to jerk a little, out of control, and her

eyes were very bright. Her breasts stood out firm and thrusting beyond the shreds of the torn pajama top. They lifted and fell with her erratic breathing.

'You almost had me,' I said. I was dazed, weak. 'Almost. You were so damned beautiful I couldn't tear myself loose. But I'm all right now. It had to come, didn't you know that? Didn't you know it had to stop someplace? I waited. I didn't think I'd make it – but I did.'

She didn't answer. There was something going on behind her eyes.

Her voice was low. 'Yes. Do you know I planned it all, darling? Do you know I planned it so that old hag would catch us doing that? Here, in this room. I planned it, knowing it would come that way. I left the windows open. I knew she'd follow us in here, if not the first time, then some other time. I aroused her suspicions until she was certain to follow us – break in on us. I planned it so I could shove her out of that window, somehow. I wanted it just to look like a fight. But it didn't come off, did it? It was too much to expect.'

I stared at her. She was crazy, all the way. It had been a good scheme, but it was going to kill her.

'Going to Verne, now,' I said. I didn't wait, but left the room. She didn't move, still stood there, with her breasts going up and down.

I went down the hall, then stumbled down the stairs. My hand was a swollen cluster of pain now and my head throbbed. I thought I heard the front door close.

Verne was behind his desk, in the study. I staggered into the room. He watched me without speaking. He seemed very calm.

'Verne.' I said. 'Verne, there's something – '

'You don't have to tell me,' he said. His voice was hollow and empty of expression. 'I know all about it, Alex. I've known about you and Petra. I tried not to believe – I've been helpless.' He motioned toward the door. 'Emmetts was just here. He told me the rest.'

'Verne,' I said. 'You don't understand!'

'I understand everything. And I'm going to kill her, Alex. You hear me?'

'Verne, for God's sake!'

He watched me very quietly. Then his gaze snapped to the study doorway and he smiled. 'Well, good evening,' he said.

I turned slowly, then rested partially against the desk. Something inside me clenched up tight like a fist, a fist of blank despair. And suddenly I saw how it all was going to end.

It was Petra. She still wore her torn pajamas, and clutched in her steady white hand was the .32 automatic. She stood with her legs apart in the doorway, her black eyes glistening like wet glass beads.

CHAPTER 24

'WELL,' VERNE said. 'We're all together again. All the important ones, that is. Emmetts doesn't count.'

'Verne,' I said. 'Believe – ' I stopped.

He didn't take his eyes off Petra. 'You killed my mother,' he said. 'Didn't you?'

'Yes,' Petra said. 'And I'm going to kill you.' Her voice was edged with hysteria.

He did not smile. 'Well. You're going to fix everything all up proper, eh?' He glanced at me. 'You certainly messed Emmetts up, Alex. He was pretty mad about that. I think he'd have come to me anyway. Folks beginning to get nosy. Too many peculiar things going on.'

Verne sounded almost under control, but I knew better. I could see something in his eyes.

He said, 'You hurt your hand on Emmetts, Alex?'

'Yes.'

'Too bad.'

The silence dragged out. Then he said. 'Tell me about it, Alex.'

Petra didn't move from the doorway. There was a half-smile across her lips. I told him everything I knew, and tried to tell him something of what I'd gone through.

'I guess I wasn't right for her,' Verne said.

'Yes,' Petra interrupted. 'Yes. You dried-up old – you husk!'

Verne recoiled with each word, but his expression didn't change. Only the look in his eyes became worse. The haunted, stricken, awful look in his eyes.

'Yes,' Petra said softly. 'Yes. Only you don't know it all. Neither of you know.' She didn't move. Her voice was so quiet I had to almost strain to hear. She leaned slightly forward, the gun in her hand quite steady. 'I've waited over a year, Alex. Trying to get you here. I had it all planned, all of it.'

Rain drummed against the windows, slashed in wild gusts across the eaves.

'You were just the type,' she went on. 'Verne told me all about you. A man of truth, honest, dependable.' She laughed. 'Didn't take me long to break you down, did it?'

I stared at her.

'I want Verne's money and I'm going to get it. I planned the old woman's death – just as I've planned yours. I'm going to kill you both. Both of you. You hear?'

I didn't move. Verne said nothing.

She looked at me. 'I knew you'd come to Verne eventually. You had to. It took you long enough, damn you! You liked it, didn't you? I was good, wasn't I?'

'I'm sure you were,' Verne said.

'Yes. Well, they'll find you both dead. You'll have killed Verne because he saw what was going on between us. Because he's jealous, as everybody knows. So you'll have killed him.' She paused, her lips working. 'And I tried to save him, but it was too late. Except in the struggle, you, Alex, got shot.'

'You're a fool,' I told her. 'It'll never work. They'll see right through it.'

'You think so?' she said. 'You should know by now I'm a pretty good actress, Alex.'

154

'What about Emmetts?'

'I'll take care of him – don't worry. I know how to shut him up.'

'It may be too late,' I said. 'Verne, say something. Tell her it's nutty. She'll never get away with it.'

'It's worth a try,' Verne said.

'Yes,' she said. 'You forget, I'm a woman. A beautiful woman, I'll get away with it.' She paused. 'Which of you will be first?'

I couldn't move from the desk. There was nothing to do. She was on the verge of squeezing the trigger and she looked as if she were familiar with the gun. I watched the small black muzzle poise for an instant on Verne, then swivel toward me. It was very steady and she was smiling. I saw her knuckles whiten faintly with pressure.

The room erupted with thunder. A steady, reverberating, monotonous crash, crash, crash. I fell back against the desk, staring at Petra.

The gun leaped from her hand, spiraled to the floor. Her mouth was a sudden gaping hole through which gouts of blood spurted. Then her right eye vanished in a blob of crimson.

She took three wavering steps into the room, hands groping. Between her breasts another hole appeared, then the tight front of her pajamas across her belly splashed scarlet. Her right leg buckled. She danced for a brief moment like a crazy doll, then crumpled into a grotesque heap on the floor, one knee raised, both arms outflung to embrace her last, her final lover – Death.

I turned slowly toward Verne. He still sat quietly behind the desk. In his right hand was an Army Colt .45. As I looked, a faint, nearly indiscernible wisp of smoke vanished above the gun barrel.

'I still hit what I aim at,' he said. 'I always did. Even with a lousy pistol. You remember, Alex?'

My voice seemed to come from someplace far away. 'I remember, Verne.'

He kept staring at Petra's body on the floor.

'She was truly beautiful,' he said.

'Yes.'

'But only on the outside. On the inside she was evil. All evil. I've waited for this moment. Knowing what she and you have done in my home.'

'Verne, I –'

He whirled. 'Get out! Get out, Alex. Quick – before I kill you, too. Alex, get out!'

'Verne!' I shouted.

He rose behind the desk and the muzzle of the gun jerked toward my stomach. My bowels writhed and I leaped for the study door.

'Don't come back!' he yelled. His voice was shrill.

Outside I ran across the rain-soaked lawn to the road.

A single muffled shot sounded from the house.

I didn't need to be told what it was; I didn't need to see. I knew there were two dead bodies in there now.

Wind and rain lashed at me as I turned down the road toward Allayne. I walked fast, then I broke into a run between the dark hills and the slowly moving shadows of the trees.

It was all over now. I knew I would have to pay for my part in it. First I had to see the police, then get back to Madge. Returning to Madge was all that mattered.

So there was hope. Without it you couldn't live. Because hope and tomorrow are the two things that keep you going. And you can always keep reaching out beyond, until that one final tomorrow. Then you don't need hope any more.

Petra and Verne were dead. I wondered if Verne had found peace. It was hard to believe that I had lived through those long days of hell with Petra. She was gone, but there would be many tomorrows before I could forget.

But I tried to forget. And then I knew I would forget.

Because I'd never again address another letter to the big red-brick house at 13 French Street.

THE RED SCARF

CHAPTER 1

ABOUT EIGHT-THIRTY that night, the driver of the big trailer truck let me out in the middle of nowhere. I had stacked in with a load of furniture all the way from Chicago and I should have slept, too. I couldn't even close my eyes. Brother Albert had turned me down on the loan, and all I could think of was Bess holding the fort in St. Pete, and us standing to lose the motel. How could I tell her my own brother backed down on me? The dream. So the driver said if I could make it to Valdosta, then Route 19, the rest down through Florida would be pie. He gave me what was left of the lunch he'd bought in Macon. I stood there under a beardy-looking oak tree and watched him rumble off, backfiring.

It was raining and snowing at the same time; you know, just hard enough to make it real nasty. The road was rutted with slush, and the wind was like cold hands poking through my topcoat. I had to hang onto my hat. I ate the half piece of chocolate cake he'd left, and the bacon and cheese sand- wich. I saved the apple.

A couple of cars roared by, fanning the road slop clear up to my knees. I didn't even have a cigarette. I figured this was as broke and low-down as I'd ever be.

My feet were already soaked, so I started walking. My feet were already soaked, so I started walking. I came around a sharp curve in the road and crossed a short wooden bridge. Then I saw the sign.

ALF'S BAR-B-Q
Drinks
Sandwiches

The sign was done in blue lights and it kind of hung like a ghost there in the dripping trees. It swung and you could hear it creak. Just the sign, nothing else.

I kept walking, feeling the change in my pocket, thinking about a cup of hot coffee and some smokes and maybe it would stop raining. Or maybe I could hit somebody for a ride.

Then I saw how I wasn't going to hit anybody for any ride. Not here. Not at Alf's. If a car stopped at this place, they'd either be crazy, or worse off than I was. There was this bent-looking shed with a drunken gas pump standing out front in a mess of mud, and Alf's place itself was a sick wreck of an old one-room house, with the front porch ripped off. You could still see the outline of the porch in the dim light from the fly-freckled bulb hanging over the door. Tin and cardboard signs were plastered all over the front of the place.

I went inside, and it was like being hit across the face with the mixed-up smells of all the food Alf's place had served for the past ten years.

'Ho, ho, ho!' a guy said. He was a big, red-faced drunk, parked on an upturned apple crate beside a small potbellied stove. He looked at me, then at the thin man behind the counter. 'Ho, ho, ho!'

'You best git on along home,' the man behind the counter said to the laughing one. 'Come on, Jo-Jo – you got enough of a one on to hold you the rest of this week and half of next.'

'Ho, ho, ho!' Jo-Jo said.

I brushed some crumbs off one of the wooden stools by the counter and sat down. Alf's place was a compact fermentation of all the bad wayside lunchrooms on the Eastern seaboard. With some additions. He had a coffee urn, a battered juke-box, two stick-looking booths, a chipped marble counter, and a greasy stove. The ceiling was low; the stove was hot.

'What'll it be?' the counterman said. 'I'm Alf. We got some fine barbecue.' His hair was pink and sparse across a freckled skull. He wore a very clean white shirt and freshly ironed white duck trousers.

'Cup of coffee, I guess.'

'No barbecue?'

'Nope.'

Alf shook his head. I turned and glanced at Jo-Jo. He was wearing overalls with shoulder straps. He was a young, rough, country lush. His eyes had that slitted hard-boiled egg look, his mouth broad and loose and his black hair straight and dank, down over his ears. Combed, it would be one of these duck cuts. He was a big guy.

I heard a car draw up outside. Jo-Jo took a fifth of whiskey from his back pocket, uncapped it, drank squinting, and put it away. He stood up, stretched, touching his hands to the ceiling, reeled a little and sat down again. 'Son of a gun,' he said. 'Dirty son of a gun.'

Alf put the thick mug of coffee on the counter. 'Cigarettes?' I said. 'Any kind.'

He flipped me a pack of Camels. I heard a man and woman arguing outside, their voices rising above the sound of a car's engine. A door slammed. The engine gunned, then shut off.

'Damn it!' a man said outside.

The door opened and this girl walked in. She hesitated a moment, watching Jo-Jo, then she grinned and stepped over toward the counter, letting the door slap.

'Ho, ho, *ho!*' Jo-Jo said. Then he whistled. The girl didn't pay any attention. Jo-Jo looked her up and down, grinning loosely, his eyes like rivets. Then the door opened again and a man came in. He stood staring at the girl's back.

'Viv,' he said. 'Please, come on, for cripe's sake.'

She didn't say anything. She was a long-legged one, all right, with lots of shape, wearing a tight blue flannel dress with bunches of white lace at the throat and cuffs. She was something to see. There were sparkles of rain like diamonds on the dress and in her thick dark hair. She half-sat on the stool next to me, and looked at me sideways with one big brown eye.

'You hear me, Viv?' the man said.

'I'm going to eat something, Noel. That's all there is to it. I'm starved.'

'Ho, ho, ho,' Jo-Jo said. I heard him uncap the bottle and drink noisily. He coughed, cleared his throat and said, 'I reckon your woman wants some barbecue, mister.'

The guy breathed heavily, stepped over behind the girl, and just stood there. He was a big-shouldered guy, wearing a double-breasted dark-blue suit, with a zigzag pin stripe. His white shirt was starched. He wore a gray Homburg tilted to the left and slightly down on the forehead.

'Come on, Viv,' he said. He laid one hand on her right arm. 'Please come on, will you?'

'Nuts. I'm hungry, I told you.'

She haunched around on the stool and smiled at Alf. 'I'll try the barbecue. And some coffee.'

'Sure,' Alf said. 'You won't be sorry.'

The guy sighed and sat down on a stool beside her. Alf looked at him, and the guy shook his head.

'You better eat something,' the girl said.

The guy looked at her. She turned front again. I could smell whiskey, but it wasn't from Jo-Jo. They'd both been drinking and driving for quite a while. They had that

164

unstretched, half-eyed look that comes from miles and miles on the highway.

I sat there with my coffee and a cigarette, nursing the coffee, waiting. They were headed in the same direction as I was. I'd heard them come in.

After Alf served her a plate of barbecue, with some bread and coffee, the guy spoke up. He'd been sitting there, fuming. 'You got gas in that pump outside?'

'Sure,' Alf said. 'Absolutely we got gas.'

'How's about filling her up?'

Alf started around the counter, nodding.

'Now, aren't you glad we stopped?' the girl said. 'We won't have to stop later on.'

'Just hurry it up,' the guy said without looking at her. 'Feed your face.'

Alf was at the door. 'You'll have to drive your car over to the pump,' he said.

I looked at him. The guy started toward the door. Jo-Jo was trying to get up off the apple crate. He was grinning like crazy, staring straight at the girl. I looked and she had her skirt up a little over her knees, banging her knees together. You could hear it, like clapping your hands softly.

Neither Alf nor the guy noticed. They went on outside and the door slapped shut. I could feel it; as if everything was getting a little tight. The girl felt it, too, because she paused in her eating and Jo-Jo made it off the apple crate and started across the room.

'Say!' Jo-Jo said. 'You're pretty as a pitcher.'

She took the mouthful of barbecue and began to chew.

Jo-Jo sprawled over against the counter, with his hair hanging down one side of his face, and that bottle sticking out, and he was grinning that way. 'Gee!' Jo-Jo said. 'Cripes in the foothills!'

I got off my stool and walked around to him. 'Come on,' I said. 'Go back and sit down. You're kind of tight.'

He looked at me and gave me a hard shove. I went back across the room and slammed against the wall.

'You?' Jo-Jo said to the girl. He held up two fingers and wrapped them around each other. He had fingers like midget bananas. 'Me?' he said.

The girl went on eating. She pulled her skirt down over her knees and chewed.

He reached over and took hold of her arm and pulled her half off the stool toward him, like she was a rag doll.

'Girly,' he said. 'I could make your soul sing.'

I nearly burst out laughing. But it wasn't funny. He was all jammed up.

'You wanna drink?' he asked her.

She was struggling. He got up close to her and started trying to paw her. She had a mouthful of barbecue and he started to kiss her and she let him have it, spraying the barbecue all over his face.

He grabbed her off the stool and went to work.

She wasn't doing anything but grunt. He got hold of her skirt and tried to rip it. I was there by then, and I got one hand on his shoulder and turned him and aimed for his chin. It was all in slow motion, and my fist connected. He windmilled back against the counter.

'That dirty ape!' the girl said.

The barbecue was still on his face. When he hit against the counter, the bottle broke. He stood there watching me, with this funny expression on his face and the whiskey running down his leg and puddling on the floor. Then he charged, head down, his hair flopping.

I grabbed his head as he came in, brought it down as I brought my knee up. It made a thick sound. I let him go. He sat down on the floor, came out straight and lay there.

'They grow all kinds, I guess,' the girl said. 'I sure thank you,' she said. 'Thanks a lot.'

'Forget it.'

She kept looking at me. She kind of grinned and lifted one hand and looked at the door. Then she turned and went over to the stool and sat down with her barbecue again.

The door opened, and the guy came in. He saw Jo-Jo. 'What's this?'

'A little trouble,' I told him. 'It's all right now.'

Alf came in and closed the door. He saw Jo-Jo. His face got red. 'What happened?'

I told them. The girl was eating again. Then I noticed she stopped and just sat there, staring at her plate. She turned on the stool and looked at the guy. 'Pay the man,' she said. 'Let's get out of here.'

I looked at her, then at the guy. I had to nick them for a ride. I had to.

'I'm awful sorry, miss,' Alf said. 'He don't really mean no harm. It's just his way.'

Nobody said anything. This guy pulled out his wallet and looked at Alf.

'The gas was six, even,' Alf said. 'The barbecue's a dollar. That's seven. Even.'

The guy counted out a five and two ones. He handed the bills to Alf and Alf took them and stood there with them hanging limply from his hand. Jo-Jo moved and groaned on the floor.

'Come on,' the guy said to the girl.

'Listen,' I said to him. 'How's chances for a lift? I'm going the same way you are. South. There's no – '

'No dice. Come on, Viv.'

I looked at her. She looked at me. 'Oh, let's give him a lift,' she said. 'It's all right, Noel.'

He gave her a real bad look. 'No.'

She bent a little at the waist and brushed at some crumbs. She looked at the guy again. Then she looked at me and winked. 'Come on,' she said to me. 'We'll take you as far as we can.'

'Thanks,' I said. 'I really – '

'You heard me, Viv,' the guy said. 'I told you, no!'

I figured, the hell. If I could get the ride, that's all I cared about. I didn't care about what the guy wanted. Then I saw the way his face was.

'He helped me out,' she said. 'You heard him say what happened, Noel. That dirty ape would have done anything. Suppose this man hadn't been here? What would I have done?'

'Ho, ho, ho,' Jo-Jo said. He was lying flat out on his back, staring at the ceiling.

I looked at the guy and he looked at me.

'All right,' he said. 'Damn it.'

The girl took my arm and we moved toward the door.

It was a Lincoln sedan. The guy, Noel, walked ahead of us, his feet splatting in the mud. He got in under the wheel and slammed his door.

'Don't pay any attention,' the girl said. 'We maybe can't take you far. But it'll help, anyway. In this weather.'

'Anything'll help, believe me.'

She opened the door before I could reach it. She climbed in. I closed the door and opened the rear door.

'Get in front,' the guy said.

She pushed the front door open and I slammed the rear door and got in. She jigged over a little and I slammed the front door and we were off like a bull at a flag.

We struck the highway, slid a little, straightened out. 'Noel,' the girl said. 'Stop the car again.'

I looked at her. She sure was a pip.

'What?'

'I said, "stop the car." So he can take off his hat and coat. He's all wet.'

The car slowed and came to a stop. The windows were closed, heater on, and you could smell the stale cigarette

168

smoke. I remembered my cigarettes back there on the counter at Alf's.

'Throw 'em in back,' she said. 'Okay?'

I opened the door and stepped out into the night and took them off and tossed them in back, beside a couple of suitcases and a brief case on the seat. Then I got in and this time she didn't shove away. In fact, she looked at me and smiled and snuggled down comfortable.

'Is it all right now?' the guy said, real evil.

She didn't say anything.

He popped it to the floor and we roared off.

I sat there without saying anything for about a mile. Just waiting. It wasn't just the cigarette smoke in this car, or the hot air from the heater, either. You could taste the trouble that had been going on between these two.

'I hope you're happy now, Noel.'

'That's enough.'

'Just remember what I said.'

'I told you, Vivian!' He let it come out between his teeth. Not loud; just hard. 'That's enough. You hear?'

She sniffed. 'Just remember.'

He tromped and he tromped. The car bucked and leveled off at eighty-three. We were flying. There wasn't much wind, but you could see that rain and snow whipping up out there.

'Thanks for the lift,' I said. 'It's a rotten night. Not many'd stop in the highway tonight. Any night.'

'One good turn deserves another,' she said, grinning.

You could almost hear him grit his teeth. He was really hanging onto that wheel. I turned and looked at her, putting one arm across the back of the seat. She tipped her head, freeing a good lot of the thick dark hair where my arm squeezed. In the dash lights, there was a sheen on her long slim legs. She looked at me then, with one big brown eye. Then she began watching the road.

169

You could smell the whiskey in the car. It seemed to have impregnated the upholstery.

'Going far?' the man said.

'Down the coast. St. Pete.'

He breathed heavily, hulked over the steering wheel. I couldn't watch him very well without stretching. He made me nervous.

She laid one hand on my knee. 'Honey. You got a cigarette?'

'There's a carton in the back seat, Vivian. You know that.'

She patted my knee. 'You know? I'm glad you're with us. Least, Noel's not cursing.'

'I'll curse.'

She hitched up and turned and got on her knees on the seat, pawing back there. The dash lights were bright. I looked away.

'On the floor, stupid.'

She came up with the carton and a bottle, turned and sat on my lap, slid off onto the seat and smiled at me again with that one big brown eye. 'Bet you haven't got a cigarette?'

I told her she was right.

She ripped open the carton and handed me a pack. 'Care for a drink?'

'Damn it, Vivian.'

She parked the fifth on my knee. I took it.

'All right,' the guy said. 'All right.'

We drove along for a while, swapping the bottle. I was hitting it hard. She took enough, too. The guy, Noel, was just touching it now and then.

The whiskey got to me good. But I sat there, propped up, smoking cigarettes and letting the night stretch out. Thinking about Bess. She was a good wife, a wonderful girl. And my brother Albert was a twenty-four carat stinker.

Everything was sour inside me. He knew he would have

got the money back, if he made the loan. I never welched yet. Knowing Albert, I should never have tried going clear to Chicago to ask him, figuring a personal talk might be better than a long-distance call.

'Roy,' he says. 'You must learn to hoe your own row. I'd gladly help you if I thought it would really be helping you. But you seem to have forgotten that I warned you not to attempt this foolish motel business.'

And Bess down home, maybe even praying. Because if the highway didn't come through by our place, as planned, we were sunk.

And that guy, Potter, at the bank. Hovering behind his desk in a kind of fat gray security. And the way his glasses glinted when he looked at me. 'We're sorry, Mister Nichols, but there's nothing we can do. We've given you one extension, and you're behind again. Another extension would only make matters worse for you in the long run. And as far as another loan of any kind is concerned, you must see the impossibility of that. You've got to make the effort to clear up your debt and meet future payments. The government stands behind you only so far, Nichols. You must do your share.'

'You don't understand, Mister Potter. Everything we own is in that motel!'

'We understand perfectly. We handled your government loan. But remember, when you went into this motel business, we all were assured the new highway would come past your place of business. It seemed a safe risk. Now it's all changed. They've suspended construction, pending the settlement on a new route. And that,' he shook his head, glasses glinting, 'put us all in a bad spot, indeed.'

'But you – '

'We have no choice, Nichols. Place yourself in our position. You're extended far beyond your means now. Either you settle to the date, or we'll be forced to – well, foreclose, to put it plainly. If I were you, I'd make every effort, Mister Nichols – every effort.'

'But the highway may still come through.'

'But when? *When?* And we can't take that risk, don't you see? Suppose you're granted a year's extension? And suppose it *doesn't* come through? What then?' The gentle pause, the clasped hands, the dull gleam of a fat gold ring. 'Surely, you must comprehend. See, here – if we make a loan to you, and you can't pay it – and there's every indication you won't be able to – what then? You'd be worse off than you are now. You'd lose your business, your investment – not only that, you'd have our personal loan to pay. And no way *to* pay. Of course, we could never make that loan. Never. I'm sorry, Mister Nichols. Very sorry, indeed.'

'My name's Vivian. Vivian Rise. This is Noel –'

'Enough, Viv. Snow's letting up. Just rain, now.'

'Teece. That's his last name. Isn't that a sparkler?'

I told her my name. 'Pleased to meet you.'

'We're going South.'

'A good time for it. How far are you going?'

I glanced down and he had his hand gripped on her thigh, giving her a hell of a horse bite. She tried to stand it. But he kept right on till you could see tears in her eyes, and she was panting with the pain. . . .

'Have some more,' he said sarcastically. 'There's another bottle back there.'

'Sure.'

I was floating. I sat there, riding up and down with the bumps, with my eyes half-closed. Trying not to remember Bess, waiting there, running up to me when I got home, her eyes all bright, saying, 'Did you get it? Did you get it?'

I held the bottle up and let it trickle down, warm.

'It's hard drinking it like that. We should have some chasers. Noel, why not stop and get some chasers?'

'Crazy? We've wasted time already.'

172

CHAPTER 2

WATER SPLASHED and gurgled somewhere. There was an odor of fresh earth and grass and wet leaves.

'Noel?' I heard her say that. Then it was still again. I knew I was on the ground and half of me was in running water. I couldn't move.

'Noel?'

Then a long silence. I went away for a time, then slowly came back again.

'No-o-*eeeel!*'

Somebody was thrashing around. It sounded like a giant with boots on, wading in a crisp brush pile. The rain had stopped. There was a moon now, shedding white on pale trees and hillside as I opened my eyes. I tried to see the road. It was hidden. I didn't dare move. We were in some sort of a gully. I lifted an arm. I turned my head. It hurt.

Something stabbed cruelly into my back. I turned, rolling away from the icy water. I was soaked. I was lying on a car door. There was no sign of the car, the girl, or the man.

Only her voice, some distance away. 'Noel.'

Shivering, I closed my eyes tight, remembering Bess like a kind of sob. Remembering all of it. And then this crazy ride with these two crazy people. Fear washed through me, and I lay there, listening, scared to stand up and look.

Finally I got to my knees. I seemed to be all right. My

neck hurt, and my right arm. I glanced at my hand, and saw the blood. I flexed my fingers. They worked.

I moved my shoulders. They hurt, too. When I put weight on my right knee, something stabbed me in the ankle. In the moonlight, I saw the big sliver of glass sticking into my ankle, through the sock. It was like a knife blade, only much broader.

I yanked it out. It hurt and the blood was warm, running into my shoe. I moved my foot and it was all right. It hadn't cut anything that counted. It would have to stop bleeding by itself. My teeth were all there and I could see and hear and move everything.

Except the little finger on my left hand. That was broken and if I touched it, it was bad.

'Mister Nichols?'

I didn't say anything. I got on my knees again, looking around, trying to find the car. Her voice had come from some distance away. Somebody kept thrashing in the brush.

A suitcase and what looked like my topcoat were lying near the door. I looked at the door and it had been torn neatly from the body. Then I saw the other suitcase and I started to get up and saw the brief case.

I kept on looking at that. The clasp was torn open and some kind of wispy scarf was tied to the handle. Only that wasn't what made me look.

It was the neatly bound packets of unmistakable money. I touched them, picked one up and saw the thousand-dollar bill, and put it down.

It was like being hit over the head.

'Mister Nichols?'

I started laughing. Maybe it was the whiskey. I needed money; not a whole lot, compared to this. But plenty for me. And right here was all the money in the world.

*

'Are you hurt bad?' I asked.

'No. Only my knee. See?'

'Where'd all the blood come from?'

'I don't know. My hand's cut – look at my dress. It's ripped to pieces.' She began to look kind of funny.

'Are you all right?'

'What'll we do?' She started away. I caught her and held her. She fought for a minute, then stopped.

'Now, for gosh sakes. You're all right.'

She turned and ran in the other direction. Her dress sure was a mess. She stumbled in circles all around between the trees. I got it then. She was looking for that brief case. She ran into the open by the stream where I had been. She splashed into the water and out and jumped over the car door.

I went on over there and held her again. 'You're all right. Now, where is he?'

'Down there. Over the edge. He's dead. I saw him. . . . No. Don't go down there.'

She ripped away from me. She had seen the brief case. She went to it, landing on her knees, kind of looking back at me over her shoulder, her hair flopping around.

She shoveled that money back in. The clasp wouldn't work. She got the scarf off the handle and wrapped the scarf around the case and tied it tight.

I went over and dragged her up. She held the brief case, pulling away from me.

'Where is he?'

She pointed in the direction of a bent pine sapling. I turned and walked over there, the blood squashing in my shoe. I came past the pine tree and saw skid marks.

I stopped at the abrupt edge just in time. The car was down there. Not too far, about fifteen feet, lying crumpled on its side, smashed to junk, in a rocky glen with the water splashing and sparkling in the moonlight.

The guy was spread out on the rocks, his feet jammed in the car by the steering wheel. The bright moonlight showed blood all over his face and his suitcoat was gone and his left arm had two elbows. He was more than just dead. He was a mess.

'We'd better get an ambulance.'

She hurried over by me and I got a good look at her face. I never saw anybody so scared in all my life. 'He's dead. What good would an ambulance do? Come on – we've got to get out of here.'

I looked at her and I thought about that money and I knew she was working something; trying to. She turned and walked away from me toward the wooded hill and the road.

A car went by up there and for an instant she was silhouetted against the headlights' glare through the trees. She looked back at me, then slipped and sat down.

I went over to her. She'd lost her shoes and her stockinged feet were muddy. She looked bad. 'Don't you see?' she said. 'We've got to get out of here.'

She tried to get up. I put my hand on top of her head and held her down.

'Whose money?'

'Mine. It's my money.'

'Awful lot of money for one woman to have. 'What about *him?*'

'Never mind about him. It's my money, and we've got to get out of here before they find us.'

'Thought you said that money was yours.'

'It is.'

I held her down with my hand on top of her head. She was so mad, and scared too, you could feel it busting right up out of the top of her skull.

These crazy people. All that money. And Bess and me only needing a little. I wanted to crunch her head like a melon.

176

I was still bleary from the whiskey and my head was beginning to ache bad. But there was something else in my head besides the ache. I kept trying to ignore it.

'It's taken two and a half years to get that money. We've got to get away from here. Nichols, whatever your name is, you've got to help me.'

'We'll have to get the police.'

She tugged her head away from my hand and stood up. She was still hanging onto that brief case. She grabbed my arm with her other hand. There was a streak of blood down the side of her cheek.

'It's stolen money, isn't it?'

'No. And we can't go to the police.' She began to rock back and forth, trying to rock me with her, trying to make me understand something. Only she didn't want to tell me about it. 'We're up the creek, Nichols.'

I kept trying to figure her. It looked like she was in a real mess.

I tried not to want any part of this. I started away from her. She came after me.

'Please – listen!'

'You're not telling me a damned thing. Look, you two picked me up and fed me whiskey. I shouldn't have taken it. But I got my troubles, too. They're big troubles to me. So now look what's happened. I'm still drunk and I don't even know you. And back there. Your boy friend's dead. How about that? I'm getting out of here.'

'Don't you see? If you hadn't seen the money – then you'd have helped me.'

'We'd go to the police. Like anybody else. You got to report an accident like this. There's a dead man down there. Don't you realize that?'

'He doesn't matter.'

'Somebody was following you, weren't they? We saw somebody in Valdosta and you'd just turned off the main southern

177

route, too. Only you turned back, and we were followed. That's why this happened.'

She looked as if she might cry. Well, why didn't I call the police then? Why didn't I do what I should have done?'

'They'll be back.'

'You stole that money.'

'You're wrong, Nichols. You've got to believe me.' She stood perfectly still and got her voice very calm and steady. 'It won't hurt you to help me. If you knew who Noel was, you'd understand that it doesn't matter about him being dead.'

There was one thing: Her fear was real.

'We'll take the suitcases and get out of here. Down the road somewhere. Change clothes. His clothes'll fit you.'

'Oh, no.'

'But you can't go any place the way you are. Look at you. Mud – blood. Neither can I. We'll clean up and get dressed. Then we'll find the nearest town and you can help me get a hotel room.'

'Lady, you're nuts.'

She dropped the brief case then, and faced me. She put both hands on my arms and looked me in the eye. Straight.

'Nichols,' she said, 'there's absolutely no other way. He's dead down there and I'm all alone. I'll bet you can use some money. I've got plenty and I'll pay you well. If you don't help me, they'll find me.'

'Let them. This is too much for me.'

And I wanted it to be too much. But the sight of that money was like catching cold and knowing it would turn into pneumonia. If only that guy had lived, then I'd have an excuse.

We stood there and the moonlight was bright on her face. Her dress was all torn, her hair mussed up, and there was this streak of blood on her cheek. There was something about it. It got me a little. She looked so damned alone and

178

afraid, her eyes big and pleading. And there she stood, hanging onto that brief case, like that.

CHAPTER 3

WELL, NEAR the edge of the town, there was this big billboard beside the concrete. It was at the bottom of a shallow slope, across a small creek. We were walking tenderly, me with the blood drying in my sock. And Vivian in her stocking feet, on tiptoe. A car passed us, but by that time we were behind the billboard out of sight.

She took off her dress. 'Turn your back, Nichols,' she said, 'and get some clothes out of his suitcase. We've got to get away from here. Hurry!'

I was afraid if I sat down I'd never get up. I staggered around, having trouble with the one sock. Finally when I yanked at it, it peeled like adhesive, but was stiff as cardboard. There was quite a hole where the glass had stuck in, and it was bleeding again. The hell with it. Only that was the whiskey still talking.

After she got through, I scrubbed off the blood and mud. My ankle kept bleeding. I fumbled in the suitcase and found a handkerchief and tied it around my ankle.

I kept glancing over there at that brief case. 'I'll help you find a room. That much.'

Still trying to convince myself. I got dressed in his clothes, transferred my wallet and stuff and put my coat and hat on again.

She bundled the old clothes together and walked away

into the trees. When she came back, she didn't have them. Her movements were still jerky. You could tell by the way she moved and looked that she was living in a pool of fright.

'No kidding, where'd you get that money?'

'It's mine.'

We closed the suitcases.

She picked up the brief case and started out around the billboard. Then she glanced back. The moonlight was on her – fur jacket, long black hair, high heels and scared.

'All right.' I grabbed the two suitcases, forgetting about my pinky. It hurt like hell. I went on after her, dressed in a dead man's clothes.

I kept trying hard not to think of what Bess would think of this business. It wasn't much good. Then I looked at that brief case in Vivian's hand again. 'You'll have to take one of these suitcases.'

'Why?'

'Because my finger's busted, that's why. I can't handle the both of them.'

She took hers and went on. I didn't want all that money. Just a part of it. Her heels rapped real loud on the asphalt. She had a long stride and she walked with her chin up.

On the road we kind of half-ran, half-walked. She kept looking behind us, and trying to see ahead. She had me as nervous as herself.

She was taking some kind of big chance.

So was I. But she knew what it was, what the odds were. I was playing it blind.

There was more to the town than I'd figured, but it still wasn't much. All the houses were asleep and her heels made terrific echoes in the still cold.

A car came down the main drag and she gave me a shove into a store front. I listened to her breathe, with her face pressed right up to mine. It was kids in the car, with the radio blaring.

181

'Off the main street, Nichols.'

We turned away from the car tracks. There was a hotel down there with a rusty-looking marquee and white bulbs saying: *Hotel Ambassador*. Three bulbs in the 'D' were smashed. She stopped under the marquee and faced me. 'You can't just leave me.'

'Why can't I?'

'You've come this far. It's not going to hurt you.'

I looked at her, saying nothing.

'Is it, Nichols? How could it?'

The wind blew down the street, dusting along the curb, blowing newspapers and small trash past the hotel.

'Look, Nichols. You can't imagine the jam I'm in.'

'That's any reason why I should be in it with you?'

'I'm not asking that.'

I looked down at the brief case, then remembered what she'd said about paying me. 'I was just on my way home,' I said.

'I know that. St. Pete, wasn't it? Well, you can't start home now, anyway, Nichols. You're tired. I'm not asking a whole lot. I can't do it myself. You'll have to help me. I've got to get out of the country.'

'Honest to God, you sound crazy.'

'That's the way it is. I'll pay for it. I'm not asking you to do it for nothing.'

'I've already —'

'That's what I mean. Listen, I'm so scared that it's all I can do to walk. If I told you, you'd understand.'

'I don't want to know.'

'But I've got to tell you.'

We stood there, and the accident and the dead guy sat there in the back of my mind. I'd already come this far, and it was a long way.

Her knuckles were white, she was holding the brief case that tight. The wind started to blow in her hair. She set her suitcase down and lifted her hand and brushed some hair off her cheek. She was an absolute knockout.

'Well?'

CHAPTER 4

IT HAD to be one room. When I said something about getting separate rooms, you could see the fear bubbling up inside her like acid. She wouldn't leave me for a second.

I felt pretty bad. I needed a drink and I was sick. Only there wasn't any chance of getting a drink, and I kept thinking more and more all of a sudden, about that dead guy back there in the gully, bloody and broken.

'I'll pay you well, Nichols.'

'Get off it, will you?'

So we were Mr. and Mrs. Ed Latimer on the register. I couldn't see as it mattered much. The clerk yawned and blinked and tossed me the keys and said, 'Two-oh-two.'

But when we went up the stairs, I glanced back and he was watching her legs from under his hand.

It sure was a dingy place.

She sat on the bed and said, 'Cripes!'

I didn't say anything. There was the bed, a straight-backed chair, a paint-peeling, battle-scarred bureau with an empty water pitcher and a pencil on the bare top. There were brown curtains on the window, and the walls were painted blue. There was one lamp by the bed with a frothy pink shade, and the bathroom looked older than the hotel.

She sat there on the bed and I stood by the closed door and it was cold. Finally she got up and went over and peeked

out the window, around the shade, and turned with her
hands clasped together like she was praying.

'They won't find me here. Not only one night.' She looked
at me, then she took off her fur jacket and hung it in the
closet. She opened her suitcase and said, 'Here.' She had a
bottle. 'It didn't break,' she said. 'Noel always had a lot of
bottles.'

'Get off him.'

'He might even have another in his bag, there.'

Something came up in me. It was like fighting, and you
get in a good punch. This punch was aimed at that something
inside me. I hadn't been able to level off. But now I had a
flash of that old white logic.

I turned and went over to the door and opened it. 'The
hell with this. I'm taking off.'

I walked out and closed the door and started down the
hall. The door opened and her heels rattled down the hall
after me. 'Nichols!'

'No.'

She grabbed my arm. I dragged her a couple of steps and
stopped.

'It's my money. I'm afraid.'

'You're lying like hell. You expect me to believe something
like that?'

'Make it business, then – let's say I hired you.'

'Let go.'

We were standing next to a door. The door opened and
a guy stuck his head out and stared at us. 'Will you two
please shut up?'

We went back into the room and I stood by the door,
holding it open, and looked at that brief case leaning against
the night table. She had the bottle. The scarf she'd tied
around the brief case was red, bright red.

She began to look as if she'd fall to pieces. It was all
jammed up inside her and she didn't know what to do. Then

185

she set the bottle on the bureau. There was a woolen blanket folded at the foot of the bed. She took it out and spread it and opened the bed.

'I'm freezing, Nichols.'

I went and sat in the chair and looked at the bottle. Then I took it and opened it and had a long drink.

I looked at her and she was standing there in the middle of the room, staring at the wall. She had her hands together like that. She kept staring, lost.

The color of the dress she'd put on was taffy. Some sort of soft material. It stuck to her. She had a lot of chin, too, and a broad soft mouth and these great big frightened eyes.

'You're going to tell me, lady. Who was it following us? What's it all about?'

'I'd better have some of that, Nichols.'

She took a sip out of the bottle, and I went over and closed the door and took off my coat and hat. She sat down on the edge of the bed and stared at the floor. I could see her getting ready to lie again. Then she crossed her legs and leaned back on her elbows. She cleared her throat, and I looked at that brief case again.

'So Noel was my boy friend. You can call it that. I've known him for three years. He took money down this way every two months.'

'Why?'

'The people – the people he worked for.'

'Yeah. But who?'

'Well.' She folded her fingers together and bent her hands back and swallowed. I took a drink, watching her. As she watched me, her eyes kind of hazed over with thinking, Can I get away with a lie? And then her eyes cleared, and she wasn't going to lie. You could see that little bit of relief in her, too. And I couldn't get that money out of my mind. She cleared her throat again. 'Well,' she said, 'Noel, he worked

186

for the syndicate. He was a courier.' She paused. 'My God,' she said, 'the things that can happen!'

'Go on.'

'I don't care. Anyway, they had him making runs through the South. The syndicate runs gambling places in the South, see? It's a very carefully controlled business. For instance, there's a place in Baltimore, and Atlanta, too. Well, every two months it was Noel's job to make the run with working capital. He carried cancelled checks, papers, notifications of change, stuff like that. Sometimes he'd pick up a part of the take, sometimes not. He never really knew what would happen till he reached each place.'

I watched her, listening, and not liking it.

She said, 'So I thought of how Noel and I could get this money. He would carry quite a pile on these trips, only they always watched him, tailed him. He never knew where, either. Listen, I was never mixed up in it. I just wanted to get him clear of them.'

'Sure.'

'It's nobody's money that'll do any hurt. I mean, it's not stealing. Not like – ' She stopped.

I took another drink. She was tight. I don't mean drunk, I mean scared, all tied up inside; frozen. You could feel it and she kept swallowing as she talked. The whiskey was reaching me, though.

I kept feeling lower all the time. I kept remembering Bess, and her wondering where I was. This was five days now. Tomorrow would be six. Damn that Albert!

She began to tremble. 'Noel said he'd maybe try it. All right. So when they got so they trusted him, then we'd take the money and leave the country together. So every trip, he'd watch how they kept track of him. And we wanted a trip where he skipped the Baltimore and Atlanta places, see? One straight through. And this was it, this one. Only they must have caught on – there in Valdosta. We were going to New

187

Orleans, along the coast and Noel made the wrong turn and one of them was waiting for that. Noel turned back, all right, but it was too late and he knew it. You couldn't explain it, see? And with you in the car, too? And then, he made the run, and that was the worst, when Noel panicked. So that's who was following us.

'Listen, they won't stop at anything now. You can't just give them back the money. It's too late for that. It's too late for the stop at Tampa. That's where he was supposed to go, and me with him. I wasn't supposed to be with him. It's too late for anything, but getting away.' She paused, looking at me, bent over a little, her eyes wide and bright. 'I've got to get away.' She shook her head. 'You can't possibly understand. But right this minute, they're hunting. It's a lot of money. It was always in cash, see? It had to be that way for them, and Noel was a trusted courier. God, maybe they've missed the car, the wreck. So that'll slow them down. But they're hunting. And they know how to hunt. They'll kill me.'

Maybe some of it was lies. But basically it was the truth, because you could see it all through her.

'Noel wanted to back out, but I kept at him. It's my fault. We'd been arguing in the car when we stopped at that place. That's half why he let you come along, I think, to – to shut me up. We were going right on to New Orleans.'

She didn't say anything for a time. I took another long one from the bottle and glanced at the brief case.

'A lot of money?'

'A terrible lot. But they've got crazy ethics. A thing like this is unpardonable. It's like any business – except you know what they do to somebody who crosses them? You know what they do to a woman who crosses them?' She looked away, her face pale and expressionless. Then she looked at me again. 'But I've got that money and I'm keeping it. It took two and a half years to get this far.'

'Not very damned far, huh?'

She put both hands against her face and turned around.

I looked at her back and I knew just why I was sticking here. It was the money, all the way. I'd seen it, and I couldn't get it out of my head. Bess and I needed money so damned bad, and there it was right by my foot, leaning against the night table.

It was crazy, maybe. She was crazy to think she could get away with it. And telling me all this, but she had nobody to turn to. In the back of my mind I began to know I was going to help her. It didn't really matter where she got that money.

I got up and went into the bathroom and found a glass. I washed the glass and filled it with water and came back and sat down in the chair again. I was drunk. I drank some of the water. It tasted like dust.

'If you're lying – I'll quit on you.'

She just looked at me.

'I been a bum. Before I met Bess. She's my wife.'

She didn't move. She was thinking.

'That's right. I was in the Merchant Marine, and the war. I been around enough to know. You think I don't read you?'

'You can get a car in the morning. I'll give you the money, so you can buy a car.'

'I met Bess in New Mexico, where her folks lived. A little town. We had that thing and we got married without a cent. I worked in a gas station and we bought a trailer, and I got hold of some dough and we bought a house. We sold the trailer. Then I couldn't make it again, so we sold the house and bought a car and came to Florida. I worked the shrimpers. We saved a lot. Then I heard of this thing.'

I was drunk and running off at the mouth. I couldn't stop. I felt sad. I was trying to convince myself out loud that this was the thing to do. It was crazy, all right. But it was happening.

'So finally I got a line on this place, a motel. Somebody'd

built it in the wrong place and went broke. Then news got around they were going to put a new highway through. It's coming right through in front of the motel. Twenty apartments. Bedroom, living room, kitchen and bath. Real nice.

'So I'd never used my G.I. loan, see? So it was tough, but I got that and right along in there Bess's old man died. He left her quite a bit. We used it all. I went into hock all around. We managed to get this place. We met the down payment. It's nice. We're happy. No money, but happy. Then payments begin to come due.'

'Mmmm.'

'We just manage, sweating out the highway. They began work, see? Then we don't manage and I had to start stalling. I got an extension from the bank, all right. But then that time went. I tried to get a job. I couldn't find one that would pay enough.' I took a long drink. 'So they suspended work on the highway.' I told her about the bank refusing a personal loan; how it was.

'Why are you telling me all this?'

'Just want you to know.'

'You don't know what trouble is, Nichols. . . . Well, go ahead. Finish.'

'Well,' I said, 'this highway will sure be something, if it does come through. We're right on it. We'll get the business. From the North, straight through to Miami. They started work, sure. Only the 'dozers sit out there and the tar vats, and nobody's working. Nothing happens, because that damned commissioner wants a different route. Meantime, if I don't have the money, we lose the place. We lose the place – I'm done.'

She leaned over and pushed her plump lips to my ear and said, 'Nichols.'

'So I went up to Chicago.' I told her about Albert.

'Tomorrow I'll give you enough for the car. We'll drive

190

on down. Then you can see about plane tickets. Or a boat, or something so I can get out. I'll pay you well, Nichols.'

The bottle was empty. I dropped it on the floor.

She reached over and put her palm against my face and turned my head. We looked at each other.

I slumped back in the chair and watched her.

She took her suitcase and went into the bathroom and when she came out I was still sitting there. She set her suitcase down and opened the other one. She was wearing a red polka-dot negligee. She found the bottle she'd mentioned and set it on the night stand and turned the light off. Then she moved by me to the window and raised the shade and opened the window. A cold wind yawned into the room. She went back and got into the bed. The sign from the hotel outside lit up the room.

I got up and took the bottle and returned to the chair. I opened it and had a drink. Then I got the glass of water and drank some and set it on the bureau. I sat in the chair with the bottle and watched her.

'You'll freeze.'

'You wouldn't understand.'

'The bed's warm.'

I took a drink and set the bottle on the bureau and fell off the chair. I got up on the chair again and watched her.

'Nichols?'

'What?'

'You can't sit there all night!'

'Shut up.'

Then she was standing by me, pulling at my arm. I stood up and fell flat on my face. The floor was grimy and there was no rug. . . .

In the morning I was hung over bad, and plenty sick. She gave me the money and I went out and found a car. I wasn't thinking yet. I couldn't think.

It was a good car. It was a Ford sedan and it hadn't taken more than a half-hour to get the papers changed. The used-car dealer took them to the courthouse himself, while I waited on the lot.

He came back, smiling through the flaps of his jacket collar, turned up against the cold. He was a tall guy with bloodshot eyes and he was happy over the sale.

'You've got a good car,' he said. 'A good car.'

'Thanks.'

'Boy!' he said. 'Everybody's running out to the other end of town this morning. Big wreck out there. Police are going out there now, I reckon. Maybe I'll run out there. Sombody spotted a smashed-up Lincoln out there. Sailed right over the damned pine trees.'

'Oh. Anybody – ? They find anybody?'

'I don't know. I'm going to run out there.'

So I looked at him, and it was like something clicked inside my head. Maybe it was just the cold morning. But I suddenly didn't want any part of this. It scared the hell out of me, just standing there. I'd gone too far, and I wanted to get home to Bess. Money or no money.

I took the papers he'd given me and put them in the glove compartment of the car. Then I turned to him again.

'Look,' I said. 'Do me a favor?'

'Sure.'

'You got an envelope?'

He went into the little office and came out with an envelope, frowning. I turned away and took what money there was left and put it in there and sealed it and handed it to him.

'Do me a favor,' I said. 'Take this, and the car. Drive the car over to the Ambassador Hotel, all right? Leave the envelope at the desk for Mrs. Ed Latimer. Got that?'

'Yes. Sure, but – '

'Better yet. Take it up to room two-oh-two, see? The

envelope, of course, with the car keys and papers. She'll tip you. Tell her you brought the car over. All right?'

'But, I don't understand.'

'You don't have to. All right?' I repeated the names. 'Take your time. There's no hurry. Wait an hour or so.'

We looked at each other. I turned away and started walking fast down through town toward the main southern route.

I wasn't on the corner under the stop light more than three minutes, when this convertible came along with an old guy and his wife. They were headed for Key West. Sure, they'd be glad to take me to St. Pete. I got in and sat quiet.

It wasn't till we were way down in Florida that I remembered I'd bought that Ford in my name. So the rest of the way, I sat there sweating with that, trying not to think about it. Then trying to think what to do about it. Nothing.

It wasn't much good, I'll tell you. The old guy and his wife knew I was sick. Getting to St. Pete didn't help, either.

CHAPTER 5

THEY LET me out on Lakeview. They were headed for the Sunshine Skyway bridge, and if it hadn't been for Bess, I'd have stayed with them. 'We'd be glad to take you wherever you live,' the woman said.

'Thanks. It's all right.'

The old guy wanted to move on. His wife wanted to talk. I grinned at them and started across the street. They started off toward their happy, unworried vacation.

I crossed to the sidewalk and began walking down Lakeview. It was off schedule for the bus, so I'd probably have to walk all the way home. It was afternoon. The sun slanted across a stately row of royal palms along the street and the air was warm. Two girls in shorts went riding by on bicycles, jabbering at each other. Cars hissed past on the asphalt. Over there between patches of green jungle, beyond cool-looking homes, you could see Lake Maggiore, pale blue and shadowed in the sun.

I moved along, trying not to think. I'd have to face Bess with this, and with the rest of it in the back of my mind. Vivian and that damned money. I'd been that close to a solution, and then turned away from it. Maybe it was wrong. I felt bad and I wanted to feel good. I'd done the right thing, it had to be. But did it matter? *What was I going to tell her?*

How do you tell them you've failed them at the last ditch?

especially when they depend on you; when they're sure of the way you do things – banking on you, like they do.

I remembered that guy, Teece, lying twisted in the wreck, and I began to feel better. I needed something to fasten my mind to. I was well clear from them both and that had to be right.

Crossing another block, it was plenty warm. I paused under a young banyan and started peeling my coat. I turned and glanced back there along Lakeview to see if a bus might be along.

A Ford sedan slid into the curb, tires scraping, steam frothing white and hot from under the fenders and hood. Vivian looked at me, pale-faced, and beeped the horn.

I looked away, shrugged back into my coat, and started walking. It wouldn't do any good. There was no place to run, and anyway, you don't run. There were about fifteen more hot blocks to my place. I heard the cars peel by through the shadows and the sunlight.

'Nichols – '

The car door slammed and I heard her running lightly across the grass and down the sidewalk after me, her heels snicking. A young guy and his girl came strolling out of a nearby house. They stopped, whispering, watching. The guy grinned behind his shoulder.

She caught up with me, grabbed my arm.

'Go away, will you?'

'You ran out on me before. You can't run out on me now.'

I kept staring down the street. In the back of my mind, I knew nothing was going to work. She'd found me, just like that – and it was only natural she would come on down here. I looked at her and she was plenty worried. Worse than before, even.

She began to laugh. It was a kind of strained, muted, hysterical laughter. 'Nichols. Come back to the car!'

'What d'you want with me?'

'You know what I want.'

I figured I should have had sense enough not to try and get away from this one.

'Come on,' she said. 'Will you?' She stood there watching me with her eyes all shot full of worry and waiting. 'The minute that man from the car lot drove up to the hotel, I knew,' she said. 'I knew even before that. I got one of those feelings.'

We went back to the car and she climbed under the wheel and sat there. You could hear the steam hissing, and the engine creaked a lot.

'I'm going to stay right at your place, Nichols.'

I turned and looked at her. She didn't bother looking at me. 'Like hell,' I told her.

'It's got to be that way. I've got to be able to get to you.' Then she turned to me and her voice had that dead seriousness she was able to get. 'How could you run out on me like that? After all I've told you?' She turned away and hid her head down against the steering wheel. She was going through plenty. Vivian kept her head pressed against the wheel.

'You can't stay at my place,' I heard myself say. 'What about my wife?'

'God, I thought I'd lost you. I got to thinking, suppose he lied to me. Suppose he doesn't live down here at all. There was no way of telling. Nichols, I'm about dead from driving. I didn't know what I was going to do. I had to find you.'

'What about my wife?'

'She doesn't have to know.'

'Your damn right. She isn't going to know. Hear?'

'Don't worry. I'm going to pay you. That's all you want – money.'

I'd made up my mind, now. 'That's for sure.' Well, all right. I'd let her stay at the motel. She'd be a customer.

Somehow. A guest. Some guest. Then I told her about how they'd spotted the wreck.

She came around in the seat like a shot. 'Why didn't you tell me?'

I didn't say anything. She started the car. It took some starting, it was that hot. Finally she got her going and you could feel the fear in her and the dead tiredness.

'Where's your place, Nichols?'

She was sitting up on the edge of the seat, staring at the windshield as if she were hypnotized. It was hard to figure her as a woman who would play it this tight. She was nice looking; more than that.

She sure had fouled me up.

I had her park the car on a side street, three blocks from the motel. The car was still steaming. I told her to get some water and she didn't say a word. I got out and leaned in the window and looked at her.

'You wait a while, then just drive up front. Give me enough time. It's the Southern Comfort Motel.'

'All right. Some name, Nichols.'

We watched each other. She had her hands clenched tight on the wheel.

I turned and took off my hat and coat and started down the block toward home. It hadn't turned out the way I'd wanted. You get caught in something like this and you get in deeper and deeper, and you begin to accept it.

Traffic had been rerouted off the main street past our place. The bricks were torn up and there was a tractor sitting silent across the way.

I walked along, alone and beat and kind of lost. Everything was cockeyed, but there was that money. I kept thinking about that. It had to work, now.

My head ached and I needed a shave and I was in a dead

man's clothes. It's real great, the things that happen to you. You don't even have to look for it hard.

> *Southern Comfort*
> *Motel*
> *Vacancy*

I could see it down there.

'*Vacancy*.' That was a hot one. We'd never once used the '*No Vacancy*' sign. But it did look good down there. The lawn would have to be mowed. I'd have to get at it right away. And some fronds on two of the plumosas needed trimming.

Walking along, I began to feel a little better. Sanctuary down there. And it was Bess who made it that way, made me feel good.

It took up a whole block. Boy! Nichols, the land baron.

Why didn't they put that highway through? I wasn't the only one, there were other motel owners going through the same thing. But most of them had been in business for quite a while. They had a nest egg.

You *could* limp along the way the road was before. But with it shut off and the detour, you had nothing.

The hedges needed trimming, too. I hadn't noticed that before I left. Then I saw the hedge that ran along the side nearest me had been trimmed about halfway.

Bess again. I'd told her never to do that. I started walking faster, unconsciously.

It was good to be home.

So then it all rushed back into my mind, maybe worse than before, like it does sometimes. Her, in the Ford, waiting back there. The wreck. The brief case with all that money. And Teece – Noel Teece, lying there dead with his two elbows on one arm.

*

Bess was sitting on the steps by the office. She had on a slipover and a pair of red shorts, just sitting there holding a broom, staring at nothing. I whistled at her.

She looked up and saw me and flung the broom and came running.

Then, watching her, I knew I'd done the right thing, after all. It had worked out right. I wasn't coming home empty-handed and I knew now I never wanted that to happen. Now she'd have what she deserved, or as near to it as I could deliver. It had been in my mind all along, I guess. If I'd come home the way I'd started, without Vivian – it wouldn't have been good.

'Roy!'

It seemed odd and sort of wonderful, hearing her call me that – after all that 'Nichols' business.

How Bess could run! She wasn't too tall, just right, and built just right, too. With light blond hair that the sun was dancing in, and bright blue eyes, her slim legs churning. And those red shorts. She came running across the lawn past the sign, and down the sidewalk.

She hit me hard, the way she always did, jumping into my arms. 'Roy – you're back!'

I kissed her and held her and we started walking across the lawn toward the office. We had the apartment behind the office.

Like I say, the sun was in her hair and it was in her eyes, too. She had on a white terry-cloth slip-over, and walking across the lawn she kept swatting me with her hip.

'Did you get it, Roy?'

'Sure.'

She stopped again and jumped up and hung on my neck, kissing me. Bess was the way I wanted it and I never wanted it any other way. Just Bess.

I dropped my hat and she let go. 'You mean, Albert gave you the money?'

I nodded.

She picked up my hat and looked at me and there was a flash of suspicion, only she chased it away. 'That's a different suit, Roy. Where'd you get the suit?'

'It's – '

'Doesn't fit you quite right.'

She reached out and flicked the jacket open and grabbed the waist of the pants and yanked. She was that way; quick as anything and I stood there, looking down at the gap. He'd been a lot bigger around the middle than I was.

'Al gave it to me.'

'Oh?'

'Like it?'

'Where's your other suit?'

'I gave it the old heave-ho.'

'But, Roy! That was your best suit.' She began to look at me that way again.

'My only. And three years old. It fell apart.'

'Oh, Roy!'

I grabbed her again and kissed her and we went on over to the office and on inside. I had a desk in here, and a couple chairs. It was a small front room.

Bess looked at me kind of funny, and took my coat. She flipped the coat on a chair and plopped the hat on it, and looked at me again.

'It's good to be home.'

'You know it.'

I took her in my arms as she walked up to me. She pressed against me, and when she kissed me, she really let me know. I got my hand snarled up in her hair and yanked her head back, looking down into her eyes.

'Gee, Roy!'

'Yeah.'

'He came through!'

200

'That's right. He's going to send the money down. Don't know what got into him.'

'You were right, then – in going up there. Instead of writing or just phoning, like I said at first.'

I kissed her again, kissing her lips, her chin, with my hand snarled in that golden hair.

'Roy, you better stop.'

I was trying to hold the rest of the bad stuff away from my mind. It was rough, because I hated lying to Bess. I remembered Vivian, and kissed her again and said, 'You son-of-a-gun!' Then I let go of her and turned around, looking at the office, rubbing my hands together. 'Boy, it's sure good to be back! Any customers?'

'A couple. Listen, you're not getting away that easy. How come you're late? I figured the day before yesterday. Where've you been?'

'Got a ride down. It saved some money. Folks coming south to Tampa, and I bummed over from Tampa.' I cleared my throat. 'For free. I drove them down, see?'

She kept looking at me. 'What did your brother say?'

I shrugged. 'Well, I laid the cards on the table. I told him what kind of a fix we were in. He saw it, all right.' I laughed. 'Wouldn't trust me with the money, bringing it down myself. Thinks I'm still wild, or something. Said he'd send it.'

She came over and put her arms around me again. 'You're sure he will, Roy?'

I nodded. 'Anything new about the road?'

She shook her head, laying her cheek against my chest. 'I missed you, Roy. And you look sick. You need a shave and you're pale. Is something the matter?'

'I'm fine. No sunshine up there. Freezing. Snowing in Georgia, even.'

I kept trying to look out the window. I knew damned well that Ford would be along any minute. She was plenty anxious. Then I got to thinking, 'What if she doesn't come? What then?' It hit me just exactly how much I was depending on that money. It was like caving in – I had to have it.

'You went and started trimming the hedge. I told you not to do that.'

'It's just started growing again. I had to do something.'

'Yeah, I guess.' I caught myself pacing.

'Roy, you sure you feel all right?'

I turned and looked at her. 'Just happy, getting home and all.'

She started to come over to me and I heard the car drive up out in the street. Bess looked at me. I didn't look out the window, I didn't dare.

'Somebody's stopped out front,' Bess said. 'Maybe business is picking up.' She yanked her sweater down and headed for the door. 'I'll go see, Roy.'

'No. You take it easy. I'll check this one.'

We stood there, looking at each other, by the door.

'You listen to me,' she said. 'One look at you, and you'd scare anyone clear down to Key West. You look like you've been shot out of a cannon. So I'll see who it is. You sit right here and relax.'

The screen door slammed. I watched her cross the lawn, her legs scissoring, the red shorts in and out of shadow.

Sweat popped out all over me. I stood watching them through the window. Vivian got out of the car and stood there, looking at the motel. When she saw Bess coming across the lawn, she kind of shrunk back against the car, then straightened and reached for her purse on the seat. She turned as Bess stepped up.

They were talking, and I sweated and sweated, sitting at the desk, my head propped on my fist, watching Bess and Vivian. Vivian was nodding about something. Her hair was real black. Bess was shorter than Vivian, standing there with her hands on her hips.

202

They both started up toward the office.

It was all wrong. I got up and walked out of the office, into our living room. I couldn't stay there, so I came back. They were talking out on the front lawn. It was enough to drive you nuts.

I had to have a cigarette. I found a pack in the desk drawer and lit up and stood there sweating and fuming. I went out into the kitchen and got a drink of water.

I didn't want to see the two of them together. Not now, I couldn't face that. Bess was too wise.

I heard the front screen door slam. I walked as slow as I could back to the office. Bess was beside the desk, counting some money.

'Two weeks!' She turned and waved the bills and smiled. 'Just like that. Isn't it swell? I gave her number six. A woman, all alone. She's a real looker, too. You stay away from her door, Roy. Hear?'

I looked at her, but she had her eyes on the money. She took it over and put it in the cigar box in the desk drawer. I felt real bad about this. Now it was beginning.

'She's coming over to register.'

The blood began to pound behind my ears. 'Did you tell her where to park the car?'

'No. You can show her later.'

'I think I'll take a shower, Bess.'

'Right. I'll take care of her. I'll fix a good dinner.' Then she left the desk and came over by me. 'It's swell about Albert. Maybe we can make it now.'

'Sure, we'll make it.' I kissed her and gave her a good smack with both hands and went back into the apartment and closed the door. In the bathroom I started to take that suit off; I'd never put it on again.

I was taking off my shoes, when I remembered the broken finger and the ankle. Bess hadn't said a word about that

203

finger. It looked like a miniature baseball bat and it was as black as midnight. She couldn't have missed seeing it.

The ankle was a mess. I took the sock off, then untied the handkerchief. When I yanked the handkerchief, it started bleeding again. I got a Band-Aid and fixed it up with some iodine and then remembered the shower.

I'd fouled things up just dandy.

'You can show her the garage, Roy.'

'All right. Did she register?'

'You bet.'

'You didn't say anything about my finger.'

'Uh-uh. I saw it, though. Did Albert bite it?'

'It's busted. Caught it in the car door, coming down. Not my fault, either. This old biddy slammed the door on it.'

She looked at it. 'You'll have to see a doctor.'

Then she looked up and smiled at me. 'You look lots better, shaved and in your own clothes. They fit, at least.'

I had on sneakers, a pair of gray slacks and a T-shirt. 'Fix some dinner, huh?'

'She's out by her car. Go show her the garage.'

I went on out there, walking across the lawn like it was a big basket of eggs. The sun was way down now, right smack in your eyes from across the street in the park, glinting between the branches of the oak trees – long slices of fiery orange peel.

'Hello, there.'

I nodded at her.

'Wonder if you could show me where to park the car?'

'I'll drive it around. Get in.'

She slid under the wheel and over to the other side of the seat and I climbed in after her. I slammed the door, not looking at her, started the engine and took it down around the block and in the drive behind the apartments.

'Nice wife you have, Nichols.'

I showed her the garage for number six. I drove the car inside and got out and stood there in the semi-dark. She got out on her side and came around and stood in the doorway, looking at me. She wasn't self-conscious.

'You've got a swell place. You're very lucky.'

'Thanks. And listen: Be careful around my wife.'

'Relax, Nichols. I'm a woman, too.'

She was telling me! 'You go that way, I'm going around the other way.'

'But, Nichols – !'

'You heard me.'

'You've got to stay by me. Suppose somebody – ?'

I left her standing there and cut around the other side of the garage. She worried me plenty. I heard her walking the other way on the gravel. It wasn't good having her here. I had to keep elbowing out of my mind who she really was, the things she'd been mixed up in, the people she knew. But that money kept chewing away at me.

I headed for the back door. Bess was waiting, holding the door for me. 'I've got my eye on you, Roy.'

I knew she was kidding. Bess was real smart, but she was usually trusting. I wondered just how far that could go. It made me sweat, the way she was standing there and the way she said that.

CHAPTER 6

WITH VIVIAN in number six, my nervous system started to
kick up. I couldn't stay still. Thing was, I didn't know what
she might do. She was scared and wound up tight and
anxious to get on the move. There was always the chance
she might crack and come running over to our place, yelling,
'Nichols – Nichols!'

That would be all I'd need.

I couldn't see any way to get to her tonight. If I took a
chance and went over there, Bess might wise up. She was
watching me like a cat, anyway. I figured she was thinking
about what I'd done up in Chicago. She probably thought
I'd got drunk.

'Last day I was up there, I stayed in a cheap hotel. Waiting
for these folks to get ready for the trip down. I bought a
bottle, Bess. I shouldn't have, but I felt like celebrating.'

She seemed to take it all right. Celebrating! That was a
hot one, all right.

'It was bad stuff. I got sick.'

'You looked pretty bad when you came home. Lots better
now, though.'

'When I saw you, I felt better right away.'

'Now, Roy, you know what whiskey does to you. You
shouldn't take the chance in a strange town. You don't have
any sense when you're drunk. Somebody tell you, "Let's rob

a bank," you'd be all for it. Whoopee!' She shook her head, standing there by the oven in the kitchen with the roast going. 'No sense at all, Roy.'

'Let's not talk about it. All right?'

We looked at each other. Then she started smiling and she laughed and it was all right. For a minute there, she had me worried. The way she looked at me.

It was a good dinner. Roast beef, mashed potatoes, fresh peas in a cream sauce, apple pie and coffee.

'Wonder what she's doing down here?'

'Who?'

'That woman I put in number six. One that came in before dinner.'

'Oh. Why?'

'All alone, like that. You don't see them like her alone. Miss Jane Latimer, from Yonkers, New York.'

'That's her name?'

'Didn't you introduce yourself?'

I shook my head.

Bess drank some coffee. 'She didn't go out for dinner. She hasn't left the place.'

'It's early yet. Who else we got aboard?'

'There's an old guy in number fifteen. He's a shuffleboard bug. I think you ought to clean off the courts. He'd play all by himself. His wife's going to join him in a month or so. They're looking for a house down here. So we've got him for a month. Mr. Hughes, he is. . . . Say – maybe I should introduce him to Miss Latimer?'

I began to wish she'd lay off.

'Then there's a couple – middle-aged. The Donnes. She drinks an awful lot, always got one in her hand. I don't blame her, though. The way her husband sits and broods. They came down from New York, so he could get some rest. They never do anything, just sit. Every day a taxi comes up with a load of papers for him. He's an editor. Some New York publishing house. Got great big circles under his eyes. He walks up and down, talking to himself. She told me she's scared he's going to crack up.'

'Anybody else?'

'Honeymooners in eleven, only here for a couple of days. Real cute. And a woman whose husband just died, in nine-teen. That's all.'

'I think that's damned good, the way things been.'

After supper I got out on the lawn and monkeyed with the sprinkler system, trying to work myself over by number six, so I could see what was going on. It was real quiet over there, but she had a light burning.

I turned the sprinklers on. I knew if I was going to speak with her, it would have to be fast, while Bess was doing the dishes.

We had the floodlights cut off to save juice, what with the electric bill we had. They turn them off on us, and it'd really be rough, but I had the lights turned on the lawn at the two corners of the block. And the sign was a big one.

What I did was turn all the sprinklers off, then start turning them on, one at a time, by hand. I followed around, working toward number six. The sprinklers ticked and swished. They looked real good. If only there was lots of traffic, and I could have put the floodlights on. It looked good from the road, but the road was like a mortuary.

'*Psst!* Nichols!'

I almost went right out of my skin. She was standing there behind one of the double hibiscus bushes at the corner of number seven.

'Get back.'

'I've got to see you.'

I just walked straight off across the lawn. I leaned against the royal palm by the sign. I heard her go back toward number six. So then I went over to the sprinklers again.

I got the one by seven going, then moved on down beside six. It was in shadow.

It wasn't good to whisper and sneak. But it wasn't good to play it straight, either. Let Bess catch me running over here every chance, she'd put the clamps on – trusting or not.

I heard Vivian breathing through the screen windows from inside number six. She had the lights shut off except for one burning in the kitchen.

'You've got to get a move on,' she said. 'I mean it. I can't stay here forever.'

'I'm not doing nothing till tomorrow. That's the way it is.'

I could still hear her breathing; kind of rough, like she was breathing across a washboard. 'I haven't anything to eat.'

'Well, go out and buy yourself something. You got enough money.'

'I can't go out, Nichols. You'll have to get me some groceries. Something. Buy me a hamburg.'

'Get it yourself.'

Her voice crackled, high and shrill, whispering through the window. 'I can't go out, damn you! They'll be watching! My God, they'll – !'

'They won't be in St. Pete.'

'But I can't take that chance!'

'All right. I'll be in front of our place. You come on over there – by the office, and ask me real loud. Hear? And bring some money. And no hundred-dollar bills.'

She started to say something, but I was already walking away toward the office.

Well, I waited and nothing happened. She didn't come and she didn't come.

'Roy?'

The front screen door slammed. It was Bess, coming around front where I stood. Now, *she* would come. That's the way it always goes.

209

'Roy, that Latimer girl asked if you wouldn't go someplace and buy her some groceries.'

'What?' It was a good thing she didn't get a close look at my face.

'She came to the back door. Not feeling well, but she's hungry. Tired from the trip down. She made a list, here. And here's some money.

'The corner store's still open. I told her you'd be glad to do it.'

So I got the Chevie out of the garage and bought her groceries and came back. She and Bess were talking out in front of the office, on the lawn. I wanted to talk with Vivian.

I came across the lawn. 'Here you go.'

'Oh, fine. Thanks so much.' She was wearing white slacks and a black cardigan sweater.

'Well, don't stand there,' Bess said. 'Take them inside for her.'

I went on across and into number six. There were the two suitcases, sitting in the middle of the floor, one of them open. I didn't see anything of the brief case. I left the groceries on the table in the kitchen, with the change, and started out.

She came in the front door. She didn't say anything. She just stood there, wringing her hands. 'I feel trapped.'

'Tomorrow. I'll do something tomorrow.'

'You've got to get me out of here fast.'

'Leave, then.'

'I can't just leave. Nichols, I've got to get a plane, or a boat, or something. And I can't do it myself. They'll have every place covered!'

'You're nuts. They can't do that. You think they got the U. S. Army?'

'It's worse than that.' She stood there, not looking at me. 'I wish you were staying with me tonight. I'm scared, Nichols.'

'Where's the money?'

'Under the seat of that chair.'

I could see the tip of the brief case and some of the red scarf. 'Why don't you fix the clasp on that brief case? Give you something to do.'

'Better the way it is. I've had that scarf for years. It's a kind of talisman.'

'What in hell's a talisman?'

'Good luck charm, like.'

Bess was coming back from the curb, brushing off her hands. She was looking toward number six, squinting a little.

'We'll work something out tomorrow.'

She turned and kind of leaped at me, both hands out. I got over by the door. 'Nichols. I'm scared.'

I watched her for a second, then went on outside. That Vivian, scared of her own shadow! How could they cover all the airports? They didn't even know she was down here. Maybe they didn't even know she existed. It was Teece they would be wondering about. And they wouldn't wonder about him for long. They would wonder about the money.

But who were 'they?' she was really frightened, there was no getting around that.

Well, I'd have to get her out of here. And I was going to hit her hard for doing this. It was costing me a few years.

I went on out and put the Chevie in the garage.

'I phoned the doctor.'

'What?'

'About your finger. You've got an appointment for tomorrow afternoon. Two o'clock. I tried to get it earlier, but he was filled up.'

Bess closed the Venetian blinds on the bedroom windows.

The next morning I couldn't get near number six no matter how hard I tried. She came out and walked around and you

211

could see the nerves. She had on the white slacks and the black sweater.

The best we could do was wave at each other. There was so much to do, I didn't really accomplish anything, what with the worrying.

The front of number twenty was beginning to peel. I mixed some paint, trying to get the same pastel shade of blue it was in the first place. When it began to dry, it was a lot darker. It looked bad.

'You'll have to paint them all, Roy. They need it anyway.'

And all the time Vivian was back there in number six, going crazy. Every time I walked past on the lawn, she'd come out on the little porch, kind of frantic, making eyes. I didn't even dare look at her much.

Roy this; Roy that. The grass needed cutting. The garage roof leaked in two places. The hedges needed trimming and the fronds were withered and brown on all the palms. The lights had gone bad in ten. The sink was plugged up in number five. Mister Hughes said his toilet wouldn't flush.

I ran around the place, getting nowhere, and then it was one-thirty.

'How'd you do this to your finger, Mister Nichols?'

'Well, Doc, you see, I caught it in a car door.'

He looked at me, blinking his eyes behind enormous black-framed glasses. He was a young guy, heavy-set, with shoulders like a fullback, with those eyes that say you're lying no matter what you say. He kept looking at the finger and shaking his head.

'Have to set it. Have to get the swelling down first.'

'Anything. Listen, just set it.'

'With the swelling, the pain would be bad.'

'Go ahead – go on.'

Well, he liked to kill me. So there I was, finally, with it in

212

a neat little cast. My finger sticking out so it would be in the way of everything.

'Bill me, Doc.'

'Well, all right, Mister Nichols. And, say – be careful of car doors after this.'

His grin was real sly. . . .

His office was alongside the Chamber of Commerce building. I went on out to the car, figuring I'd have to see Vivian if I was ever going to get my hands on any of that money. I climbed into the car and started her up.

The sun was bright and hot.

I looked back to check traffic and happened to glance over toward the front door of the Chamber of Commerce building.

It was like being shot in the face. But it was no mistake. I would never forget that face.

Noel Teece was limping across the sidewalk.

CHAPTER 7

I SAT THERE, staring, with my foot jammed against the gas pedal, my hand just resting on the gearshift. The engine roared and roared without moving.

Teece was limping badly, dressed in a white Palm Beach suit. His left arm was in a big cast and sling. One side of his face was bandaged, so he only could use one eye.

I didn't know what to do. All the things Vivian was afraid of were beginning to come true.

He walked right by the front of the car, starting across the street. Then he looked directly at the windshield, and you could see him frown with the way the engine was tearing it up. I let go on the gas. He turned away. The sun was on the windshield, so he hadn't seen me. Then he went on across the street, limping, moving in a slow slouch.

He was real beat up and in pain. You could tell.

I watched him go on across the street and stand on the corner. He stood there arranging the sling, kind of staring at his arm as if it was something foreign. Then he patted the bandages by his left eye. He was wearing a Panama hat and it rode on top of the bandages on his head. He kept trying to pull the brim down.

I had to tell Vivian. When I did, there was no telling what she'd do. I sure didn't like seeing Noel Teece – alive.

Because I knew why he was in this town.

'You get your finger fixed?'

'Yeah.'

I had tried bringing the car around to the garage, figuring I'd be able to sneak over to number six. Bess must have seen me coming, or else she was just waiting back there. Anyway, she watched me park the car in the garage.

'That's good.'

'The doc set it. It sure hurt.'

'Tough,' Bess said.

I looked at her. She had on a two-piece white swim suit. She'd been working in the back lawn while I was gone, and she was wet from the sprinklers. Only there was something else in her eyes. She had some mud on one hand, and she wiped her face and some of the mud smeared off.

We stood there watching each other. Finally I started for the house. Somehow I had to get to Vivian, because Noel Teece knew my name. I remembered telling him in the Lincoln. All he had to do was check a little, and he'd be along.

'Where you going?'

'Inside. This damn finger. You wouldn't think a little finger could hurt so much.'

She came along behind me, her feet swishing on the grass. 'Roy?'

I stood there holding the screen door open, half inside the kitchen. You could tell it from the tone of her voice. She had something on her mind. 'A letter came for you.'

'Oh?'

'It's in on the desk.'

'Well, fine.'

She just stood there. She didn't say anything.

I went on into the kitchen and let the screen door slam. It was like everything had gone out of the place, all life. There just wasn't any sound at all.

I kept thinking of Vivian. I went in and the letter was on

215

the desk. There wasn't another thing on the desk. Just that letter. Now, I knew Bess was pulling something.

It was from Albert, and it was open.

I started reading and I heard her coming. It was short and sweet, just like that creep. Explaining everything, just fine.

'Why did you lie, Roy?'

'What in hell else could I do?'

'You could have told me he wouldn't give you the money. I didn't mean to open it. I thought it was all right. I thought it was the check.'

Albert had said how sorry he was about not giving me the money. The same old line all over again. Hoe your own row. Maybe some time ten years from now. . . .

'Roy?'

'Huh?'

'You didn't answer me. Why'd you tell me he was sending the money?'

I stood there with my mouth open. Vivian was walking across the front yard. She went over by a palm tree and stood there. I could see her gnawing her lip.

'You want a telescope, Roy?'

'Cut it out!'

'Answer me, then.'

I had to get Vivian back into the apartment. My God, what if Teece came along now? She didn't even know. All day long she'd been waiting for me to do something and I hadn't even been able to talk with her.

I turned to Bess. 'I had to lie to you. How could I tell you the way he acted? It was lousy – crumby. You never saw anything like it. My own brother!'

'You don't have to talk like that, Roy.'

'Well, damn it, it's true. I didn't know what to do.'

'So you let me get my hopes up. And the suit, Roy. Did he give you the suit of clothes, too?'

'Sure, he did. Certainly. My gosh, Bess!'

'Don't blame me. I don't know what to believe any more.'

She came over and perched herself on the corner of the desk. Her hair was all messed up and there was that mud on her face. 'Take it easy, Bess.'

'I'm taking it easy. I'm just so damned mad I could choke you.'

Vivian was staring over here at the office. Then she started back across the lawn toward number six. She paused and glanced toward the office again.

'You notice? She cut off her slacks and made a pair of shorts. She's got nice legs. Hasn't she?'

'Bess, for gosh sakes!'

She came off the desk and started toward the kitchen, and whirled and stood there. 'You saw him four days ago. Where were you all that time, Roy?'

'I told you – waiting for a ride down here. Listen, I didn't have much money, you know that. The hotel bill took everything. I had just enough for that damned bottle. So I bought it. Not enough dough to get home, even. I didn't even eat, Bess. Last night was the first meal in two days.'

'All right,' she said. 'I'm sorry.' She walked up to me and put her arms around me. She was soaking wet, but I held her tight and kissed her.

'Forgive me, Roy?'

'Sure. What's there to forgive?'

'I shouldn't be that way. Only you were gone so long, up there in Chicago. And I know Chicago, remember? I thought all sorts of things. Then to find this out – that you didn't get the money.'

I kissed her again.

'What are we going to do, Roy?'

'I'm figuring something. But I can't tell you now. Something'll work out.'

'All right. I'll lay off. I'm going to take a shower. I'm sorry what I said about her, too. But she's been walking around

217

in those home-built shorts of hers. She cut them so close up
it's a wonder they don't gag her.'

'Go take your shower.'

The minute I heard the water running behind the closed
door, I started over toward number six.

Hughes was a fine-looking old gent. He stopped me right
outside the office. I tried to let him know I was in a hurry,
but he wasn't having any nonsense.

'Mister Nichols?'

I nodded and tried to brush by.

'Wait. I want a word with you.'

'What is it?'

He was tall and thin and stooped a little; the scholarly
stoop. He had on a gray business suit and a red bow tie and
his eyes were like a busy chipmunk's. 'It come to me that
you should do something about that shuffleboard court of
yours, there. Now, if you like, I could get to work and clean
it up just fine. We could – '

'All right, you just go right ahead and do that.' I could
still hear the shower going, but it wouldn't be for long.

'Now, there's one thing – '

'I'm sorry. I've got to run.'

'Well, it's just – '

I whacked him a light one on the shoulder. He darned
near collapsed, but I was already cutting across the front of
the apartments.

'Teece is alive.'

She was sitting there in a chair, with a newspaper in her
hand. It was shaking like crazy.

'I knew it,' she said. 'I knew it.'

'I saw him. Downtown.'

'Oh, God – Noel.'

'You'd better stay inside and not go out.'

She dropped the paper on the floor and Bess had sure been

right about those shorts. Then she grabbed the newspaper up and shook it at me.

'It's in the paper about the wreck. They found the Lincoln, Nichols. Only they didn't find anybody in it. . . . Nichols! What in God's name am I going to do?'

She stood up and threw the paper down. I picked it up and she pointed to the little news item.

According to the report, there'd been blood all over everything. The pine trees were sprinkled with it. They'd found a smashed whiskey bottle, and that was supposed to account for the wreck. There had been no sign of any of the car's occupants. They located a trail of blood leading up along the bank of the stream to the road and down the road, only it stopped. They had no idea what happened, but decided the person or persons involved had picked up a ride on the highway.

Vivian was breathing down my neck, trying to read it again over my shoulder, trying to thoroughly digest the bad news. Then she stepped away, flopping that thick black hair around. 'You've got to get me out of here, Nichols.'

'Relax a minute, will you? Let me think.'

'There isn't time to think. Noel's after that money, now. He's out to find me. He'll be here. You *know* he'll be here!'

'Quiet.' I remembered Bess. I had to get out of the apartment. 'We can't talk here. You just stay inside. There's nothing to worry about. If he comes, I'll talk with him. He may not even come.'

'Stop it!' she said. 'Will you please stop it!'

'Well, we can't talk now. If my wife spots us together and thinks anything at all, she'll have me boot you out of here – and quick.'

She had her hands folded the way she did, praying again. 'If I didn't move you out, she'd call the cops.'

She shook her head. 'Oh, no, Nichols. I'd tell her you

slept with me night before last. In that hotel. How would she like that?'

'You think she'd believe you?'

'Nichols, we've got to hide the money. At least you can do that much?'

She had me going. It was like my mind had shut down like a door. What she'd said about telling Bess had jarred me. Because Bess would believe it, the way things had been going. I tried to calm down inside, so I could think straight. I couldn't do it. I was all tied up and everything was going wrong.

She'd never let me try to ditch her and back out on this now. And Teece was alive and he knew me.

I had to take the chance of Bess finding me here, so I told Vivian I'd help her hide the money. I didn't know what good it would do. But if Teece did raise any hell, at least he wouldn't get that money.

'You know,' she said. 'It's not just that brief case any more, Nichols. It's me, now. And it's you. Noel's not dumb. He's probably worked it out, what's happened.'

We hid the money in the bureau. I took the top drawers out and wedged it in against the back of the bureau. The drawers wouldn't close all the way, so I took some of her clothes and dribbled them over the drawer. It looked like the drawer was jammed with black lace.

'Now, I've got to scram.'

'Nichols, Nichols.' She got her arms around my neck and slung herself against me. 'I'm scared.'

I pulled her off and checked the back way from the kitchen door. No sign of Bess. I went on outside and started toward our place. Bess stepped onto our back porch from the kitchen, and looked at me. She had on a bright-colored skirt and a peasant blouse. Her hair was brushed to a soft gold.

'Where've you been, Roy?'

'Just checking the paint on the rest of the place. Sure needs a paint job.'

'Wait, I think I heard a car stop out front.'

It felt as if the porch steps began to rock and heave.

'Roy, you're pale as a ghost. What's the matter?'

'Nothing, honey. Nothing at all.'

I pushed past her on the porch. She followed me through the house and I was sweating all over. Sure enough a car had stopped out front. It was a big black baby, a Cadillac, and the sun shot off it like a mirror. It was huge.

I stared till my eyes watered. Then a man got out and stood there a minute, staring at the motel sign. It wasn't Teece.

'Look at that car. It's like a hearse.'

I didn't answer. My heart gradually began to slow down and we stood there together, watching him.

'Think he's coming here?'

He was. He threw a cigar away, turned and started up across the grass. He was a big guy, wearing a single-breasted powder-blue suit and a light gray felt hat. I didn't like it, the way he came at the office. His head kept going back and forth, his gaze checking.

'Could it be somebody from the bank?'

'I don't know.'

'Well, go out and meet him, Roy. He probably wants an apartment.'

'His kind don't stay at motels.'

I went on outside and waited. He saw me and his face didn't change expression. Then he grinned and paused by the porch steps. I came down a step.

'Roy Nichols?'

'That's right.'

'My name's Radan; Mister Nichols. I've just come over here from Tampa. That mean anything to you?'

'No. Why?'

He pursed his lips and lifted one foot to the first step of the porch. Then he took off his hat and held it in both hands on his knee and watched me. His hair was immaculate. It was black hair and it was perfectly combed. His eyes were level and steady. There were tiny nips at the corners of his mouth and, standing there, he gave an impression of great leisure.

I heard Bess moving around inside. 'Looking for a place to stay?'

He shook his head gently. 'Nothing like that. Not yet, anyhow.'

'Well, what is it?'

'That's not the question, Mister Nichols.'

'Maybe we'd better talk inside?'

'That's up to you. I believe perhaps it might be best that we talk alone, privately. At least, for now.'

'Oh?'

He took his foot down and lightly banged his hat against his leg. He seemed to be waiting for something.

I stepped down beside him. He edged a little toward the front lawn, looking at me with his head a shade to one side. Then we both walked out on the lawn.

'Is that your wife inside, Mister Nichols?'

'Yes.'

'I didn't want to embarrass you.'

I didn't say anything.

'I understand how these things are, Mister Nichols. Now, where is Vivian?'

'Vivian?'

'Yes. Vivian Rise. You know what I mean, Mister Nichols.' He cleared his throat carefully. Unless you *would* rather go back inside and discuss it with your wife.'

'I don't get you.'

'I'm sorry about this,' he said. He kept his voice low and his manner was apologetic. 'But I can't do anything about it.

222

You see, I've been sent over here to clear this up. You recall Noel Teece, don't you, Mister Nichols?'

The screen door slammed and I heard Bess coming toward us. 'Roy? Could I be of any help?'

The guy turned and jerked his head in a neat little bow. 'We'll see, Mrs. Nichols. We'll see.'

CHAPTER 8

BESS SMILED at this Radan. She had slash pockets in her skirt. She jammed her hands into the pockets and stood there, smiling and rocking back and forth on her heels.

Vivian might not know who Radan was. More than likely she'd never heard of him. So all she had to do was wander out here now, in those shorts of hers and make things just right. I got a tight feeling at the base of my skull, as if somebody'd put a clamp on there and was screwing it tighter and tighter.

Radan cleared his throat. 'You have a very nice place here.'

'Thank you. We love it, don't we, Roy?'

'Oh, yes.'

Radan looked at me and smiled pleasantly. He banged his hat against his leg. He looked at his fingernails. He banged his hat against his leg. He looked at his fingernails, and then at the apartments. He checked the roofs, glancing at Bess from the corner of his eye.

'Thinking of staying in St. Pete?' Bess said.

He frowned at her.

I glanced over at number six. There was no sign of life. But I knew she was there, behind the Venetian blinds, watching, waiting.

'Let's see around back,' Radan said. 'I'd like to have a look at your garage, Mister Nichols.'

I started to say something and changed it fast. I didn't
want him to see the Ford with Georgia plates. If he got a
look at that, there was no telling. I didn't know exactly who
he was, but I had a good enough idea. I wished to God I
was out of this. But there was no way out right now.

'All right.'

'Sure,' Bess said. 'We'll show you.'

'Well – Mrs. Nichols.'

'Bess, you know – ' She stared at me.

I tried to give her the eye, making it look as if this guy
was nuts. As if I didn't know anything about what he wanted,
one way or the other. I winked at her.

'Guess I'll see about dinner, Roy.'

Radan nodded and Bess went back inside.

We walked on across the grass toward the far side of the
block, over to the edge of the apartments. 'I'm afraid you're
in over your head, Mister Nichols. I don't think you have
any idea what you're really mixed up with. Or have you?'

I didn't say anything.

'You understand?'

'I don't believe so.'

He paused and got in front of me and lightly tapped the
brim of his hat against my chest. Then he pursed his lips
and turned and walked toward the corner of the apartments.
The shuffleboard courts were just beyond, under some pines.

'Come along, Mister Nichols.'

We went on past there. I had this one court. Hughes was
on his hands and knees on a pad, scrubbing the cement with
a G.I. brush. He was working with a pail of soapy water,
wearing khaki shorts. He kept coughing as he worked. There
was soap and water all over everything. He was really
scrubbing.

'Now, Mister Nichols,' Radan said. 'You've got to understand that we want to know where this girl is.'

Hughes saw me. He got up, straightening like a rusty

hinge, and came toward us, stooping. He waved the brush and a string of soap and water dribbled wildly. 'Mister Nichols?'

'We'd better go the other way.'

Hughes reached us. Radan sighed.

'How you like that, Mister Nichols? Getting her really cleaned up around here.' Hughes' eyes sparkled. He waved the brush and a long stream of soapy water sprinkled on Radan's suit. Radan kept on smiling, brushing at it with his hat.

'I'm sorry,' Hughes said. 'Excited, I guess. You can't blame me, getting the courts all fixed up and all.'

Hughes moved in closer and stood there, holding the brush so it dribbled gobs of soap on Radan's shiny right shoe.

'I'll have her cleaned up in a jiffy. Then I can play. We'll get up a game, right, Mister Nichols? You and your wife can come out and we'll have a fine time. I think the Donnes are becoming interested in the sport.' Then Hughes nudged my arm, looking at Radan. 'Is this somebody new – going to stay here, Mister Nichols?'

I shook my head.

'I'm afraid not, sir,' Radan said. He walked toward the rear of the apartments, past some benches I'd put beside the shuffleboard court.

'Mister Nichols?' Hughes called.

We kept going. At the corner of the apartments, Radan paused. He got out a handkerchief and bent down, rubbing at the soap and water on his shoe. It took all the shine off. 'I don't exactly go for this,' he said.

'Sorry.'

He straightened. 'You smash your finger in the wreck, Mister Nichols?'

'What wreck?'

'That won't do any good. There's no use pretending. We

226

know all about it. Either you take action, or we take action. That's the way it is.' He was still very apologetic.

'You haven't made yourself clear.'

'Whether you like it or not, you're mixed up in it now, Mister Nichols. I don't believe you realize that.'

'I still don't understand.'

'Yes. You do. Don't be foolish. We don't like to get rough. It's silly, this day and age. You should understand that.'

'Are you threatening me about something?'

'Mister Nichols, for Lord's sake! Now, look – you certainly wouldn't want to see your place burned down, would you? Your motel, I mean? Now, would you?'

He talked very pleasantly. He was almost pleading, and very matter-of-fact about everything. Looking at him, talking with him, you would think he was some kind of a businessman. He was obviously prosperous. But there was something about him.

'We just can't let it go on, Mister Nichols.'

I could hear Hughes working on the cement with the scrub brush, and his dry, papery cough.

'All right,' Radan said. 'I take it that I have your answer. Right?'

I still said nothing.

'All right,' he said. 'You've had your chance. I was told to give you ten minutes, and I have. You've used them up, playing this all wrong. Now, where's Vivian Rise?'

'Never heard of her.' He was beginning to make me mad, now. Damned if I'd tell him anything.

'Have you seen Noel Teece, Mister Nichols?'

I didn't say anything.

Radan put his hat on. He watched me levelly. 'You've had it, Nichols.'

He turned and walked rapidly away. I started after him. He walked on past Hughes, then paused and stepped over beside the court. Hughes was on his knees, scrubbing the cement.

Hughes looked up and saw Radan and smiled and bobbed his head. Radan looked at him for a long moment, then he lifted his foot, placed it against the old man's head and shoved. Hughes slipped down onto the soapy cement.

'Listen here!' I said, going after him. Radan paused and looked back at me, turned sharply and cut across the lawn. He reached his car. I stood in the middle of the lawn by the sign and watched him get in the car.

Radan took a last look at the motel, started the engine and made a fast rocking U-turn on the broken road. He vanished around the corner, the engine hissing.

I went over to Hughes. 'I'm sorry about that.'

'It's all right, Mister Nichols. I could tell he was a sorehead when I spilled that soap on him. He didn't hurt me. There's all kinds in this world. Now, listen – I think the court should be renumbered. Have you any white paint? I'm really good at lettering.'

'You'll find some in the garage for number one.'

He nodded happily and I started back toward the office. I had to see Vivian again, but I didn't know how I was going to get to her.

This Radan was a beaut.

'Roy?'

'Yes?'

'What did he want?'

'Oh, that guy? Kind of a funny character. Says he, well – wanted to build a motel. Comes from over in Tampa. He's been riding around looking at motels. He likes this one. Asked me a few questions, that's all.'

'Sure peculiar.'

'I know it. Hard to figure. Wants to build a motel. He

sympathized with us, being stuck the way we are, with the road not through yet. He mentioned taxes.'

'Please. Don't even speak of them. What'll we do, Roy? What are we going to do about money?'

'I'll think of something.'

We were in the office and she was standing in the doorway leading to our living room. She turned and went back into the kitchen.

I wished I could think of something to send Bess out for, so I could go talk with Vivian. But there wasn't a thing I could do. And there she was in the doorway again. When Bess looked at me, it was in that funny way that I didn't like.

'Roy, you look sick. Honestly, I never saw you look so bad. Try not to worry about things. Everything'll be all right. You wait and see. Hasn't everything always worked out all right?'

'Sure.'

'Or is it just that you had a hot time up there in Chicago?'

'Nothing like it. I just got drunk, that's all. But it was bad stuff. Maybe I can't take it any more.' I had to get away from her and think. Try to.

'You don't suppose that man had anything to do with the bank?'

'No.' She was so worried, and there was nothing I could do to straighten her out about things. Not now. I wanted to and I couldn't.

'Maybe they've put the place up for sale, or something. Without telling us about it.'

'Stop it, Bess!' My voice was hoarse. 'They can't do a thing like that. You know that.'

'What's the *matter* with you, Roy?'

I went outside and stood on the porch and looked down across the lawn. There was no sign of Vivian. I knew that was no way to act if I wanted to keep Bess quiet. I went back inside. She was standing by the kitchen table with both hands flat on top. She didn't look up as I came in.

'I'm sorry about that.'

'It's all right.'

'Everything's got me down. Trying to figure a way out of this mess.'

'I know.'

Oh God, I thought, if she only did know. . . .

A few minutes later she was in by the desk; checking the bills. 'Roy – that man just drove past again.'

I went over by the desk. 'What?'

She turned and looked at me, frowning. 'The man in the hearse, Roy. I've seen him go by the place twice now.'

I stared out the window. It was quiet on the street, but I knew she had seen him. And I began to know she would keep on seeing him.

CHAPTER 9

'MRS. NICHOLS. I've got to see your husband.'

'Oh, hello, Miss Latimer.'

'Is Mister Nichols around?'

'Yes. He's in the other room. What is it?'

'Well – I think he'd better have a look at my stove. There's something wrong with the stove.'

'What seems to be the matter?'

I went on out there. She was on the back porch, talking with Bess. She was still wearing the shorts and she looked wild. Her hair was like she'd been combing it with her fingers. She had on lots of lipstick, but the rest of her face was the color of flour.

She saw me over Bess's shoulder and her eyes got kind of crazy. Bess heard me and turned, holding the door open.

'Miss Latimer's having trouble with her stove.' She gave me the eye.

'Well, all right. You want me to have a look?'

'Would you?' Vivian said. 'I hate terribly bothering you like this.'

'Sure.' I brushed past Bess. Vivian went off the porch onto the grass and Bess stepped after me. I didn't dare say anything. If Bess came along, there was nothing you could do.

'Think I'll see how Hughes is making out with the shuffleboard courts,' Bess said.

'Every time I light the gas, it pops,' Vivian said.

'Air in the line.'

Bess went off along the rear of the apartment.

'God. Nichols!'

'Wait'll we get over there.'

As soon as we were in her kitchen, she whirled, and it was like somebody was running a knife in and out of her. 'I saw him, Radan! That's Wirt *Radan!* I know about him. I know why he's here. You don't even have to tell me. He's famous, Nichols – famous! I met him once in New York. He moves around the country. You know what he is?' She was breathing quickly, her eyes very bright, and she had her fists bunched tight against her thighs. 'He's a killer.'

'Cut it out. . . .'

'Sure. You wouldn't believe that. I knew you wouldn't, you're such a damned square. But it's true. That's his job. He's one of them that works to a contract. You think they don't do that any more? Do you? You're crazy, if you think that!'

'Take it easy.'

'Noel told me about him just a few days ago.' She paused and turned and held her back to me that way, and her shoulders began to shake. She whirled on me again and I thought for a second she was going to yell. She didn't. She just kept talking, with her voice held down in her throat, and she was really scared now. 'Noel said Wirt Radan was getting so tough the men are afraid to work with him, even.'

'And you told me you weren't mixed up in any of this.'

'I'm not. I was Noel's girl. That's all.'

'Only that wasn't enough.'

'Nichols! You've got to get me out of here!'

I wanted that as much as she did. Only, how? 'Did you

ever stop to think of the mess you've got me in?' I said. 'Did you?'

'I'm paying you. Remember?'

'Vivian, all you think about is that money. Money can't take care of everything.'

'You're thinking about it, too! Plenty. True, Nichols?'

'All right. How do you want to work it?'

'I want plane tickets to South America – Chile, probably. You'll have to get me to the airport, see me on the plane. Somehow. Then you'll get yours.'

'Why not just get the tickets? Can't you get them yourself, for that matter? You can drive to the airport yourself. It's not far.'

'Can we still get them now? You think it's open, downtown? The ticket office?'

'I guess so.'

'Then let's get going. I can't go alone. I know they'll be at the airport.'

I just stood there. She turned and rushed out of the room and I heard her in the bedroom, yanking the bureau drawers. I went in there.

She had the brief case. She got her suitcase off a chair, snapped it shut without putting anything extra back inside, and looked at me. 'Let's go, Nichols.'

She was off her rocker. She wasn't thinking; traveling in some kind of a vacuum, she was like a hound dog on the scent, flying like the crow.

But I thought about that money, and not only that – if I could get her out of here now, I could tell Bess I'd taken her downtown. Tell her anything. Because she'd be gone and there wouldn't be any chance for argument.

She glanced down at her shorts, turned abruptly, dropped the brief case and opened the suitcase and whipped out a blue skirt. Her anxiety was almost comical, except you knew how real it was.

233

I heard Bess call to me from outside.

'No,' Vivian said. 'Please – don't go.' She grabbed me. 'Tell her something – anything. You know I've got to leave here now.'

I shoved her and she went windmilling across the bedroom and landed against the wall. I beat it out into the kitchen and Bess was just coming up on the porch. I opened the door. Bess tried to look past me. I let her look.

'Did you fix her stove all right?' There was a slight touch of sarcasm in her voice. But as she looked at me, she began to smile.

I grinned at her. 'You go fix dinner. I'll be along.'

She turned and went back toward our place. Vivian came out of the bedroom wearing the blue skirt. That wild look was still in her eyes. There was something about the way she held her mouth, too; a tenseness that told you a little about what went on inside her. Just a young kid, really – only not a kid – and her life all twisted out of shape. And she was trying to save her life in the only way she knew. Watching her, I felt a sense of hopelessness.

'All right. Let's get going.'

She picked up the brief case and the suitcase and I saw the filmy red scarf fall softly, lazily, from the brief case to the floor. She jammed the case under her arm and we went out into the kitchen.

'Wait'll I check.' I looked outside. Nobody. 'All right. You get in your car. I'll be along in a minute, so it won't look so bad. Make it fast, now, to the garage.'

'Yes.' She gave me a quick harried look, turned and went outside. I watched her cross the grass swiftly and slip between the garages toward the drive, her shoulders held rigid, as if she were trying to hide behind them. Twinkletoes.

I waited another moment. I knew it was better this way. She'd be gone, and the worry would be gone with her. She'd carry that part wherever she went, but it would be off my back. Somehow, I knew it was going to work out all right.

I stood there, trying to get my breath evened out, and then I went on outside and closed the door and started across the grass. She came running at me.

She tripped, stumbling, and the suitcase fell out of her hand. She made a wild grab for it, missed, and came on, her mouth open and her eyes stricken and sick.

'Get back!' She kept running. 'He's out there. Radan just drove through the alley!' She came past me and rushed inside.

I went on out and got the suitcase and made it back to the porch. I entered the kitchen and looked at her. 'Did he see you?'

'No. No, he didn't see me.' She kind of turned and bent over like an old woman, and let her head hang, and went into the living room, moaning to herself. She still had the brief case plugged under her arm.

'Did he stop?'

'No. I saw him coming. I was right out in the drive, there. He'd just turned in off the street with that big black car. I could see his face – looking. Not at me, though. Oh, *damn it!*'

'That's bad.'

'I'll never be able to get out of here now. He'll watch, and he'll watch.' She flopped down into a chair, hugging the brief case and she began to cry. It was wild, angry, hurt crying.

'The money. We'd better hide the money again,' I said. 'But not in the bureau. I got a better place. Come on.'

She just sat there. I went over and grabbed her arm, pulled her up, and she leaned against me, shuddering. She was an awful sight and I felt sorry for her.

'The apartment next door's empty. That'll be a better place – just in case. We'll have to run for it again. The front way this time. So come on.'

235

We went outside, and there was no sign of Radan. The sun was beginning to dip. Another day gone, and things just that much worse.

We went in next door. It was hot and stuffy. It hadn't been aired in weeks, and our footsteps were loud on the floors. 'Suppose somebody moves in here?'

'They won't. I'll see to that. Listen, I'm going to drain the tank behind the toilet, shut it off, and we'll put the brief case in there.'

She was lost again, praying. I got the brief case and there was an immediate thrill, knowing what was inside it. It was heavy and full and it made you want to run some place, hanging onto it. I took it into the bathroom, turned the water off, flushed the john, and put the money in the tank.

'What are you doing over here, Miss Latimer?'

'I – we – he's checking the stove for something.'

I came out of the bathroom, dodged into the kitchen and stood there sweating. Bess was talking in the living room now, about it being so hot. I went out the back door and let it slam real hard. I went over to number six, and stood there fiddling with the stove, turning it on and off, hating every minute of this and wishing I didn't have to treat Bess like a stranger. I could hardly see the stove.

Pretty soon they came along. Bess entered the kitchen first and I didn't look at her. I got out a match and lit the stove, and the gas caught just fine.

'Hi. She's okay now.'

'That's fine,' Bess said.

'Thanks so much, Mister Nichols. Honestly, I hate all this trouble I'm causing.'

I looked at Bess. Boy, was she sparking! Vivian moved past us, on into the living room and stood by the front window.

'You just call me if there's any more trouble.'

Bess and I went outside.

'You're sweating, Roy.'

236

'Roy. She's got a man's suitcase in there.'

'What?'

'Miss Latimer. She's got a man's suitcase, and it's full of a man's clothing.'

'What've you been doing in her apartment?'

'I just looked in, that's all, while you were next door. I saw it. What would she be doing with another suitcase, like that?'

'Darned if I know. Maybe it's her husband's. Maybe she's married, just doesn't want to say anything. Some women are like that.'

'She acts pretty queer, if you ask me. Has she said anything to you about being married?'

'No.'

I had to shut her up, or get away from her. I couldn't take it, because I knew now that I was in on everything with Vivian, and I was scared. Just plain scared. I didn't know what to do. With Radan skulking around like that. Only you couldn't call the cops. Not on a thing like this, not even if you did want to back out of the bad part.

Besides, that money. It was there, and I *had* to have some of it. Somehow. It was the only way I could see – even if it was a wrong way. When the taxes for this property came due, we'd really be in the soup. I didn't want to lose this motel. I wasn't going to lose it. I couldn't let Bess take it on the chin any more. She'd never had any peace, never – all our married life, it had been like this. From one thing to another, never any peace, and by God, she was going to have peace and some of the things she wanted.

One way or another.

Even if I had to get hold of the brief case myself, and run. . . . God, I was in a sweet mess and I knew it. But something had to be done.

'Roy,' Bess said, 'I hate to keep at you like this. But I know darned well something's the matter with that woman. You must have seen that. She's afraid of something. We've got enough around here without somebody tossing their troubles in our laps.'

'How do you mean?'

'I don't know. I can't figure her out, but I do know something's wrong. You think I should ask her?' I knew Bess had been doing a lot of thinking. There was no way of her catching onto the truth, but I didn't like her this way. It was my problem, not hers. She said, 'I'll bet she's in some kind of trouble, Roy.'

'Well, maybe so. But let's not stick our noses in, huh?'

'Yes. I know you're right.'

I went into the bedroom and lay down. I finally dozed a little. Once I heard Bess come in, very softly, and stand there looking at me. I didn't open my eyes. She went away.

I woke up and it was dark. I could hear Bess breathing quietly. I rolled off the bed carefully, so as not to disturb her and stood there in the dark. It was after midnight by the clock ticking away on the dresser. I had conked off for sure. I hadn't even eaten and Bess had let me sleep. The poor kid was plenty worried about everything.

I started to undress, then looked at her again. She was really knocking it, breathing deep and heavy.

I left the room. In the office, I looked out through the window. The sign was still lit up and I sat down at the desk for a while, trying to think of something. I got nowhere.

It was real quiet, inside and outside. And it got real lonely.

I finally got up and went and looked into the bedroom again. She was sleeping quietly. There was a dim shaft of light down across her face, from where one of the slats in the Venetian blinds was tilted open. She looked worried, even in sleep. I knew she was catching on to things, to something anyway, and it troubled her plenty, even if she didn't know what it was. She knew me too well, and she trusted in me too much, and God, I loved her and I wanted her to be happy.

I left the room and slipped out of the back door and around between the apartments. It was quiet over at number six, but there was a light inside. I went up onto the porch and kept checking out there on the lawn. I opened the door and stepped inside, and closed the door.

'Yeah,' Noel Teece said. '*Yeah*. Here he is now.'

They were sitting there. She was on a chair, with her hands clenched in her lap, holding her thumbs, staring up at me, round-eyed and hopeless-looking.

Teece was humped on the studio couch. He was all bandaged up, the way I'd seen him. His hat was on, jutting above the bandages on his face.

CHAPTER 10

TEECE HAD an evil-looking eye.

That eye watched me, blinking under the hat brim, and you kind of wished you could see the other eye, too. But the bandage covered that. The eye that watched me was bloodshot and tired, yet kind of frantic and steady, even behind the blinking. His cheek was mottled and his lips were pale and thin and he needed a shave. He just sat there, blinking that damned eye at me.

'Noel just came in. He sneaked in the back way,' Vivian said. 'Noel, honey – we thought you were dead. You know we thought that.'

He kind of laughed. It sounded a little like he was crying inside.

'You two been happy?'

Neither of us said anything. I didn't like the looks of him at all. Like I say, there was something frantic about the way he looked. As if he was out of hand and knew it and didn't care. He was breathing pretty fast.

'All afternoon I've been trying to get in here, you two. Now, I'm here.'

His eye was watering. Vivian just sat there, holding onto her thumbs.

'Thought I was dead, did you? Well, I'm not dead.'

Still we didn't speak.

240

'You know why I'm here?'

Vivian began nodding slowly.

Teece stood up. Now I could see what it was. The man was scared. He was so scared he didn't know what to do next. It was knocking the hell out of him, the way he was.

'I talked with them on the phone,' he told us. 'I can't go see them. They'll kill me. Oh, yes. But if I get that money back to them, maybe I can swing it. Maybe they'll understand.'

He said it like that, but you could tell he didn't really believe himself. He knew they wouldn't understand. That's what you could read in the half of his face that showed, and in the way he began prowling up and down the room.

'All right. Where's the money, Viv?'

She looked across at me.

'We haven't got it,' I told him. I heard myself say it and went along with it. 'They beat you here, Teece. You worked too slow.'

He was like an animal. His mouth came open and the way I'd said that had hurt him. He stood there, blinking, with the light gleaming in that bloodshot eye.

'We gave the money to some guy called Radan.'

'Wirt Radan?' He turned on her and she bobbed her head fast.

'That's right, Noel. He came and we gave the money to him. We had to.'

'But, he's – '

'Radan said they were going to get you, Teece.'

'You lie! Both of you lie! You and Viv, you think I can't see through this? You're planning it together. But you're not getting away with this. Now, where's that money?' He reached into his coat and came up with a gun. It wasn't very large, but it wouldn't have to be. Only he wasn't sure of himself. He wasn't certain that we were lying.

'That's not going to do a damned bit of good. I told you,

this fellow Radan came here today. This afternoon. He drives a big black Caddy. He knew all about everything – you, the accident, the works. We gave him the money, and that's it.'

He moved his head slightly from side to side.

'It's the truth, Noel.' She came up out of the chair, with an imploring look on her face. It was a real art, the way she did it. 'It's true, Noel.' She stood there, looking straight into his eye. 'He told us what they were going to do. There wasn't any other way. *You know Radan.* Sure, I was going to try and get away with the money. Wouldn't you have done the same thing? What else was there to do?'

He kept on moving his head from side to side.

'Noel, honey. We thought you were dead. I did the only thing I could do. I've been trying to get Nichols to help me, see? So I was going to pay him to help me get out of the country. He needs the money for his motel, here. Can't you understand that?'

The gun began to droop a little and the head-shaking slowed down almost to a stop.

'So, then Radan came here this afternoon. He burst right in here, Noel. He saw the brief case we had the money in – remember? I gave it to him. There was nothing else to do.'

A crafty look came into the eye. 'Radan just took the money? Didn't he do anything else?'

I said, 'He threatened a lot of things. Maybe it's all still up in the air. He hasn't been back. That's why I came over here now, to ask her what we should do.'

He wheeled on me with the gun, and it scared me. I made a pass at the gun with one hand. It connected. The gun clattered on the floor.

'Don't!'

He came at me with that one arm, his head back, cursing. It was comical. Him with his arm in a sling and his head all bandaged up and that scared look in his one bloodshot eye. But he swung, just the same.

242

I tried to hold him off. Then I took a poke at him, shying away from his face. I hit him in the chest. He staggered back toward the door and the door opened and Bess stood there, blinking sleepily and hitching at her housecoat over her pajamas.

'I heard a noise,' she said.

He fell against her. She shoved him off and looked at us. He turned and saw her and his face reddened.

'What's going on?'

'It's nothing, Bess. It's all a mistake.'

Teece eyed me and swallowed and looked at Bess.

There was the gun on the floor, but Bess hadn't seen it. Vivian saw the gun and she stepped over and stood just beyond it, so Bess wouldn't be able to see it even if she looked down there.

'But, Roy – ' Bess said.

'Yes,' Vivian said. 'Sure. Look, this man – ' she motioned toward Teece – 'is a friend of mine. Mister Nichols must have heard something and made a mistake.'

'That's right, Bess. I couldn't sleep after I woke up. I went out to get some air and I saw this guy snooping. I thought he was a prowler. Actually, I guess all he was doing was looking for Miss Latimer's apartment. I'm sorry I was so bull-headed.'

Teece's eyebrow shot up.

'He'd planned on coming down,' Vivian said. 'He was supposed to meet me here. He met with an accident on the way. Maybe you've noticed how worried I've been? Well, this is why. Mister Nichols thought he was doing the right thing. He came to help me.'

Bess stood there and took it all in. Then she turned and stepped out onto the porch. 'I'm sorry,' she said through the screen door. 'You coming, Roy?'

'Sure. Just a minute.'

She went away and we looked at each other.

'The money,' Teece said.

'We told you. Radan's got it.'

Teece went over and picked up the gun and looked at it. He put it away.

'Radan, huh?' he said, and there was this funny new look in that eye of his. He stared at Vivian for a second and she looked right back at him, nodding slightly. Then he turned away and went outside. He disappeared along the side of the apartment, back toward the garages. I started for the door.

'Don't leave me alone!'

'I've got to get out of here.'

I opened the door and stepped out on the porch. She came up to the door and stood there, scratching her fingernails on the screen.

'Don't you see?' she said. 'I can't leave now. I can't leave!'

I went down off the porch and around toward the garage. I heard a car start up out in the alley. It drove away fast, showering gravel. I listened to it until I couldn't hear it any more, then I went back to our place. . . .

'Roy, I'd like you to ask Miss Latimer to leave. I'd appreciate it if you'd go over there now and ask her to pack her things.'

'Bess, don't be silly. I know how it looked. It bothered me, too. But everything's all right now.'

'I'm sorry. But I'm asking you to do this for me. I don't like it, the way things are over there. Are you going to do it for me?'

'Look. Let her stay till morning.' I reached out and drew her close, and kissed her, but she was kind of cold about it.

'Morning?'

'All right. In the morning, you go over there the first thing, Roy.'

CHAPTER 11

IN THE morning I figured she forgot about what she'd said. Either that, or maybe thought better of it. I didn't get much sleep. I lay there thinking it through, but trying to stay away from the real part – how it was working out. I kept trying to figure how I could have got my hands on some of that money, or all of it, without this mess. There was no use telling myself I didn't want that money. There were too many reasons why I needed it.

The big thing I kept figuring was that it was crooked money to begin with. Somehow that made me feel better. I kept coming back to that, trying to figure some way. And then I remembered that was how Vivian had talked in the hotel room. It wasn't money that really belonged to anybody, she'd said. Or to that effect. And she was right.

But, there was no way. Not unless I went over there and took it and got out of here. I thought about that. How I could grab the money and run. Then I could mail Bess enough to pay off the motel, and . . . only it wasn't any good. It didn't have that part I wanted – the peace of mind part.

Because without the peace, you had nothing. And you couldn't buy that, either.

Anyway, all I wanted out of this world was Bess and the motel. The motel. That was a laugh, and I lay there with

Bess asleep beside me, thinking of her, and how I could make some decent kind of life for us together. . . .

I figured I'd done enough to belong to a part of that brief case, anyway. Not a big part. Just enough to take care of immediacies. Where did that come from?

And then I saw that Radan's face, like it was hanging up there on the ceiling of my mind. And I knew what kind of a guy he was. I didn't want to mix with him.

It was all real crazy. Albert, and the Lincoln and Vivian and Noel Teece, and now Radan, like a parade through the bloody twilight. And the brief case with that red scarf tied around it. Only she'd dropped the scarf. Talisman.

'Go to sleep, Roy.'

'Yeah.'

What in hell was I going to do? The emptiness got filled with a kind of frantic rushing and my heart got to going it, lying there. I wanted to yell and crack my knuckles, or sock somebody.

Because it was all closing in. I could tell.

You recognize the landmarks, because you've seen them before, if you've been around enough. You go along trying to hold it all gutted up and hard and ignoring it all, then one fine day it busts wide open. And there you are. You got to do something, and there's nothing to do. You can't think even.

Southern Comfort Motel – crawling with fright.

That Vivian was a dilly, sure enough. Getting herself messed up like she had. Shooting the works to Teece, and so scared now with what she'd done, she could hardly stand up.

It was like I didn't quite know them and I didn't want to. Just that brief case. A piece of that. . . .

So I finished breakfast and she didn't say a word about anything. My second coffee, I said, 'Maybe mow the lawn today.'

She clinked the plates and coffee cups to the sink. She ran the water. She shut it off. She had on a kind of blue-flowered housecoat and she looked nice, only worried.

'Roy?'

'Yeah?' Here it was.

'Have you forgotten what I said last night?'

I kind of ran my hand across my face, trying to remember what she meant, letting her think that was it.

'You know what I mean. About Miss Latimer. I want you to go over there and ask her to leave.'

'I figured that was just a pipe dream.'

'It's no dream. You want me to do it? If you won't, I will.'

She sure had me there. Now what was I going to do? Tell Vivian that, and she'd freeze over there in number six, and you couldn't get her out with a derrick.

'Well?'

'You'd have to give her back her rent money.'

'A pleasure.'

She left the ktichen. 'We can't have people like her running around, Roy. She'll hurt the name of the place. Imagine, that wreck of a man coming in the middle of the night. Maybe she picked him up off the street, how do you know?'

I tagged along and she went into the office, to the desk, and counted the money out of the cigar box and looked over at me.

'I'd appreciate it if you'd do it, Roy.'

I took the money. 'Can't we give her a little more time?'

'You want her staying here? That it? With her nice tight shorts and everything?'

I looked at her.

'I'm sorry I said that, Roy. Honest. I didn't mean it.' She stared down at the desk, then up at me again. 'It's just she worries me, being here. She isn't right, and you know it.'

'Okay.'

I left the office and let the screen door slam.

247

I came along by number six and looked it over. It was quiet. What was I going to do? I had to tell her what Bess said, but there was no saying how she'd take it. I knew how she'd take it. It had to be Bess's way.

Well, she sure had that red scraf tied around her neck.

Vivian was right there on the floor in the doorway between the living room and the bedroom hall. She was all crumpled up in a twisted knot, the blue skirt up to her belly, and her face was a hell of a color. Her eyes bugged and her mouth was open, her tongue all swelled up like a fat pork chop.

I turned around, wanting to run, then stopped. The scarf was tied around her neck so tight the flesh bulged around it. I got over there, still holding her refund money in my hand, and I touched her.

She was cold.

CHAPTER 12

WELL, VIVIAN was gone, all right. Only it wasn't exactly the way Bess had wanted her to go.

I knelt there for a long time, dizzy and half sick. Her shirt was torn at one shoulder and there were bruises on her arms. She was crumpled on the floor like paper gets crumpled.

That red scarf. Vivian's good luck. Her talisman.

Then I remembered the brief case. I got out of there, still carrying the rent refund wadded in my hand. I shoved it into my pocket and cut over next door. I kept thinking. What now – What now – ? I went next door, let myself in and headed for the bathroom.

I got the lid off the tank and there was the brief case. All I could think was, maybe she told whoever did this where the money was. I got it out of there, and the money was inside. I put the lid back on the tank, turned the water on and headed for the rear of the apartment.

I had to hide it again. But where?

I got out in the garage and stood there, wondering what to do with the brief case. So finally I climbed up on the hood of the Chevie and grabbed a beam and snaked myself up there where I had some lumber piled. I crawled back into the corner under the eave and shoved the brief case under some of the boards. You wouldn't find it unless you knew it was there. They'd tear the whole motel apart first.

They? They – who? And it kept hitting me that the law would be in on this now. There wasn't anything I could do about that. I climbed down onto the car again, and hit the dirt. There was no sign of anybody. I made a run for it, down between the garages and to the back door of number six. It was open. I walked through the kitchen, and she was still lying there on the floor.

'Roy?'

It was Bess. She called again from out front. I stepped past the body and walked through the living room fast, and out the door. I stood on the porch.

Bess came across the lawn. She'd been talking with Mrs. Donne who was settled in her beach chair, a half-filled drink in her hand.

'Well, did you tell her?'

I didn't say anything.

'All right. *I'll* tell her!' She tried to push past me. I got hold of her and held her still. She had on a white dress and she looked fresh and lovely, but I couldn't remember ever seeing her look so worried. Her eyes had that kind of not-quite-looking-at-you way they get.

'Don't go in there, Bess. Bess – ' I couldn't bring myself to say it.

'I certainly *am* going in there! I'm going to tell her. Didn't you say anything to her at all? What'd you do, just stand there?' She pulled away from me and started for the door of number six. I turned and went after her. 'Is *he* still inside?'

'No.'

'Then, what – ?' She knocked lightly on the door, brushing some hair away from her forehead.

'Nobody's going to answer,' I said softly.

Bess opened the door and went on inside. I followed her, thinking, What am I going to do? Bess just stood there,

staring and I could see her start to yell. If she yelled, that
was her business. She didn't. She cut it off and turned and
looked at me and blinked. 'She's dead.'

'Yes.'

Well, she just stood there, staring. She didn't cry or scream
or carry on at all, like a woman might. And I was proud of
her – that she was my Bess. Then she looked at me again
and swallowed.

'Well,' I said. 'That's the way I found her.'

She shook her head and went over and slumped into a
chair. I got over there and pulled her up and held her. She
was trembling a little. I held her tight.

'What d'you suppose happened, Roy?'

'That's better.'

I wondered for a moment if she'd thought I'd done this.
Sometimes they can cook up some weird things in their
heads.

She looked over there again and whipped her head away.
'It's awful!'

She didn't even begin to know how awful. It was just
hitting her, what had really happened. You could see it come
across her face. A shadow of fear, and something like hate.

'Mrs. Nichols?'

I whirled and it was the young girl who was on her honey-
moon, in number eleven. We hadn't seen anything of them,
but now here she was. Her yellow dress was one of these
fluffy things, and she had brown hair and brown eyes and
she smiled and said, 'Mrs. Nichols.'

'No,' I said. 'Wait.'

But she was already coming through the door. Bess started
toward her with one hand out.

The girl said, 'I was just looking for you. I saw you come
in here, so I – ' and she stopped. She saw that over there
on the floor and she screamed.

She put both hands against her face and filled her lungs

251

and let it rip. It rocked the house. She really had lungs. Her face got red and she kept on screaming. She turned and ran smack into the screen door, and got it open and went outside, screaming and running for number eleven.

I looked out the window. Mrs. Donne was standing out there by the beach chair. She held the glass in her hand, but it had all spilled down her front. She watched the girl run across the lawn, trying to brush the spilled drink off her dress. Then she looked over here at number six.

'We've got to phone the police.'

'Wait.'

'What d'you mean, wait, Roy? We can't wait.'

'Wait, anyway.' I went and sat in the chair and held my head. I felt blocked. I knew there was something I could do. There had to be –

'We've got to phone the police right now. Is there any reason why we shouldn't?'

'Wait.' I didn't want her to call the cops. I couldn't help it, I just didn't want it, and there was nothing I could do about it.

'Roy, let's get out of here. I don't want to stay in this place.'

'Yeah.'

She came over and grabbed my arm. I stood up and we walked over to the door. 'What's the matter with you, Roy?'

'All right.'

The girl from number eleven was standing down there by her porch. She was talking with her husband through the window, waving her arms around. I quit looking at her, but I could hear her damned piping voice talking and talking.

We got over to the office and Bess sat down at the desk. 'What'll I say?'

I stood there watching her.

'Roy!'

'Just go ahead. Call them.'

252

So she did. . . .

'How long d'you think it'll take them to get here, Roy?'

I sat there on the couch, staring at the floor. I could see Bess' feet going back and forth on the rug, back and forth. She walked up and down.

'Roy. You just sit there.'

I stared.

'Did – did you touch her?'

'Yeah. She's cold.'

'What could have happened? It must have been that man, the one with his arm in the sling. This is awful, Roy! It can ruin business here, too.'

Business. Business.

'Here come the honeymooners.'

I looked up and they came along and knocked on the office door. Bess went over and started to open the door, then decided against it.

'We're leaving,' the guy said. He was a tall, thin guy, dressed in a gray suit. He had red hair and freckles, and the girl stuck close to him. 'We were going to stay another week, but now we want this week's rent back. We've decided to move along. That's how – '

'All right,' Bess said. There was a kind of a sting to the way she said it. 'Come on in.'

'No,' the girl said.

They stood there, shuffling on the doorstep. Bess looked at them for a moment, then went and counted some money out of the cigar box and looked at me and went over and opened the door. She handed the guy the money.

They turned quickly and walked away without a word. The girl was talking like crazy the minute they were on the front lawn. I sure didn't envy him his married life with that one. A few more years and she'd really be a dilly.

'I wish they'd come.'

'They will, don't worry.'

'Roy. Who d'you think she was? Murdered – murdered right here in our place. I didn't hear a thing. Did you hear anything after we came back from over there?'

'Nope.'

I got up and went out into the kitchen and washed my hands in the sink. I dried them on the dish towel. Then I took a glass down from the cupboard and filled it with water and stood there drinking. You could taste the chlorine, and the water wasn't very cold.

'What are you going to tell them, Roy?'

'What *can* I tell them?'

She was in the doorway. She came over and stood by the kitchen table. I didn't want to look at her. At the same time, I wanted to tell Bess everything I knew, all I'd been through with Vivian.

'You're spilling water all over the floor, Roy.'

Well, I took that damned glass and I let her go. It whizzed across the room and smashed against the cupboards and busted, and water and glass showered.

She didn't move. Just stood there, watching me.

'Honey,' she said, 'what's the matter?'

'It's all right,' I said. 'It's nothing. I'm sorry I did that. It's just things, that's all. *Just things!*'

CHAPTER 13

WE STOOD there for a time without saying anything. It began to scare me a little, understanding how easy it is to start a canyon of doubt between two people. We'd been as close as any two people can get in every way, and now I could sense the separation because of doubt, and because I couldn't, or wouldn't tell her about things. I couldn't. And then I knew I wouldn't ever let it be like that.

'It's nothing, Bess. I'm just wrought up, I guess. Not getting the money from Albert, and then I went and lied to you about it all, and he writes. All the money we owe, and I can't see my way clear.'

I went over to her and put my arms around her. She was kind of stiff, then she let loose and laid her head on my chest and it was like old times.

'And now this,' I said. 'Can you understand how I feel?'

'It scares me, Roy.'

'It's damned well enough to scare anybody.'

'I mean the way she looked. She was beautiful, Roy.'

'I guess maybe she was.'

'How could anybody *do* a thing like that? And us finding her. Why? Why?'

I patted her head and squeezed my hand on her arm. I wanted it to be right with us. But how could it ever be right from now on in?

So finally I let her go, and went in and flopped down on the bed. And I kept seeing that face, red and black. With the tongue.

Well, you either win – or you lose.

'Roy, that man in the car like a hearse drove by again.'

'Oh? Yeah? Him?'

'He just keeps driving by. It's the third time I've seen him today, Roy. Maybe he's gone past other times. Just driving by, like he's going around and around the block. I wonder what he's up to?'

'I don't know.'

'Well, he's sure up to something.'

'Maybe.'

'Please don't act that way, Roy!'

I lay face down on the bed, with my head buried in the pillow.

'I wish the police would come. Why don't they hurry up?'

They came quick enough for me. They came to the office and Bess went out there. I stuck with the bed. She told them about number six and they went over there. You could hear them, like elephants.

You could hear them talking.

There's something about the voice of the law. It's a jumble of solemn and righteous sound. It reached me all the way in the bedroom and I lay there, listening, wondering what I was going to do. What would I tell them? My mind was all cluttered up with that brief case, and how it had been for the past few days. I kept being with Noel Teece and Vivian in the Lincoln, off and on, cracking up on the Georgia road. And then the hotel room, and the brief case again, around and around.

'Roy?'

I didn't move. She came into the bedroom and over to the

bed. After a little while, she sat on the bed and put her hand
on my shoulder. What did she figure was the matter with
me? I'd make a fine crook, all right – running off and trying
to hide my head like an ostrich.

'They're still over there,' she said. 'One of them says he
wants to talk with you. He said he'd be over here.'

'Okay.'

'They're going to take the body away. They've been over
there an awful long time.' She paused, then said, 'I think
you'd better come into the office – kind of show yourself.
That one, he said – '

'I heard you.'

'Don't snap so.' Her hand rubbed on my shoulder, the
fingers squeezing. I rolled over and looked at her and she
grinned at me. So I grinned at her, and it was like she'd
come back to me, after she'd been away a long time. And
then I knew she wasn't really back at all. Because she still
didn't know. But she was with me. That much of it paid for
a lot.

I sat on the edge of the bed. 'Okay, honey,' I said.
'Thanks.'

We watched each other, and she put her hand on mine
and I took her hand and squeezed it and it was almost as if
she knew everything and was with me. So I knew everything
was all right, even if she didn't know.

'What are you going to tell them?'

I kept looking at her, kind of drinking her in. Then I
grunted and got up and went into the bathroom. When I
came back, she was still sitting there on the bed.

'They took the body away. I told them we found it
together.'

'But, Bess – we didn't.'

'I told them that, though.'

'Well, all right.'

257

'I haven't seen him drive by any more, Roy – not since the police have been here.'

I looked at her and she looked at me, then down at the floor, then up at me again. I grinned at her and turned and went into the office and sat down at the desk. I felt plenty shaky inside. Maybe she really thought I did it. She was acting funny. Acting good, but – would they think that?

I heard her come through the hall. She leaned against the jamb in the doorway, with her hands together just the same way Vivian used to do. 'Here he comes, Roy.'

'Okay. Everything's going to be all right, now.'

'*Shhh!* Here he comes!'

I stared at her. Her eyebrows were all hiked up and my God, I didn't know what to do. Really, I hadn't done anything, and yet she suddenly had me feeling so guilty and I was rotten with it. And then I knew it wasn't her fault. She was trying to do right by me, and I was kicking her for it. . . .

Knock – knock. . . .

Bess went across the room, stumbling once on the rug, and opened the door. 'Yes, Officer?'

'Mrs. Nichols, hate to bother you again. Is your husband awake yet?'

So, I'd been asleep. Great.

'Yes, Officer.' She held the door open, stepping out of the way, and he came into the office and took his hat off. He stood in the doorway, so she couldn't close the door. He looked over at me. 'Mister Nichols?'

'Yes?'

He stepped into the room and she closed the door and leaned back against it. I could hear old Hughes talking from outside.

The plain-clothes cop was a little guy, not big at all. His voice was very soft, kind of like purring. He wore dark-brown pants and a light sand-colored jacket, white shirt, and a clean maroon tie. The tie was clipped halfway down with a silver sword and his coat was open so you could just see the hump and the edge of the butt of his holstered revolver. On the left side, for a cross draw.

'Could we talk for a little?'

'Sure thing.'

He had a moon face and it was buttered like a bun with sweat. There were little pouches under his eyebrows, and his eyes looked at you through slits in the pouches. Brown, bright eyes. This was the man whom I'd deal with.

I couldn't help staring at him. I'd been waiting to meet him for a long time. Almost ever since that Lincoln picked me up on the Georgia road. . . . His hat was brown, like a chocolate drop.

'I'm Ernest Gant.'

I got up and went around the desk and stuck out my hand. He transferred his hat and we shook once and dropped clean. He had a waistline shake, palm down.

'Well, I guess I'll be in the kitchen,' Bess said.

'That's all right, Mrs. Nichols. You needn't leave.'

'I just thought – '

He smiled at her, then looked at me. 'I wonder if you'd just step over to the other apartment with me a moment, Mister Nichols?'

'Sure thing.'

He grabbed the door and held it open and grinned at Bess again. The grin went away and we were outside and the door was closed.

'What do you think?' I asked him.

He didn't say anything. We walked across the grass. A uniformed cop hurried across the lawn toward an official car parked by the curb. The Southern Comfort Motel had become a busy place.

Gant was nearly as tall as I was, after all – it was just that he seemed smaller, somehow. He wasn't, though. Not really.

We went inside number six. There was nobody there. The body was gone.

'Your wife tells me you found the body together?'

I started to go along with that. Then there was something in the tone of his voice, in the way he looked at me. It gave me a queer feeling and a certain respect for him, too. 'I want to clear that up. She said that, but it wasn't quite that way. I came in first.'

'I understand.'

He went over and stood by a chair. Then he sat down. His actions seemed to be thought out beforehand. He put his hat over his knee and patted his pockets. He came up with a crumpled package of cigarettes.

'Smoke, Mister Nichols?'

'No, thanks.'

'Sure?'

'Well, all right – I guess I could.' I took one and fumbled for a match. By the time I found one, he had a Zippo going under my nose. It was nice and steady with a big flame. He went over and sat down again.

'Why don't you sit down?'

I got over on the couch. I kept looking toward the hall doorway, the area drew my gaze. They had cleared the body away and there wasn't a trace.

Somebody came clomping heavily through from the back way. I looked up and it was another harness cop. He walked into the room, his leather creaking, and stepped around the place on the floor where the body had been.

'You want anybody posted outside, Lieutenant?'

'You stick around, all right?'

'Burke's with me.'

'Tell him to stick around, too. I'll let you know. They're finished with the floor?'

'I guess so.'

The cop looked at me. He was a man of perhaps thirty-five and there was nothing at all in his look, the way they look at you. He had very pale blue eyes, and his cap was on very straight. 'We'll be out in the car, then.'

Gant nodded and went on smoking. He had very dark hair, parted neatly on one side and brushed straight back. 'You came in first?'

'That's right.'

'When was that? What time, about?'

'This morning.'

'This is this morning. Could you narrow it down some?'

'Well.' I didn't have any idea about time. Time was suddenly all run together like syrup. 'Maybe nine?'

He smoked. He would come back to the time later, after I'd thought about it a while. He really had me thinking about time now. When *had* I come in here?

'And your wife? When did she come in?'

'A little after I came in.'

'Oh. I see. Let me get this straight. I thought you both came over here together, and you came in first. But she – ?'

'No. That's not right. I came over alone.'

He nodded. 'That's straight enough. Then your wife came along. That it?'

'Well, she – yes. That's right.'

'You just kind of – well, waited around until she decided to come and find the body, too – huh?'

I looked at him.

He held his hand up. He grinned. The grin went away and he began to smoke again, really working on the cigarette. He would take a drag and inhale, and hold it and then let it out, and stare at the cigarette, and do it all over again. The cigarette was finished, with that treatment. He held the lungful of smoke and ground the cigarette out in a standing ash tray. Then he let the smoke out in a long sigh, down into his shirt.

I was getting mixed up, and it made me mad.

'What did you do when you found the body of this woman – girl – in here?'

I started to blurt something, then paused, and that was all he needed. I could see it in his eyes, no real expression, just a shadow. I wanted to cover it, he was thinking. You couldn't cover it. You make your slip just once and it stands there, laughing, sneering at you for the rest of your life.

'Did you touch it?'

'No. Of – yes. Yes, I did.'

'Why?'

'I don't know why, I just touched it, that's all. Wouldn't you touch it?'

'*I* would. But then, that's my job. It doesn't matter, Mister Nichols. Don't misunderstand, please. I've got to get everything as straight as I can. You see, your wife was rather, well – nervous? She tried not to be, but she was. A normal reaction.'

I nodded.

His voice was soft, like velvet. Honest, it purred like a little well-oiled motor. There was nothing sleepy about his eyes. He just seemed to be holding cards, that's all. He hadn't said anything to make me know that for sure, but I couldn't help believing it. I was guilty of a lot of stuff that had to do with this crime, and it was stuff I didn't want known. I had to catch hold of myself, and keep the grip.

There was something about Gant . . . I didn't like him. So what could I do about that?

'Was the body cold?'

'Yes.'

'Then what?'

'How do you mean?'

'What did you do then?'

I started to say something and he leaned back in the chair and held up his hand and cleared his throat. 'Wait. I mean, let's get back a little bit. Why did you come over here?'

'Didn't my wife tell you anything about – ?'

'Just answer the question.'

'I don't have to answer anything.'

He sighed and stared down into his lap. He lifted his hat and rapped it on his knee and looked out the window. Then he tipped his head a little to one side and said, 'Would you really mind answering a few questions, Mister Nichols? You'll have to sooner or later. Why not now?'

'I didn't say I wouldn't. I just – '

'Fine! That's the way to talk.'

I could feel the shaking start in my stomach and spread. 'No reason in the world why I wouldn't answer some questions.'

'Look,' he said. 'I have to go about this in my own way. This is a serious thing.'

'I know it.'

'This woman was murdered. Somebody choked her to death with a silk scarf. She took quite a beating, too.'

'I know.'

'Oh. You know.'

'I saw the bruises.'

'Mister Nichols, don't you think you'd better put that cigarette out? It's going to burn your fingers. It makes me nervous.'

CHAPTER 14

'LET'S RELAX. All right?'

I jammed the cigarette into the dirt around the cactus plant on the table by the couch. I wanted to relax. I had to get hold of myself, but it wasn't working right. Like if I tried to lean one way, I'd really be leaning in the opposite direction. I looked at my hands and they seemed steady, yet I could feel them tremble. The shaking was all through me. I couldn't control it.

If I refused to answer his questions, it would only make things worse.

'You have a nice place here.'

'Thanks.'

'Been here long?'

'Oh, not too long.'

'Must be expensive, the upkeep.' He shook his head. 'Especially now. Must be a headache, with the highway all torn up. Hasn't that done something to your business?'

'It's knocked it off a little.'

He wasn't looking at me. Then he did. 'Mrs. Nichols said something about a man's suitcase being in here.'

I didn't say anything.

'Did you see it?'

'I didn't really notice.'

'Did Miss Latimer mention anything about a man?'

'No.'

'Nothing like her being married, anything like that?'

'I didn't talk with her much.'

It troubled me that he thought her name was Latimer. I didn't know why. Then I began to realize just how snarled up things were. With me smack in the middle. And I was already off on the wrong track with Gant. There was nothing to do about that, either.

'What about this man who was here last night?' He had left it open. I didn't know what to say. 'You met him, didn't you?'

'Yeah – I met him.'

'How did you happen to meet him?'

I told him how I'd thought he was a prowler and had gone to see if Miss Latimer was all right. Telling it to him that way, it came out easy. Then after it was out I sat there and felt the sweat. Every word I said, it got deeper. Why couldn't I just tell him? Tell him everything?

I knew why, and it was hell. That money hidden in the garage. There was no reason why the law should ever find it, because they knew nothing about it. It didn't concern them. The only thing they were after was the killer of Vivian. I couldn't tell them that, either. Sooner or later they'd find out. And I hadn't killed her, so I was all right.

'Were they arguing, Mister Nichols?'

'Who?'

'This man and Miss Latimer. Did you notice whether or not they got along – seemed to?'

'Oh, sure. There might have been some argument.'

'Your wife said something about it. When she came in she said you – '

'Oh, that. Well, the guy sort of resented my bursting in like that. You understand.'

'I see.'

All I had to do was keep that brief case hidden the way it

was and everything would be all right. Even if Gant was a snoop, and I was pretty sure he was. Then I remembered something.

I looked at him and it came to me and I almost fell off the couch. I had never had any thought hit me this hard.

'What's the matter, Mister Nichols?'

'Nothing. Pain in my stomach.'

'Oh?'

'Cramp, like.'

I put my hand on my stomach and made a face. 'Listen, would you excuse me a minute?'

He looked at me and frowned slightly.

All I could think was, The car. The Ford. With Georgia plates taken out in my name. It was beautiful.

'I won't be long. Just wait right here, Lieutenant. I get these pains every once in a while. There's some stuff over at the house.'

'All right.'

We got up and stood there.

'I'm not through talking with you, though,' he said. 'I'll be out front in the car.'

'Fine.'

I went on out quick and cut toward our place. He walked across the grass to the police car at the curb. When his back was turned, I started down between the apartments, toward the garage. I ran.

Sure as the devil, they'd trace those plates. If they found them in my name, how could I explain that? If I could just hang on long enough, I felt sure something would turn up. They'd find Teece; they'd find who she was and they'd get him for it. If I could just hang on and keep them off my neck, so I wouldn't have to spill about that money.

They'd never say anything about that money to the law. They wouldn't dare, not a one of them.

I reached the garage for number six. Her car was there,

all right, with the door closed and nobody'd been around yet. Her car hadn't been mentioned. Maybe they thought she'd come down by train, or plane. Maybe they wouldn't ever ask about her car.

Don't be a complete idiot, I told myself. You know better than that. But they might play it out that way. Worse things have happened than the cops slipping up.

I worked as fast as I could. I was so excited I really did begin to get cramps.

I went along the front of the garages to our garage and got back in there by my work bench. Under the bench I knew I had a last-year New York plate. Some folks had left it here. There was week before the time expired in Florida, so it would still be okay down here.

I couldn't find the plate. I got down under the bench and rummaged around in the junk box. It wasn't there. Then I got up and saw it sitting on a side beam, like a decoration. I grabbed it and headed for number six garage.

I had to come back for a pair of pliers and a screw driver. I was kind of sobbing to myself by then, soaked with sweat, running against time. He'd begin wondering where I was and I didn't want him to wonder.

The Georgia plate came off easy. They had it snapped on with a kind of coil spring deal, so I didn't need the screw driver and pliers, after all. I flung them across the alley into a field beside a house. I got the plates changed and stood there with the Georgia plate.

I started back for number six and Bess came around the corner of the garage, emptying the garbage. She had the little tin bucket from the house and she was just taking the lid off the big garbage can by the garage, when she heard me.

'Roy.'

I had the plate jammed into my belt, in back, up under my shirt.

'You through talking with the detective?'

267

'No.'

'What are you doing back here?'

'I was just – oh, hell – I had a cramp.'

'What?'

'Stomach-ache. I don't know.'

I started past her.

'You want me to fix you something?'

'I was just coming over to the house. I'll have to get back there. I told him I'd be right back.'

She looked back down the line of garages, then at me. She didn't say anything. I kind of grinned at her and patted her shoulder. I left her standing there and went for the house. As soon as I was around the corner of the garage. I ran again.

In the house, I had that damned plate. I didn't know what to do with it. I had to hide it. There didn't seem to be any place and Bess would be back in a minute. I heard her coming across the yard, then, the handle on the kitchen garbage bucket squeaking and her feet hushing on the grass.

I went into the office, still with that plate cutting into my back. I looked outside. He was leaning against the car, talking with them, watching the office.

The kitchen door opened.

I went over to the studio couch, lifted a cushion and jammed the plate down in back. I pushed it as far as it'd go and something ripped. I jammed it down in there and put the cushion back and sat on the couch to see if it was all right. It was, and I was plenty tired all at once.

'Your stomach any better, Roy?'

'It'll be all right. I was just going.'

'Be glad to fix you something. Bicarb, maybe?'

'No. Never mind.'

She stood there watching me and I could see she wanted to help, only I couldn't let her do anything. I didn't half know what I was doing. I got up and went out and across to number six. Gant saw me and started back over the lawn, walking with a kind of head-down shuffle, holding his hat.

I waited for him, trying to ease my breathing.

'Feel better, Mister Nichols?'

'Lots better. Thanks.'

Then I saw the front of my T-shirt, and my hands. There was dust on my shirt and my hands were black with dirt and grease. He hadn't noticed yet, but he would.

'Wait a second. I'm going to turn on the sprinklers.'

He looked at me and frowned with that nice way he had. I paid no attention, went down by the main faucet and turned the sprinklers on. Then I turned on the spare faucet that I used for the hose, and washed my hands the best I could and splashed some up on my shirt. I saw old Hughes walking around the corner of the apartments, toward the shuffleboard court.

'Can you talk now?' Gant said.

'Sure. Fire away.'

'Let's start from where we were.'

'Shall we go back inside?'

'Let's just stand out here.'

I didn't like the tone of his voice now. It had changed; there was something new in it. It was no longer so soft. 'This man who was in the apartment with Miss Latimer. You didn't happen to hear his name?'

'Not that I know of.' It came out like that and I wished I hadn't lied about that. But I couldn't correct myself, not without making it worse, so I'd have to let it ride.

'What did he do? I mean, when you came in. Did he want to fight you?'

I laughed. 'He couldn't fight so well. He had one arm in a sling. His face was all bandaged up.'

It made me feel good to tell the truth for a change.

Gant went over and leaned against the wrought iron railing

269

on the small porch of number six. He looked like a man who had maybe worked hard at his studies, always treating everything very seriously, and now he was exactly where he wanted to be. He seemed certain of where he was going now, and what he was going to do. He was a thinker, keeping everything peacefully and quite seriously to himself.

'Did he want to fight?' Gant said.

'Well, yeah. I guess he did. I took a little jab at him, just to warn him.'

'Your wife said you almost warned him right through the door.'

'Well, it might have been harder than a jab. I mean, he was off balance.'

'Mister Nichols.' He looked at me and took his hat off again, then put it on again, fooling with the crown until he was satisfied. 'This is no way to go about things. Honest.' He shook his head. 'I know you don't feel well, but you've got to get your thinking arranged better than this. You keep making me think things.'

I didn't say anything.

'The way you act, anybody would think you killed that Latimer girl.'

'I didn't.'

'All right, then. Why don't you make at attempt to help me? This is my job, and I like it. But you're making things tough for me.'

'I'm just answering your questions.'

'No. You're not. You're thinking just as fast as you can, and you're saying the first thing that comes into your head. Are you trying to cover up something? Because, if you are, it won't do any good. We *always* find out, Mister Nichols. It'll just save lots of time if you'll play it straight with us.'

'I'm not covering up anything. What right have you to say that?'

'There you go again.' He sighed and stared down at his

shoes. 'We deal with things like this all the time. I'm with Homicide, and sometimes we have to talk and talk. But I can't recall ever having talked with a guy just like you, Mister Nichols. You say one thing and you must know your wife has told me different. Why do you do that?'

'Well, I don't know. I didn't realize it.'

'Are you trying to shield your wife from something?'

'No. Listen, I've got a motel to run. There's a million things – '

He held up his hand and stepped closer. 'I don't want to have to run you down to headquarters, Mister Nichols. But if this keeps up, we'll have to. We question a little bit different down there. And you wouldn't be able to take care of the motel by remote control.' He looked around. 'Anyway, there's not really much to take care of. Your wife says business isn't good at all. I don't see many people around.'

He began to scare me now.

'Now, try not to get excited,' he said. 'I never saw anybody get so excited and pretend they aren't.'

I didn't dare say anything. I wanted to either poke him or walk away. I didn't do either, because I was beginning to see how I looked to him. From his side, I'd either done this thing, or I'd done nothing. I was just a motel owner, a guy who was a near-witness to a murder, and he was trying to learn what he could from me. But with the amount of lying stuff I had inside me, it was difficult to act right. I *was* trying to think every minute – I *was* saying the first thing that popped into my head. And now I knew it couldn't be any other way.

'Your wife says Miss Latimer drove down here in what looked like a Ford sedan. That right?'

I nodded, and the world seemed to tilt a little. 'That's better. What say we have a look at the car?'

I motioned with my hand and we started walking toward the garage. Boy, it was that close. If only I wouldn't make any slips now. He wasn't fooling me now. He scared me some, but I was still ahead of him. And I had to keep it that way. That brief case was Bess's and mine, from now on straight down the line. It had to be.

Now, just take it easy . . . easy is the way.

Because the thought I kept on hanging to was that *I hadn't done anything*. Not anything real bad. Of course not. . . .

'You're sure lucky, Mister Nichols. Having a place like this. I'd give my eyeteeth for something like this.'

'Thought you liked your job.'

'Well, sometimes it catches up with me.' He didn't look at me when he said that. We came around by the garages and walked up to number six.

'You always leave the garage doors open?'

'I guess she must have left it open. I didn't check.'

He nodded and we stood there and looked at the Ford. The New York plate on the back bumper would knock your eye right out, it was that bright. He looked at that and went up and flicked it with his fingers. It clanged. Then he stretched his neck to look into the back seat through the rear window.

'Don't touch the car. We'll have to dust it for prints. No use messing it up any more than it probably is.'

'Oh.'

'Probably won't find anything. Hardly ever do. We'll have to check it, though, just the same.'

'I understand.' Sure, with my prints all over it. 'I drove it around here and parked it in the garage for her.'

'Oh, well, that won't matter. Person would have to be in the car for a time, to really lay any prints worth while. Anyway . . .'

He didn't finish that.

He looked the car over, looking in every window, hanging his head in the open windows. He kept looking at me, now and then. I just stood there and waited, thinking about things.

272

His attitude was lousy. He had no right acting the way he did, saying those things he'd said. He was getting me on the defensive and keeping me there. He didn't have anything on me. There was something speculative in the way he'd look at me, kind of like he was trying me out on things.

I turned away and walked along the garages. He could come and get me when he wanted me. The hell with him, and the hell with everybody.

'Nichols?'

He called from back there. I waited for him and he came up.

'Didn't you hear a thing last night?'

'No.'

'Well, this is a hell of a one, all right. It must have been that guy who was here last night. But why?'

'She said she'd been waiting for him to show up. She didn't say he was her husband, anything like that. Just waiting.'

'And your wife claims she saw a man's suitcase in the apartment before he came?'

I waited while he thought that over. He shoved his hat back and scratched his head, looking at me through those slits of eyes.

'Look,' he said. 'There's something I've got to check on. Then I'll want to see you again. So don't go away.'

'What did he want?'

'Just questions, honey. He thinks he's a hot-shot.'

'I didn't get that impression.'

I went into the bedroom and sat down on the bed. Then I flopped back and lay there looking up at the ceiling. She came in and sat down on the bed. I wished she would go away. Then I cursed myself for even thinking such a thing.

'Roy,' she said. 'You got to tell me if there's something troubling you.'

273

I didn't say anything. I reached out and patted her arm and let it go at that.

Gant had left things hanging, because he was planning something. I knew damned well that's what it was. There'd been a crafty look in his eye and he'd practically run back out to the curb to get in the car. What could it be? I had to stay a jump ahead of them.

'If there's anything you think you should tell this man, Gant, Roy – I wish you would.'

I cocked my head up and looked at her. She had on her red shorts now, and a yellow blouse. She looked real good and she was smiling at me. Her eyes were very bright.

'What d'you mean?'

'Nothing. Just that you should try to help all you can.'

'What do you mean?'

She shrugged. I sat up and grabbed her arm. 'You mean something. You're trying to say something.'

'No, I'm not, honey. You're reading something into what I say.'

We watched each other. She kept on smiling and I began to feel better. I'd thought for a minute there – but I'd been wrong.

'Roy?'

'Yeah?'

'Why do you think somebody killed her?'

'I don't know.'

'You don't even like to talk about it. Do you?'

I didn't say anything.

'Roy, I hear somebody.'

She started up. I heard somebody step on the office porch and then the rattle of knuckles against the door.

'You answer it, Roy. It's probably Gant again.'

Somehow I didn't want to answer that door. I did, though. It was Wirt Radan.

CHAPTER 15

RADAN STOOD there in the doorway and looked at me. He didn't smile; he didn't do anything. His face was without expression and he was wearing a gray suit and a blue hat, this time. He had switched colors, but he looked as natty as ever – and the threat in him was as quiet and contained as before.

'Hello, Mister Nichols.'

I waited.

'Would you mind opening the door?'

I opened the door and went on inside. I heard Bess come into the office and glanced back.

'Hello, there, Mrs. Nichols,' Radan said. He touched one finger to his hatbrim and the corners of his mouth pinched up a little.

'Oh,' Bess said. 'It's you.' She smiled at him. 'Won't you come in?'

'He wants to see something outside,' I said. We went out onto the lawn. Bess stood by the screen door, then I heard her walking toward the rear of the apartment.

'Well, well,' Radan said. 'Here we are again.'

'What is it this time?'

'It's like this,' he said. 'I saw them take her out. Feet first. She was here and Teece was here. What do you figure you'll do about this?'

'Take who out?'

'Let's get away from here,' he said. 'Come on.' He started down toward the rear of the apartments. 'Come along, Mister Nichols.'

I followed him and he had that same jaunty walk as before. His shoulders leaned forward just a shade with each step, and he didn't look around to see if I was coming.

He paused by some bushes. 'Where's the money?' he said.

'You killed her, didn't you?'

'Be careful how you talk to me, Nichols,' he said, and something peculiar came into his eyes. It was only there for an instant, then it was gone. Something had come over his face, as if the skin had shrunk in that brief moment. Then it relaxed. But I'd seen all I needed to see. I knew that if you touched him, he'd be like a piece of steel ready to spring. There was that warning emanating from him, from the way he looked at you and the way he stood. It hadn't shown so much before, but now it did show. Just enough to let you know. He didn't seem to have any satisfaction about it, either. It was, as was everything else about him, quite matter-of-fact, edgily contained.

'You're learning,' he said. 'Aren't you?'

I wanted to get away from him. I'd read about them, the way he was, but I'd never really met up with one. He was a killer, and in no joking sense. It was written in every line of the man. He was woodenly conscienceless.

'Where's the money?' he said.

I still didn't say anything, but I moved slightly away to not say it.

'We can save time, Mister Nichols – and energy. Your energy, if you'll just tell me quickly.' He sighed and shoved his hands into the pockets of his jacket and stood there looking at me with his shoulders hunched. 'You know,' he said. 'I've never met a guy just like you.' He shook his head.

'You know who I am, and why I'm here – yet you act this way. It's a dumb way to act. I wish you wouldn't do it.'

I grinned at him. He didn't move.

'Was she here when I was here last time?'

'Did it ever occur to you I won't be pushed?' I said.

'No.'

I didn't say anything.

He took a single step, bringing him up close to me. His eyes were very clear, the whites as clear and innocent looking as a baby's. 'Mister Nichols,' he said. 'You know the kind of a man I am, and you know the job I'm on. I'm paid very well for this job, believe me.'

'So?'

'I'm going to kill you right here in your own yard, if you don't tell me what I want to know.'

He waited. That's all there was to it. You knew absolutely that he would do exactly as he said. It would be, to him, like turning around and walking away. A single movement.

'We gave the money to Teece. You're too late.'

'You're not lying?'

'It's the truth. I swear it. We gave it to this Teece. All right, yes – she had it. I didn't. I didn't have anything to do with this. She told me about it – wanted me to do some damned thing for her. She gave it to Noel Teece. It was in a brief case.'

He kept standing there like that, watching me. I saw the skin on his face shrink up again and stay that way, and his color under the tan was pale. There were tiny pinpoints of perspiration on his nostrils. Otherwise, he didn't change at all. He didn't move.

'What did she tell you about it, Mister Nichols?'

'Nothing. She just wanted me to help her.'

He thought about that for a time, watching me steadily.

'This is something that has to be cleaned up right away,'

he said. 'You can believe that, can't you? And it's not getting cleaned up – not at all. It's getting gummier all the time.'

'The hell with you, Radan.'

'You can say that, yes.'

I turned and walked away from him.

'All right,' he said, from back there. 'I'm going to move in.'

'What?'

'I want her apartment. Number six.'

I paused, then went back to where he was standing. 'The hell you say!'

'I'll take the one next door, for now. As soon as the law's through, then I'm moving into her apartment. You can understand what that means, of course?'

'You can't do that!'

He laughed quietly, reached out and tapped me on the arm. 'Come on,' he said. 'Will you show me the apartment? Or shall I take care of that myself?'

I just had to stand here and take this, along with all the rest. And it was getting to be too much. Wouldn't the law know him? Apparently not. He wouldn't be here if they did, and he was damned certain I wasn't going to say anything. He had me over a barrel.

'Let's do it right,' he said. 'Like any decent landlord, Mister Nichols.'

He started walking out toward the front of the motel. Then he turned. 'You going to change your story, Nichols?'

'She gave Teece the money. Honest to God she did. He did something, threatened her – listen, she wanted me to help her get out of the country. That's how I got mixed up in this. It's all over now. It's done, can't you see? Teece is probably in South America, by this time. Can't you go away and leave us alone?'

'Nobody got that money, Nichols. You're lying.'

'I'm telling you – '

278

'All right. I'm moving in. We'll see. I'll have to work it out.'

Well, he moved into number seven. And the first thing he did, with me right there, was walk into the bathroom and lift the lid off the toilet tank and take a look. He clanked it back on and didn't say a word.

'I have some things out in the car,' he said. 'Come on, help me carry it in.'

'You can go to hell.'

'All right.' He shrugged and went out, whistling. He got into the car and started it and drove off. My cripes, was he leaving? I rushed out there and watched him drive along and turn the corner. I waited. He turned into the alley and I heard the plump tires of his Caddy on the gravel back there and I heard him stop at the garage for number seven. The door squeaked as he slid it open. He drove inside.

Pretty soon he came along, carrying two great big suitcases, so he'd figured on something like this. He walked past me without looking at me and went on into number seven.

I went after him. I stood in the doorway. He had taken the suitcases into the bedroom, and he came back into the living room and glanced at me, then went over and opened the blinds.

'You can't stay here,' I said.

'Why don't you prevent me?'

'I told you all I know.'

He began to whistle. It was shrill and harsh on the ears, tuneless. Just ceaseless, endless, hard. He walked around and put all the blinds open, took off his hat and set it on an end table, with care. Then he took his jacket off and went into the bedroom. When he returned, he wasn't wearing the gun, either. It had been a big gun.

'I like these assignments, Nichols. Everybody knows what's going on, and only one is lying or not lying, and eventually you find out.'

He wasn't sure about believing me. I could tell the way he looked at me. His instinct told him I was lying, and his instinct was right. Only he had to believe me.

'Too bad I can't have a dame around here,' he said. 'But I'm traveling under orders, like I said. Too bad. It'll be lonely – unless something happens. And it probably will.'

We stood there and watched each other. He reached up and loosened his tie, stretching his jaw, his eyes never leaving mine. Where his shoulder harness for the gun had been, his shirt was wrinkled. It was no light harness, either; it was thick-strapped and Radan was a tried gunman. You knew it, you didn't have to be told. And there didn't seem to be any fear in the man, and he wasn't ignorant.

'There a phone in the office, Nichols?'

'No.'

He shoved by me and went on outside. I had thought about shoulder pads in his suit jacket. It wasn't so. Radan's shoulders were broad, pushing at the seams of his shirt. He was loaded with energy, and very fit, and I felt that in his own secret way, he was very proud of this. So far, I hadn't seen him smoke. I wondered if he drank.

He started across the lawn toward the office. I went after him and caught up with him.

'Listen: Be careful what you say over the phone. My wife's around.'

He didn't bother answering. He stepped jauntily up on the porch and opened the door and called, 'Mrs. Nichols – I'd like to use your phone. Will it be all right?'

Bess came into the office. 'Why, hello, there.'

'I've moved into your motel, Mrs. Nichols.'

She looked at me and I nodded. 'Number seven.'

She swallowed and said, 'You've probably heard what happened here this morning.'

'Wipe it straight off your mind. The phone?'

She pointed to the desk and he went over and picked it

up and dialed once and asked the long-distance operator for a Tampa number. Then, waiting, he looked first at me, then at Bess.

Bess tugged at my arm. We were bothering him, and after all, when a person's phoning, you should have the common decency not to listen in. 'Hello,' he said into the phone. He waited as somebody spoke on the other end. 'Yes,' he said. 'All present and accounted for. I moved in. Yes.' He hung up, turned and grinned at Bess.

'Thanks,' he said. He stood there by the desk and said, 'How much for a week? I figure a week should take care of it.' He looked at me when he said that.

She told him and he paid her, and he went outside, whistling. 'He's rather nice, in a funny way, isn't he?' Bess said.

'Yeah, sure.'

'What did he say when you told him about what happened?'

'Nothing, Bess. It didn't seem to trouble him.'

'You think they've caught the man, yet?'

'How's about fixing something to eat?'

She hesitated, watching me. Her eyes were soft and blue. I looked at her and there was this expression of patience on her face, in her eyes, and she smiled at me. Then she came up to me and put her arms around me. I held her tight, wanting to crush her, loving her maybe more than I ever thought I could love her. I was lost and all these things were crowding me. I didn't know what to do now. And she didn't know what it was all about and I couldn't tell her. That's what hurt most, I guess. I wanted to tell her – but I never could. She believed in me and trusted me, and I'd slipped up.

Only the money was out there, and it was our money. I wasn't going to lose that now.

Her lips were warm and I kissed her temples, feeling the soft golden hair against my lips, and her forehead and her chin. I pulled her tight against me.

'I love you, Roy.'

We stood there like that.

And him over there in number seven, with his gun and his suitcases, waiting for God knew what. And Gant. And Noel Teece.

Remembering Teece brightly was like a kind of added pain.

Maybe if I could talk Bess into taking a vacation. Just close the place down, kick them all out, and go away. Let it all blow over. We could take what money we had and just leave that brief case. When we came back, Lieutenant Gant would have the murder solved, and we could . . .

After we ate, I went around trying to catch up with things. Trying to keep my mind off what was happening – what could happen. It didn't work. I'd be in the yard and find myself sneaking around the apartments to have a look at the outside of the garage. Six or seven times I went into the garage, for nothing. Just to find myself standing there by the Chev, staring up there at the beams where that brief case was. Or I'd look over at number seven, and sometimes he'd be standing on the porch with a tall glass in his hands. He'd look across at me and I'd turn away.

Once he waved and called, 'Hot, isn't it?'

I began to quit trying to duck everything, and face it up instead. I'd have to, sooner or later. And maybe right then, for the first time, I really began to understand what I was up against. I'd thought I had before. Now it all came up into me like a big choke. These people who had sent Radan over here weren't fooling, and I'd been kidding with it. And Radan had said he had a plan.

What kind of a plan? I didn't want to think about that. I began to get scared, more than ever before in my life, and I knew I had good reason. Bess was in there and what was she thinking? And Gant, what was he going to do – would he be back today? I went back inside our place and just sat.

Bess would come and look at me, then go away. I didn't care what she thought. It didn't matter.

I felt empty inside, as though there wasn't anything left – no place to go. Yet, I had to hang on. If I weakened now, then it was all shot and we wouldn't have anything. It was the chance I had to take. All down through the years there'd never been anything but fight, fight, fight – for nothing. Whenever we got anything, we'd lose it.

Now, just this once . . . !

I'd sit there and Bess would come in and look at me. Sitting on the couch in the office, waiting. I didn't know what for. For the guy over there in number seven to do whatever it was he was going to do – or for Gant to come back and shackle me and I'd still fight, and if I fought, I'd have to lie. And that would put me in deeper and deeper, only I couldn't stop.

It happens that way sometimes. If you ever have it that way, then you'll know what I mean.

And there was a deep concern in Bess's eyes; something I couldn't quite read. It bothered me, but what was I going to do?

'Come and eat, Roy. Supper's ready.'

'All right.'

I went into the kitchen and sat down and stared at my plate. I didn't want to eat. There was this rotten black feeling all through me and I couldn't shake it.

'Eat something, Roy. What's the matter?'

'Nothing. I just don't feel so hot.'

I wanted to go over and take this guy Radan and knock the hell out of him. Only I knew I wouldn't. You know when it's not ready; you know when something's going to happen.

Something had to happen. It was like before a big storm, with the black clouds out there on the horizon. Everything goes calm and dead, and then . . .

283

It happened about four o'clock in the morning. It was still dark when somebody began pounding on the office door.

I got up and wandered around, kind of hazy, there in the bedroom. They pounded on the door. I didn't want to go out there. Finally I put on a robe and went.

I opened the door and a cop stood there, his face shining in the darkness. I saw a car out by the curb, with the headlights gleaming cold and brilliant on the road.

'Get some clothes on, Mister Nichols,' he said. 'Lieutenant Gant wants you to come along with me.'

CHAPTER 16

WE WENT out to the car. There was nobody inside. The motor was quietly idling and the door on the driver's side was open. He sure didn't give a hang about the city paying for his gas. I went around and climbed in and he got in and we slammed our doors at the same time.

He started up and we went down the street and took the turn at the corner and headed toward Tampa Bay. He drove along through the quiet Southside residential section, his face turned rigidly front.

'Well,' I said. 'What's up?'

He didn't answer.

It makes you feel like hell when they act that way. They get that superior air and I suppose they teach them that. Only I was a taxpayer, at least on the books, and I paid his salary.

'Lieutenant Gant, eh?'

'Look, Mister Nichols. It won't do you any good to keep asking. I'm not going to tell you anything. Those are my orders, and I reckon I'll keep them.'

We turned left on the street along the park by the bay and he stepped it up a bit. You could see the reddish halo of light across the bay, over Tampa. Like a hooded, glass-enclosed Martian city, maybe – or just a pale hell on the not-too-distant horizon.

The park looked shadowed and quiet.

Then it changed.

There were some cars parked along the curb up there. Men were grouped in three or four places and they wore dull uniforms upon which sparks of light winked. Two spotlights were shining a silvery wash down there in the park, focused on the ground just beyond a tremendous live oak. The light was somehow off-white, bringing that odd cast of known green but seen gray to the brain and eye. The two cars were parked down there in the park on the grass.

We rolled along and he put on the brakes. He scraped the curb with the tires and we stopped.

'Get out, Nichols.'

I got out and waited, looking across the park where the spotlights were. A man detached himself from a group down there and the group dispersed. The man came along with a kind of head-down shuffle.

He came along and flipped his hand at me. 'Something I want you to see, Nichols.'

It was ominous and I didn't like it. This Gant was too somber. He motioned to the cop and the cop went around and got behind the wheel of the car and drove off. For a moment Gant and I stood there. The palms along the road sent crazy shadows leaping from the streetlights. 'Come on,' Gant said.

I started along with him, down through the park. There was nobody down there where the spotlights from the police cars shone. I couldn't see where we were going, because there was a huge bush in the way.

We came into the beams of the spots. We rounded the bush and Gant looked at me, waiting.

Well, it was Noel Teece.

He had been what you might say torn limb from limb. A long streamer of bandage from the cast on his left arm lay tugging and fluttering in the wind, up along the grass. The

286

cast on his arm had been smashed. His eyes were half-open. The bandage had been torn off his face and it was all scabs. He was lying flat on his back, looking up into the dark sky.

Then I saw how he'd been slit up the middle with a knife, or maybe an axe. I turned and walked around behind the bush and was sick.

When I came back, Gant hadn't moved. He was standing there, looking at Teece.

'Like a fish,' he said. 'Just like a fish.'

'What'd you bring me down here for?'

'Don't you know?'

I couldn't look at him again.

'Go ahead,' Gant said. 'Look at him. That's Noel Teece, Nichols. He's the man who was down to your place, visiting that Latimer dame. Recognize him?'

I still couldn't say anything.

'He's a little hard to recognize, I admit,' he went on. 'But that's him, all right.' He turned and looked at me and frowned. 'Do you say it's him, Nichols?'

'I don't know.'

'Well, make up your mind. We brought you down here just to make sure. Not like there's two of them running around, dressed the same – and with a broken arm and a patched-up head. What do you say?'

'It might be.'

' "*It might be!*" You – ' He paused and rubbed his hand across his face. 'All right. We'll bring your wife down here. She saw him, remember?'

'I guess it's him, all right.' I still didn't look down there again. 'I'm sorry. I don't know why I said that.'

'Thanks. For nothing.' He turned and started away, then whirled and came up to me again. 'Why do you do this? Why do you act this way? Isn't it enough – ?' He shook his head, breathing hard, real mad.

287

I felt like hell. I wanted to help him. But if I helped him, I'd be helping myself right out of that money.

Then I thought of Radan and it was as if the back of my neck turned to wood. He'd done this, as sure as hell – Radan. So why hadn't he come to me? If he did do this, he sure would head for me right after, because by now he'd know Teece didn't have the money. And that was all Radan wanted.

I could hardly move, the way I felt.

'What's the matter, Nichols? What's cooking in that peaceful little mind of yours?'

'If you knew who this guy was, why'd you bring me down here? What's the point of that?'

'Nichols, I wish to God you weren't what they call a citizen! I'd run you in and I'd work you over.'

'Why don't you? I'd like to know what you're getting at. You act like I've done something.'

He went absolutely still. His mouth hung open and his eyes got wide and he shoved his hat back on his head. Then his eyes went normal again. 'Done something,' he said. 'You're lying, Nichols. You know something. You're scared. There's something inside you that's eating at your guts till you can hardly stand it. It's going to bust out, too. Wait and see.'

'You think I did this to that guy?'

'I don't know.' He turned and walked away again. I went up by him and he turned and stopped me with his hand out. 'Why don't you come clean, Nichols? This is getting you no place. *What is it you're trying to hide?*'

'You've got it wrong. A woman was murdered at my motel. Now you think I'm mixed up in it.'

'We're running lab tests, Nichols. What are you going to do then? Because I know we're going to find something. All right, suppose this one killed the Latimer girl. Then who killed him? And why? Why at your place? Why do you act so scared? Why do you lie about things that don't matter, that couldn't matter to you? I'll tell you – it's because they somehow *do matter*. Do you know who that dead man is? Noel Teece. Do you know who *he* was? We know, Nichols. We know all about him, and why he was going to end up this way, for sure. You think it's going to take long to find out all the rest of it?'

'Who was he?'

He just made another face and I was plenty sick about the whole thing. You're damned good at this,' I said. 'You've got it all straight in your mind, haven't you? You've got the guilt all leveled at me. You can do that fine. What do you do about protecting the public from things like this?'

He cursed in a soft whisper, watching me. 'Yes,' he said. 'You'd say something like that, too. But I'll tell you – even you, and you know what I'd like nothing better than to do to you, Nichols – even you . . . I have two men stationed by your place all night – just waiting. Know what they're there for? For your health, Nichols – so you won't get hurt, because we might be wrong, and you might be right, and that's the job the way I see it. I have to do that. And it was done because you were a suspect in the killing of that girl, too.'

Now I saw why Radan hadn't been around. Radan would be half nuts with wanting to get at me. I hadn't seen any guards by the house, but Radan would know. It explained a lot of things. And now what was going to happen when I got home?

Radan wouldn't move too quickly; haste could mean a big bill of waste in this instance. He had orders to get the money. He knew I wasn't going any place with the law barking down my collar. So he would wait until everything was clear. Then he would move in on me, because he knew now that I'd lied to him about the brief case.

'Nichols?' Gant said. 'You aren't listening.'

'What?'

'I said, "What happened to your finger?" '

289

'It's broken.'

'That's damned enlightening, I mean, how broken?'

'I caught it in a car door.'

'When?'

'What's that to you?'

'See, Nichols? See what I mean?'

We stared at each other.

'Nichols, there's hardly a thing I can ask you about that you don't get scared and want to run. *What is it!* God, I'll bet you can't bring yourself to tell me about that finger, even. Not the truth. You can't force yourself to tell me how it got caught in what door, or when, or where? Right?'

I didn't say anything. He had me really going. I wanted to pile into him, and I couldn't. And that was bad, because I knew I was the one who was wrong.

He was doing his job. He had every right to be this way, and I could see that much of it clear now. And I was withholding the very grains of knowledge he had to have.

'Nichols, all I have to do is ask your wife.'

My neck got hot. If he asked her, she'd tell him about my going to Chicago. I felt trapped.

'Well?' he said. 'Where *did* you bust your finger?'

There was a kind of gleeful tone to his voice, as though he was really enjoying this, or maybe a little crazy or something. And I knew he wasn't enjoying it.

'A car door.'

' "A car door." '

He turned sharply and started up toward the road, muttering to himself. I watched him go with this tight new feeling of being trapped inside me. If he went to Bess, what then? I hadn't done anything! I wanted to yell it at him. If he really had anything on me, he'd have run me in fast. I knew that. So I was all right. I was still ahead of them – 'way ahead.

Only how long would they keep it up?

All I had to do was tell them. Only I couldn't tell them a thing, and they didn't know that. And by keeping my mouth shut and lying, it looked as if I was really mixed up in this. Maybe even committed murder.

I started on up across the park toward Gant.

So Vivian was dead. And now Teece, too. And it struck me what Radan might be doing, and I was damned well scared. I wanted to get home. . . .

'I'm going to haunt you, Nichols.'

'Listen, if I could help you, I would. There's nothing I can do to help you. You think I know a lot of things that I don't. You're reading a lot into this that isn't there. I mean it. Why should I want to stand in your way?'

He turned to a cop standing about ten feet off on the curb. 'Pete, will you run Mister Nichols home?'

'Listen,' I said, rapping his arm. 'You didn't answer me.'

He looked at me and grinned. 'I'm going to haunt you,' he said. Then he turned and walked off across the park toward where the spotlights were focused.

'Coming, Mister Nichols?' the cop said.

'Yeah.'

Way off there toward the Gulf, you could see the pale, gray-pink line of dawn, blurring the horizon.

I headed for our place in a hurry. I hoped that Gant still had his guards posted. But it could be that Radan would wait to make certain about everything.

Bess lay there in bed with her eyes closed. But she was awake. Already the gray morning was probing through the Venetian blinds. Still fuzzy with sleep, she sat there on the bed, staring at me, her pale golden hair mussed, and looking as warm and cozy as crackers.

'Wh-what did Gant want in the middle of the night?'

While I undressed, I told her about Teece, and she put her hand up to her mouth, her eyes round. 'Roy,' she said, and her voice broke a little, 'I've had all this on my mind and I can't stand it. . . .'

I could feel the sudden tensing behind my solar plexus.

'Will you tell me? Will you?'

'What, Bess?'

'You're mixed up in something, I know you are. How long do you think I can go along with you like this? You knew that girl, Roy – I know you did.'

'I don't get you at all.'

'Listen, Roy. I've been playing dumb, for your sake. But it can't go on. I live with you. I love you. I can't help feeling things – knowing something's wrong. All I know is this – you're in trouble and you won't tell me what kind of trouble.'

'Listen, Bess,' I said finally, 'if there was anything I had to tell you, I would. I didn't know that girl, and I'm not mixed up in anything. Now, just relax, and let's try to get a little sleep before we have to get up. Huh?'

She turned over and didn't answer. I could tell she was mad, and she knew darned well she was right about a lot of things and all of it was eating at her. Just like things were troubling me. . . .

Well, just for now, to hell with them. I was real beat, and I had to get some rest in, because God knew what was coming up in a few hours. Before anything else, I had to check the garage. Just an hour or two of sleep. . . .

CHAPTER 17

MAYBE WHEN you get in more real trouble than you can handle and get dead beat-out the law of subconscious gravity or something slides the whole load off somewhere. Anyhow, I didn't know a thing until dark, and Bess brought me some stuff in on a tray, like I was an invalid. It made me feel worse than ever, and now all the things were catching up with me, and I got dressed, and carried the tray out to the kitchen. But I couldn't eat. I had some black coffee and all the worries were crowding me again.

I was telling Bess that she should have gotten me up, when someone knocked on the office door up front. I went over and swung it open.

Gant stood there. He nodded at Bess, who had come up behind me. He gnawed his lower lip and thrust his hands into his pockets. 'Mind if I step inside your place for a few words? The two of you together?' He looked carefully at me when he said that.

'Sure.' I stepped aside and he came in.

'Shall I go make some fresh coffee?'

We both looked at Bess and Gant smiled pleasantly. He took his hat off. 'That would be nice. But would you mind waiting a moment?'

She nodded and her gaze sought mine.

There was something in the air that I didn't like. Something smug about Gant and the way he spoke. He walked across the room and stood by the studio couch.

'Sit down,' he said. 'There are a couple of things I'd like to clear up.'

'But,' Bess said. 'I don't understand. About what?'

He smiled. 'Please, sit down and take it easy.' And he sat down on the couch and there was this *clang!*

He stood up immediately. The *clang* had come from behind the couch. I knew what it was right off; that Georgia license plate, and my world quietly exploded.

'What could that have been?' Bess said. She went over by the couch. It had been much too loud to be ignored.

Gant frowned and stepped away from the couch. He was watching me. His interest wasn't behind the couch.

'Let it go,' I told Bess. 'Probably just a spring busted.'

'No; it wasn't that. Here, help me move the couch.'

Gant frowned and frowned.

I went over there like a sleepwalker and helped her move the couch. She skinned behind there, up against the wall, and bent over and came up with the plate. 'Why, it's a license plate. It slipped through the back, where the lining's torn.'

Gant was already halfway over the back of the couch. He snatched it from her and looked at it and started nodding his head. I went across the room and sat down. Bess put one hand against her face and stared at me. She came out from behind the couch and shoved it back with her knee, as easy as anything, and stood there.

Gaunt looked at me and sighed. 'This shouldn't take long to check, should it, Nichols?'

I sat there and stared at him. I felt this grin form on my face and I couldn't erase it. He tapped the plate against his other hand and stepped over to the telephone.

He called police headquarters and asked them to run an immediate check on that plate and he read the numbers.

'How ever did that get there, Roy?'

I didn't bother answering that. Gant hung up and moved to the couch again and sat down. He laid the license plate across his knees. 'Bright and new, too. Hardly used at all. Odd.' He patted his pockets and came up with a package of cigarettes. He didn't offer me one. He took one and lit up.

Bess watched me closely and I hated seeing the look in her eyes. She didn't know what was up, but she knew that whatever it was, it was no good.

'Mrs. Nichols, why don't you go make that coffee you mentioned? I reckon I could go for some I reckon we all could.'

'Sure thing.'

'We may have a little wait, here.' He paused and glanced my way, not quite meeting my eyes. 'All of us.'

She left the room, her heels smacking the floor.

'Well, Nichols. You want to say anything?' He had lowered his voice and I liked him for that.

'No.'

'All right. We'll just wait. You see, Nichols, it's a funny thing. License plates was exactly what I came to see you about. We checked that New York plate through.' He shook his head and smiled to himself. 'Thought we had it all in a hat. Boy, how wrong can you get? Where'd you think it would get you? Never mind, you'd lie like hell, anyway – we'll find out.' He shook his head again. 'That New York plate was owned by people living right here in town, Nichols. They were staying here at your motel a while back and they bought their Florida plate and exchanged them in your garage. Maybe you even helped them, hey?'

'No.'

'Boy, you've got a real stubborn streak, haven't you?' He stood up. 'Second thought, I'm afraid I'll have to take you downtown. Might have a long wait and I don't think this is the best place.'

He waited. I stood up. 'Whatever you say, Lieutenant. You're the boss.'

'How right,' he said. Then he turned and called to Bess. She came into the hallway. She was very pale.

'Your husband and I are going to run down-town for a while. I'm sorry about the coffee. All right?'

'But – Roy?'

'It's all right. I'll be back.'

'Sure,' Gant said. 'Sure.' He looked at me.

'Roy.'

I didn't look at her. I moved across the office and out the door and he came with me. Bess ran over to the door and called my name again.

'It's all right, honey. I'll be right back.'

'Good-night, Mrs. Nichols.'

We walked out across the lawn. He kept banging that license plate against his leg. We climbed into the car and he started the engine and drove off.

'You want to hold this, Nichols?' He handed me that Georgia plate. 'You're not going to try anything, are you, Nichols? You're not *that* crazy, I hope.'

I just sat there, trying to think.

'Gee. It's sure something, isn't it, Nichols?'

It was a small room, not much larger than a good-sized closet. There were no windows and only one doorway, with no door. At one end of this room, there was a platform perhaps ten inches high. On the platform was a straight-backed chair, nailed to the floor.

I was on the chair.

Over my head, swinging about a hand's breadth, was a 150-watt bulb, with a green tin shade. Nobody had touched the bulb, hanging from the high ceiling by a black length of wire, but it never stopped swinging and their shadows leaned and lengthened and shortened against the wall, breaking up against the ceiling. And my shadow was on the floor. It was crazy, any way you looked at it.

Gant had brought me in here, and for quite a while I sat alone, brooding. Then one by one they came and looked at me. They would stand in the door, with their uniforms all creased and their harness creaking, and just look at me.

They talked in the other room. Now and again one of them who had looked in once before, would come and stick his head in and then step away again.

Gant finally came into the room and stood against the far wall, watching me. It was a little hard to see him, because of the light. The light was hot, too. Then another man in plain clothes joined him. This was a big one, smoking a stub of cigar and he looked like the nasty kind. He was in his shirt sleeves.

'This is Armbruster,' Grant said. 'Armbruster, meet Nichols.'

'Hello, Nichols.'

I nodded.

Armbruster smoked his cigar, standing there. He had a red face, round and beefy, and when he breathed it made quite a noise. He had a barrel chest and it was like he had a pain in his stomach. He would kind of groan a little to himself every now and then.

'You want to say anything, Nichols?'

'What in hell is there to say?'

'Still chipper,' Armbruster commented.

'Oh, he's chipper.'

They stood there. Armbruster smoked and Gant just leaned against the wall, looking at me. It's pretty bad when people just stand and stare at you, like that. It begins to annoy you. You itch. You try to look away. You can't do anything. You begin to sink into the chair. You sweat. You think of a million things to do, all of them wrong.

'They've traced the plate,' Gant said.

297

'Oh?'

'Yes. It didn't take long, did it? The Ford car was in your name. Roy Nichols.'

'Isn't that something?' Armbuster said.

I swallowed. I wanted a drink of water, but I knew better than to ask for one.

'That's all there is to it. Just that quick. We made it with two phone calls. Now, what do you say, Nichols?'

'Hell, man,' Armbuster said. 'Don't be a damned fool. Tell us about it.'

A uniformed cop ushed past Armbuster and looked at me. 'Why'd you do it, Nichols?' he said. 'Why'd you kill Vivian Rise?'

He went away. I stared at the space where he had been. They knew her name.

'Yes,' Gant said. 'Vivian Rise. Did you know a girl by that name, Nichols? Or did you just know her as Jane Latimer? Or are you really Ed Latimer? Or what?'

'Or what?' Armbuster said.

'Come on, Nichols,' the cop said, sticking his head in the doorway. 'Why did you do it?' He looked at me for a minute, his face without expression. Then he stepped inside the room. He took a package of cigarettes out of his pocket. 'Have a smoke, Nichols?'

'Thanks.'

'That's all right.' He lighted my cigarette, put the lighter away, stood there a moment, then left.

'Well, Nichols?' Armbuster said. 'Are you Ed Latimer, late of the Ambassador Hotel?'

Gant looked down at the floor. 'Come on. Let's not be here all night long.'

Armbuster looked at Gant. They both left me sitting there.

The cop came in, the one who had given me the cigarette. He stood in the doorway, smoking and looking at me. 'We

298

know you didn't kill her,' he said. 'But how about the other one? Did he make you mad? That it? Was he going to tell your wife about her? That it?'

I looked at him and opened my mouth. He turned quickly away and I heard him walk across the room.

They began talking out there. I couldn't make out what they were saying. I dropped the cigarette and stepped on it and sat there, staring at my hands. What to do?

That money. I had to keep it. Somehow.

It beat like a very small drum in the back of my head. A small and very distant drum. . . .

CHAPTER 18

ARMBRUSTER CAME and stood in the doorway.

'Tell Lieutenant Gant I want to see him.'

'Sure thing, Nichols.'

He went away. A telephone rang. I could hear them talking out there. I was in a terrible sweat and I was going to tell it – my way. I had to tell something, and it would look all right. Anyway you looked at it, that money was still up there in the garage.

Gant came into the room and stood there.

'All right,' I said. 'Here's the story.' I told it to him straight. All of it. Only I left out the money and I left out Radan. 'I don't know why she wanted me to help her. She wouldn't say. She just said she'd pay me. That's all. I needed money. I need it bad. So I told her all right, it was a go.'

'You thought this Teece was dead?'

'Yes.'

'Did you check to make sure?'

'He looked dead. I thought he was dead, that's God's truth. Lieutenant. But he wasn't, that's all.'

'It could happen. Then why in hell did you keep on lying after she was dead?'

'I don't know. I was scared.'

'Oh, hell, Nichols. You don't scare that easy. I can tell.'

'It's the truth. I was scared for Bess – my wife.'

'And how about when you saw Teece dead?'

'I didn't know what to do. I figured you thought I'd killed him.'

'Hey, Ernie!' one of them called.

Gant left the room. Pretty soon he came back. He looked at me for a long time. 'You telling me the truth, Nichols?'

I could sense something. It smelled good. But I had to doubt it.

'Yes. It's the truth.'

'Get out of the chair and come on.'

I stood up. My back was stiff. I followed him through the other room, past Armbruster and three cops who were standing there. They didn't look at us. I followed Gant and he led me out and into a hall. We walked down the hall, our heels echoing on the marble floors.

We reached the front doors and the street was out there, with cars going up and down. A girl and a guy walked along the street out there, holding hands. He kissed her on the cheek and she laughed and they walked along out of sight. A truck went by, backfiring.

'All right,' Gant said. 'Go on home, Nichols.'

I looked at him. 'But, what in hell?'

He turned and walked back down the hall. And I smelled a rat. A great big dead rat. But I went on through the doors, and onto the street. It was like just waking up in the morning.

Down the street I hailed a cab and went home. During the ride, I sat there and I was numb. I couldn't figure it. And I knew I had to do something.

It was crowding me hard. I knew it wasn't over.

Not yet . . .

'You're back, Roy!'

'Yeah. I'm back.'

Bess had been sitting on the studio couch, waiting. When I opened the door and saw her, she looked up, scared to death, with worry all over her face. Then she ran across the room and jumped into my arms, like the old days.

'What did they want you for, Roy?' Her voice was tight.

I held her away, looking into her eyes. 'About those two murders. They thought I was implicated.'

'But you weren't – *you weren't!*'

'No. Listen, Bess – I've got something to tell you. Something I should have told you long ago.'

'Yes?' She was smiling. I grabbed her and held her as close as I could. Then I thrust her away again and led her over to the couch. We sat down.

'I'm not asking you to forgive me,' I told her. 'But I've been lying to you, Bess. Up and down and crosswise. I'm in a terrible jam. But I want you to know the truth. All of it. The police already know.'

'You've told them?'

'Yes. Only not all of it. Not the part I'm going to tell you.'

And I told her. I gave it to her straight and hard, without any holding back. The whole business, from the very beginning on the Georgia road when the truck driver let me off, to the barbecue joint and the Lincoln. The hotel room. Vivian and me, in that room, and the money. I told her everything and she sat there, listening, with no change in expression and her eyes got wet just as I finished. 'So, I'm not asking you to forgive, unless you can. If you can't, I understand. I had to tell you. I just found out I had to tell you, coming home tonight from the police station. I was sitting in the cab and I knew you had to know. That's why I've been like I've been. I couldn't stand it. That girl – it was only the one night, I want you to understand that.'

'You were drunk, weren't you?'

'It makes no difference. I'm not making excuses.' I wasn't. She had it in her lap now. All of it. 'That guy Radan, he's right next door.'

The only thing I didn't tell her was where the money was.

302

'All right, Roy.'

She got up and turned her back to me and I saw her shoulders stiffen a little. She walked over to the hallway, turned and looked at me. She wasn't saying anything. Her eyes were a little cold now. I couldn't blame her. It was bad, but she had it straight, anyway.

'I've known something was wrong for a long time,' she said. 'I just didn't know what. You told the police about the money?'

'No.'

'But Roy – !'

'It's our money, Bess,. You're not going to tell them, either. I've been through too much for that money. It's got to be somebody's money, and it's ours.'

'No, Roy.'

'I mean it.'

'Where is it?'

'I'm not saying. If you tell the cops, Bess, I'll say it's all the bunk. I'll lie up and down, all over again. They'll *never prove different*. I mean it, honest to God, I do.'

'Yes. You and that girl. Yes.'

I watched her put her hands to her face. But she didn't cry. She brought her hands back down and came over to the couch and stood there in front of me.

'You've got to tell the police, Roy. You've got to!'

I shook my head. 'I'm sorry, Bess. I can't do it. I've had that out with myself. It means too much for us, and they don't know anything about that.'

She turned around and stood with her back to me. I looked at her hair, falling thickly to her shoulders, and the line of her back and her legs and her feet. I saw her hands along her sides, the fists half-clenched and she was perfectly still. I wasn't sure how she was taking it, or what she was thinking.

'All this time – ' she said.

'That's right. I've lied, and I've lied.'

'When that girl was here, Roy. Did you go over to number six and be with her? Did you?' She turned and looked at me, then. 'Because, if you did – if you – '

'No.'

'I believe you. God only knows why.'

I couldn't look at her face. I didn't feel any better, having told her. I felt worse, because it was hurting her. I didn't want that. Yet, she had to know.

'Roy,' she said. She came to the couch and sat down and looked at me. Her voice was pitched low. 'You've got to tell them. We don't want that money. It'll stand in the way of everything for the rest of our lives. We'd never be happy with it.'

'We'll never be happy without it. We've been without it all along, and it's not going to be that way any more.'

'Roy, I'm telling you – you've got to listen.'

'I'm not listening.' I stood up.

'For me, Roy.'

'Not for you – not for anybody. The money's ours. It stays that way.' I leaned over and looked her in the eye. 'I went through a lot to keep it. And now we've got it.'

'Not "we", Roy. You. You've got it.'

I turned and walked out of the office, and down the porch steps. On the grass, I half expected her to come after me. She didn't. I looked back in the screen door and she was sitting there on the studio couch, staring vacantly at the wall. I walked away from there.

I heard the hiss of feet on the grass and somebody grabbed my arm, whirling me around. 'Nichols.'

It was Radan.

I was mad and I went straight into him. He stepped back and I saw the gun.

'Take it easy, will you?' he said softly.

I stopped, watching him.

'Come on, now,' he said. He stepped up to me and

rammed the gun into my back. 'Move. Over to number seven.'

In the apartment, he closed the door and looked at me. He needed a shave, and he looked harried and I realized he'd been drinking a lot more than he should. But that gun was very steady, and so were his eyes.

'What do you want?'

'You know what, Nichols. You're going to tell me where that brief case is. You're the one who hid it, and we know that. You're going to tell me – all alone – just me.'

'That's what you think.'

'So. At last you admit it.'

We watched each other. He stepped in toward me and brought the gun down. It raked across my face. I grabbed his wrist and he grunted a little and his other fist flashed around and I saw the brass knucks.

I went down and sat against the wall. My face was ripped open and bleeding from the knucks.

'All right, Nichols. Tell me.'

CHAPTER 19

He stood up there looking down at me with the gun in one hand and the brass knuckles in the other. I was seeing Wirt Radan for the first time. I brought my hands down, braced against the wall and pushed. He wouldn't use the gun, I was sure.

I hit him hard in the legs. He didn't fall, but his fist did. The gun bounced off my skull and the pain flashed through me. I raked at him with my arms and got a leg and pulled. He fell on top of me.

I felt the quick impact of the knucks against my head. *Once – twice – three* times and I got groggy and lay back on the floor, staring up at him. He brought his foot back and let me have it hard in the head. My teeth jarred and I bit my tongue. I tried to catch his foot, but it was like working in slow motion. My head was one great big knot of pain and the pain shot down in my chest.

Then it was quiet and I gradually began to hear him breathing. I looked up and he was over there, sitting on the edge of the couch, resting, holding the gun, and the knucks glistened in the dim light from the lamp on the end table. He still wore his suit jacket and his tie wasn't even out of place. His breathing began to slow down.

'Where is it, Nichols? You may as well tell me. I think you understand that by now?'

I didn't say anything. I just lay there, looking up at him, trying to get my breath and let the pain chip away. The pain came into my head in great sheeting waves, and my eyeballs hurt. Finally I began to get up. He rose quickly and stepped over and lashed out with the gun barrel, hitting and raking, back and forth. He did it mechanically, without emotion – as you might swing a hammer at a nail. I tried to catch his wrist.

I caught it and the knucks landed again. I was on the floor, flat out again. He was killing me. He was quick and I knew he wanted that money, and if he got it he would kill me, and that would be that.

It was quiet. I heard water dripping in the kitchen sink and the sound of our breathing whispered harshly in the room. There was no other sound. It was as if everything was dead and gone and there was only this pain, throbbing inside me.

'You'd better tell me,' he said. 'You're going to, you know.' He cleared his throat gently. 'Honestly, you really are, Nichols. Can you believe that?'

I watched him. 'I gave it to Teece.'

'No, you didn't. I killed Teece, Nichols. Just as I'm going to do to you. He told the truth, I know that. He was crying and pleading like a small child. He said he didn't have the money. Those were his last words, Nichols.'

'He lied.'

'We know he didn't. I've been sent on this job, and I'm going to finish it. I always do. It's my turn for the brief case now.'

'The double cross from you?'

'Only halfway. They aren't sure how much is in that brief case.'

I came up off the floor and at him fast. I got him. I sank one into his gut and chopped with my other fist and he started to go down. I saw it in his face, the hanging on. Those damned knucks flashed again.

I lay there. He leaned down and smashed at me with the gun. Then he stood up and cleared his throat. Then he waited.

'All right. I wasn't going this far, Nichols. But now I am. I'm going to tie you up and I'm getting your wife over here. Then you're going to watch something. And you'll talk, Nichols. They always do. It's the last thing we try. We don't have any other way. But it's a good way. It produces.'

I looked at him and I knew he meant it. There was nothing to do.

'O.K., Nichols? You know I would?'

'Yes. All right. I'll show you.'

'One wrong move. That will be all.'

'It's all right. I've got the money.'

'Get up.'

'I can't, yet.'

He waited. After a time the pain began to drift away and I got to my knees. Finally I got up on my feet. The blood was in my eyes and I rubbed my hands across my face, knowing it was all done.

I'd let myself down. And Bess, too. I should have got Radan before, on my own. It had been the only way, and I'd missed it.

'Coming, Nichols?'

We went on out the door. I staggered off the porch and nearly fell. He stood back. He watched while I hung onto the porch railing, trying to see right. I couldn't see right.

'Around back, Radan.'

We started down between the apartments. It was a cool night and the wind washed against my face. Everything was a big blank, and I had drawn it. There was no use.

We came around behind the apartments. I still couldn't walk right. Something inside my skull kept crackling, and my teeth hurt bad. I knew I was spitting blood and I didn't give a damn, not any more.

We came by the garage and I reached up and grabbed the door and flung it open. 'You climb on the hood of the car. Then pull yourself up by a beam and the brief case is up there under the far eave, under some loose boards.'

'Stand right there, Nichols. Remember, I've got a gun. I can see you against the light. Don't go away.'

I didn't say anything. I stood there waiting. I knew I was waiting for a slug. It was almost as if I didn't care about that, either. He would kill me as sure as the night was dark. Then I thought, Maybe he won't.

He was up on the hood of the car. 'Stay right there,' he said. 'I can see you.'

I watched him pull himself up. Now was my chance to run. I didn't. I waited. I heard him up there, prowling around in the darkness. He was on the boards, over against the eave.

'God!' he said. 'I've got it.'

He came down fast, in a single leap from the beams to the car's hood to the ground. I turned and started walking toward the house.

'Nichols!'

'The hell with it.'

I started up along the side of our apartment, heading toward the office door. I heard him coming fast on the grass.

'Nichols!'

Somebody else said, 'Hold it right there, Radan!'

I whirled and saw him lift his gun and fire at the dark. He fired twice and I flattened myself against the side of the house and he came by me, running like hell.

He took a shot at me as he passed. It *thocked* into the wooden side of the house. A car moved along out in front by the curb and a spotlight blinked on, coming slowly bright and it picked him up.

I ran out after him. I saw him stand there on the front

lawn all alone, with that brief case swinging and he fired at the spotlight and missed.

'Stop – *Radan!*' I recognized Gant's voice.

Radan didn't stop. Somebody fired rapidly twice from down by the corner and Radan turned and knelt down and fired. Somebody fired from the car out there in the street. Radan stood and whirled on the car and his gun clicked empty.

The front sign went on, bright and glowing. Then the floodlights came on and it was like daylight out there on the grass and he stood there holding his empty gun. He drew his arm back and flung the gun sailing at the car. He turned and started across the lawn, running toward the far corner and I saw the brief case come open. That broken clasp. Money streamed and tumbled out as he ran.

They shouted for him to stop. They gave him every chance.

But he didn't stop. They cut him down. He skidded into a pile right by one of the floodlights, landing on his face.

Then everything became still. It had been sudden. Now it was over. I walked out across the lawn.

'You all right, Nichols?'

'Sure.'

It was Lieutenant Gant. He came across the lawn in a steady shuffle, putting his gun away. I walked over to Radan, lying on the ground. There was nothing left inside me.

We stood there and looked at him. About six slugs had nailed him. He was crumpled over on his face, with his grip still tight on the handle of the brief case, only most of the money had spilled out. He'd left a scattered green trail of it all the way across the lawn.

A cop started toward us, picking up the packets of money, softly whistling through his teeth.

'Well?' I said.

Gant looked at me. He shrugged. 'It was your wife. She knew about that money, Nichols. She saw you put it in the

310

garage. She checked and found the money, only she didn't tell us until just now, when she phoned. We'd freed you, thinking maybe you'd lead us somewhere. She wanted you to find it in yourself, to straighten it out without any help. That's why she never said anything to you about the money. I don't know. The hell with it. You know how women are. You should know how your wife is.'

'Yeah. I know.'

'She's over there. I'm not sure whether she wants to see you, though. Can't say as I blame her.'

Bess was standing there by the royal palm at the near corner of the sign. She was watching me. I lifted one hand toward her and let it drop. She didn't move.

Three officers came across the lawn.

The one who'd been picking up the money went over by the dead man and got the brief case loose from his fingers. He began packing the money inside the case, still whistling through his teeth.

'I'm afraid you'll have to come along with us,' Gant said. 'We know Teece killed the girl and Radan killed Teece, all that. We couldn't move in any quicker because we didn't really have anything on Radan, see? We've wanted him for a long while, Nichols. As I say, you'll have to come along, too. There'll be some sort of a trial. Maybe you'll get a suspended sentence. Maybe not.'

I turned and walked over by Bess. There was just nothing left inside me, but her. And she didn't want any part of me.

We looked at each other.

'Lieutenant Gant says the highway's coming through,' she said. 'He told me that tonight, when we were talking about you. Why you did all this.'

'I'm sorry, Bess.'

She looked up at me. We stood there that way for a second or two. Then I saw Gant coming toward us.

'It's all right, Roy.'

311

I didn't know what to say. It was all over.

'It's all right. I'll be here, Roy.'

Gant touched my arm. 'Coming, Nichols?'

We started off across the lawn toward the curb. 'There's a few things you'll have to clear up,' Gant said. 'I don't exactly get it all yet.'

'Me either, Lieutenant.'

As we got into the car, I looked over across toward the sign. Bess was still standing there. She waved her hand.

Gant slammed the car door. His voice reached me through a haze. 'You care for a cigarette, Nichols?'

b l u e   m u r d e r